Elle ____

CALM BEFORE THE STORM

EVAN'S SINS

VOLUME 2
RUTHLESS
STORM TRILOGY

Acknowledgements

Many thanks to all the wonderful people who helped make Calm Before the Storm Evan's Sins and the Ruthless Storm Trilogy possible. A special thank you to Whobeda A.K.A Marcha Fox for all the astrological charts and their meanings.

Volume II Ruthless Storm Trilogy

Books by Elle, Inc.
Published by Books by Elle, Inc.
225 College Dr. #65504
Orange Park, FL 32065
www.elleklass.weebly.com

Author's Disclaimer

This book is entirely fictional. No one was hurt during the making of this book. Any characters, most places or events/hurricanes are purely figments of the author's imagination. No part of this publication may be reproduced, transmitted or redistributed either in its entirety or in part without the author's express written consent.

Other books by Elle Klass

As Snow Falls

Baby Girl Series:
Book 1-In the Beginning
Book 2 - Moonlighting in Paris
Book 3 - City by the Bay
Book 4 - Bite the Big Apple
Book 5 – Caribbean Heat
Book 6 – Return to the bay
Book 7 – Prison of the Past
Baby Girl Boxes Set Books I-IV

Ruthless Storm Trilogy
Eye of the Storm Eilida's Tragedy Volume 1
Calm before the Storm Evan's Sins Volume 2
In the Midst of the Storm Tommy's Deception Volume 3

Evan's Girls
Scarlett
Emily

The Bloodseekers: St. Augustine Novellas
Book 1 - The Vampires Next Door
Book 2 – The Monster Upstairs
Book 3 – The Ghost Within

hidden journals
Isandro Volume 1

Zombie Girl
Book 1 – Premonition
Book 2 – Infection
Book 3 - Retribution

The Calm Before the Storm: Evan's Sins

Some people suffer unimaginable pain and angst. Their stories spread across the globe. Others suffer alone in unbearable anguish.

Elle Klass

Volume II Ruthless Storm Trilogy

Prologue

Snores louder than the thunder outside mingled with high-pitched whistles sounded from Evan's father, passed out drunk in his well-worn recliner. The sour alcohol stench made Evan's nose twitch in disgust as he walked past the recliner towards the hallway. He scrutinized his mother laying naked and asleep in her bed, a pillow tucked beneath her right side. The night light from his eight-year-old brother's room shone beneath the partially closed door – he refused to sleep with the door shut all the way as 'monsters may get him'. Evan chuckled at the thought. The only monsters in the house were the people who lived inside it. He peeked his head through the open sliver of the door and nodded as his brother's gentle snores told him the child was asleep.

Evan didn't check on his sister as the creaking caused by opening her door may waken her. At two years old she slept in a crib - *baby jail*. Convinced his family was asleep for the night, he padded to the kitchen in his socks and unscrewed the metal cover to the wall vent. He fingered inside it. Cool air rushed at him, sending a chill over his exposed legs. He grabbed hold of a pouch.

He laid the pouch on the tiled kitchen floor and opened it. Traces of light glinted off the contents. Evan lifted a butcher knife, touched his finger to the blade then wielded it through the air. Unsatisfied, he grabbed his father's hunting knife, sliding it from its sheath. He stole the knife months earlier… *he never hunted anyways.* He got a whipping from daddy's leather belt when he couldn't find his knife. *Worthless piece of crap who stayed drunk, handing out whippings like candy instead of protecting me from her.* His body did an involuntary jerk at the thought of his mother's daily assault on his body. A cyclone of hatred swirled inside his head.

He poked his thumb onto the tip of the knife. Drops of blood bubbled and trickled down his thumb. A smile creased his face. His eyes grew dark as visions of his future danced across his brain. *With his own knife,* he thought.

Lightning cracked through the darkened sky, brightening the room. His father still snoring, drool trickling across his cheek. Evan edged closer and chanted in his head *one monster at a time, one monster at a time.* In front of his father, he leaned in just far enough and ran the blade centimeters above the skin of his father's throat, a practice run.

He slit his father's throat, short and quick with a steady hand. His father opened his eyes for a brief second while choking on his own blood. It coursed from his throat and drenched his clothes, covering the recliner. Evan's lips curled into a sneer, his eyes glowed from the rush of watching the big man gurgle.

Evan went into his brother's room and slit his throat as savagely as he had his father's. Again, the blood flowed and soaked into the bed surrounding him. Horror filled his brother's eyes for a few seconds. "Eva... Evan... hel... " The boy reached for Evan who took a step backwards. He refused to do anything for the boy whom he loved and hated. He adored the way he followed him everywhere as if he was an idol, yet mommy never *touched him* in the bathtub. *Why? Why only me?* The storm inside Evan eased with every kill, the winds lessening as the rain-blood loosed around him, and the pressure inside his broken soul released. *You never knew suffering...*

Unable to stop the release he went into his sister's room, but she wasn't in her crib. His black eyes scanned the room looking for her tiny presence. He'd come back for her. She wasn't his main concern. He ached to give the *monster* in his family a piece of what she gave him. He wanted to share the fear and horror he endured every day - *one good turn deserves another.*

Evan lingered in the hallway outside his parents' room observing his mother sleep, remembering the horrible details of her actions. The woman who made his baths a nightmare. Her fingers fondling his male part, *stroking, licking*, making it do things he didn't want. That was only the beginning before she made him go to bed with her where she did things his brain wanted to black out. She didn't even have to sneak because daddy was always drunk! The rage inside him boiled to the surface, and he ran towards her.

Across the street, Mrs. Zander woke with a start, bolting upwards from the emergency beep originating from the TV. She placed her hand over her chest until her breathing returned to normal. She searched the couch for the remote, unable to find it she stood and crept towards the TV. As she pressed the off button, a bolt of lightning shot from the sky illuminating the house across the street. The image from their living room locked into her mind. Mr. O'Conner lying in his recliner, covered in blood.

She did a double take but, in the darkness, saw nothing. Her conscience played at her as she contemplated whether the scene was real or her mind playing tricks. Against her better judgment, especially since she didn't like the man. She never saw him without his flask and treated the oldest son, Evan, horribly - whipping him with his belt, screaming at him *piece of shit bastard!* Even if he was dead she had a moral obligation.

Mrs. Zander grabbed hold of her husband's heavy duty metal flashlight, slipped on her raincoat and boots then headed across the street. The rain pelted hard against her gear. She sloshed through the front lawn. When she stood close enough to the window, she shined the beam of light towards it and gasped. Her eyes in disbelief at the bloody sight before her. Frozen in place, she couldn't move. Every part of her screamed *run, run, run*. She felt stuck inside a horrible dream where her voice disappeared and her body refused to move.

In an instant, Evan ran into his mother's room and stopped when he reached the bed. Visions of her taking his hand and placing it inside her area. The area he didn't want to see or touch. He wrapped his hands around his head and doubled over as if in pain. In a sudden movement, he lifted his head, seeing nothing but blackness and hate, without hesitation he slid the heavy knife across her throat, again and again, then screamed. If she was still alive he never knew it.

A loud primordial shriek startled Mrs. Zander, her body unfroze and she ran, stumbling on the mushy ground, falling to her hands and knees. She crawled to the street, stood and ran to her house, throwing the door open in panic. She didn't stop running until she reached her bed and fell onto her husband. "Fra… Fra… across… the…"

He sat up, perplexed at his wife and her disheveled appearance. "Honey, what?"

"Dead, across street, Mr. O... O'Conner, police. Call."

"Mr. O'Conner is dead?"

She nodded her head yes. Mr. Zander had seen his wife upset but never like she was at the moment. He knew his wife of sixteen years had witnessed something horrible. He picked up his cell phone and dialed 9-1-1.

The pressure inside Evan was lessening. He closed his eyes, allowing the release to consume him, then with the impulsivity of a young boy, waited no longer. He needed to rid himself of her and transfer the years of torture she'd passed to him back to her.

With both hands and no patience he chucked the knife, paying no attention to where it landed, took off his pants, tossing them across the room. Inhaling in the metallic smell of her blood, he climbed on top of her, shouting, "Is this what you want? I *loove* you!" Her blank eyes stared back at him. Tears overwhelmed him as he buried himself into her corpse.

Evan's little sister huddled with her blanket underneath the dresser in her room.

Sirens blared from all around and the police trooped the suburban house. They pulled Evan off his mother as he screamed, "How does it feel? Are you enjoying this? Isn't it always what you wanted?" As the police removed Evan's body off his mother, he struggled and bucked against them. His release so good, too good. He needed more - hungered for it! They forced him inside the awaiting police car, rain pelting the windows and dripping from every orifice of his body, and carted him off for psychological evaluation, then to the county child mental facility.

The police coaxed his sister out from under her dresser and took her to Child Protective Services.

Evan's mind grew furious at his sloppiness and noise which no doubt alerted the neighbors. The gale force squalls inside him came and went, they weren't steady - a partial release. Next time he'd be more careful. Next time he'd take them out the way he'd planned.

"Well ain't that Somethin'"

June 30th 1992

enry's Bar and Grill flashed in orange neon lights. Pickup trucks and small cars filled the parking lot. The air inside the bar was laden with cigarette and cigar smoke. Evan sat alone at the end of the half-horseshoe bar. His untamable blond ringlets stood at attention, his expression a solid poker face - normal for him.

Female servers pounced about serving drinks while the bartenders stayed busy making them and chatting with the customers. A cute young woman took a seat beside Evan. Her ebony skin accentuated by her deep brown eyes and a figure shaped like an hourglass with taut legs and stomach. Evan had no interest in the bouncy young woman and thought her annoying.

His mind replayed the night he slaughtered his family and the pent up rage he felt spending a decade in Windy Oaks. He dwelled on the childish mistakes he made. *From now on I will be quick, in and out.*

His mother mocked him: *Baby, come, let me love you only the way I can.* He tried as always to drive her out of his head. To erase her from existence. He battled with his subconscious as his mother slowly forced herself on the young woman beside him. His inner beast raged to break after years of dormancy.

He focused his energy on his drink, not willing to give in to stupidity. Drink after drink, his defenses grew weaker until he no longer saw any of the young lady beside him, but his mother. "Baby, I've waited so patiently for you. I want you," said his mother as the young woman beside him or at least that is what his corrupt mind heard her say. Really, she said, "Do you have a light?" as she lifted a cigarette to her mouth.

The young woman swam back into focus. "I asked, do you have a light?"

"No, I don't smoke." A pile of matchbooks lay on the bar to his right. He grabbed a book and lit a match, holding the flame to the end of her cigarette.

"Good looking and a gentleman. Not often both come in one package." She flirted. "I'm Gala." She held out her hand for him to shake.

Evan knew how to be pleasant, even charming. Ten years at Windy Oaks had taught him. He also knew better than to give his real name. "Kevin," he replied, meeting her hand with his and giving a gentle shake.

Gala's lips curled into a smile and a slight dimple graced her left cheek. "So Kevin, you don't look like a trucker. You're too young and…" She stumbled over the words, not wanting to sound immature or stupid. She liked his blond curls and even though he wasn't particularly handsome, she found something dark and tempting in him. "Educated."

C⋆C⋆C⋆C⋆C

Their conversation continued and Gala couldn't help but enjoy his polite but unmistakably mysterious presence. To match his fake name he fed her a fake story she believed. "A college man. What's next?"

"I start my bachelor's degree this fall."

She did herself good and decided he was a keeper. He'd be able to take care of her unlike her father who hadn't held a steady job in several years. Gala tilted her head in an alluring pose, hoping to trap his attention. "So… are you on break?"

His eyes drifted forwards to the TV behind the bar. *Tropical Storm Chloe gained stamina although meteorologists still predict it to make landfall south of the islands.* Evan predicted it would stall, gain strength and plow straight into the islands. Predicting hurricanes became a hobby of his during his stay at Windy Oaks. "I have family owns a house on one of the islands." *They just don't know they're family yet.*

17

The Calm Before the Storm: Evan's Sins

Gala spied the night's cover band come in and set up the stage. There was no time to waste, she needed to work her magic quick before the music became too loud for her to converse with Kevin anymore.

C*C*C*C*C*

All the while Evan fought against envisioning Gala as his mom. She nagged and pleaded with him to take her on the spot with everyone watching. She enticed him with her gentle stroke, which was in truth his hand in his pocket, and coaxing voice. His mother's persistence drove him wild. He thought to stop her drabble. The alcohol, mixed with his mother's annoying presence, swelled inside him and he needed to finish what he started so long ago, tonight!

The band started their set with the classic Don McLean song *American Pie* as she and Evan headed out the door. Gala was giddy and loaded with heat and desire. She wanted this strange college boy, desired to show him what a gem in the sack she was so he craved no one else. She yearned for a man to take care of her. Unable to take her eyes off the huge bulge in his pants, she led him to her car. Liquid turn-on ran down the side of her leg as proof she wanted him.

In her drunkenness, she stumbled to her car, opened the back door and plummeted forward into the seat. Her skirt fell over her backside revealing her round ass with a thin thong slid between her cheeks. He unzipped his pants and pulled out his awaiting hardness, ripped her thong off, tossing it on the floor of her car and pounded into her awaiting rear. An observer would have seen Evan's five-foot-four stocky frame, fully clothed ass moving in quick thrusts from the doorway of the car. Not an unusual sight for the bar's parking lot.

He wrapped one arm around her waist as he pressed and thrust into her, with the other he felt in his back pocket for the blade he purchased earlier in the day. Finding its tough, ivory handle and grasping it firmly he pressed the button to release the steel sharpness he yearned to run across his mother's throat once more. His release was coming soon. His tension subsiding. The memory of her blood rushing in pools on the bed beside them as he gave back the pain and fear she gave him. As his thoughts drifted to the moment of his mother's death he became more and more turned on. He grabbed Gala's hair and pulled her head upward. The blade edging near his mother's - Gala's - throat. His excitement building with each hard stroke inside her. His release beckoning him to slide the blade. Now!

The Calm Before the Storm: Evan's Sins

As Gala fell into the car face first she attempted to turn herself around, but found herself unable as a thick arm wrapped around her waist and his trunk plowed into her warm, wet, awaiting vagina. Only she no longer wanted this rough man who, moments ago, she considered as sweet, polite and a gentleman. She tried to scream, "Stop, No!" Her voice muffled in the fabric of the seat. She kicked to free herself from his clutch, but his strong grasp paralyzed her. Tears filled her eyes and poured down her cheeks. She didn't want it like this. Suddenly his hand let go of her waist and pulled her up by the hair. Something cold pressed against her neck and she knew her life was ending.

Release Gone Awry

His release, only seconds from erupting inside of Gala, wouldn't come. The conditions weren't right. He needed his father, brother, even his skittish little sister, the one who had got away. No! They were absent. He flipped the blade back into the handle and used it to give the girl a quick, firm whack on the head.

Without buttoning his pants, his shirt dangling over the huge rock between his legs, he walked back to his motel room in excruciating pain. His balls pleaded for discharge. He closed the door behind him, rested his back against it as his hands sought to relieve the pressure, stroking hard and furious.

☾ ☾ ☾ ☾ ☾

Gala awoke to a blistering headache and a huge knot on the back of her head. Dried blood caked between her legs. Sharp pains forced their way from her vaginal area to her chest in waves. Hanging her head over the side of the seat, vomit spewed from her mouth in unforgiving torrents, covering her purse, thong and the floorboard of her car until dry heaves consumed her. Every inch of her body ached with pain - her soul severed.

A single thought raced through her mind. *I want to go home.* She fumbled through the thick vomit until she found the keys in her purse. Tears rolled down her cheeks as the entire scene played over and over in her mind. Slowly, using every bit of her strength, she lifted her body upwards and fell back against the seat. *He's gone. I'm alive.*

With each deep breath her mind swam into focus. Her eyes scanned the empty parking lot, surveying the darkness surrounding her. With a burst of energy she locked her doors. With every move she made, the pain from her head shot down through her body, rendering it immobile. *He might come back.* She knew she needed to find the strength to leave before he did, or next time he'd kill her for sure.

Gala's fear of her attacker kept her from opening the door. *He might be waiting. He might be right outside the car. With the doors locked, he can't get inside.* She threw her keys into the driver's seat. Gathering her energy, she forced her legs between the front seats. Straddling the hump, she grasped both seats and heaved her body forward. She stopped to regain her energy, leaned her pounding head against the driver's seat headrest and scanned the parking lot again. She saw more perched on the hump. The darkness around her, lighter than moments earlier, surrounded the bare parking lot. *Morning, it's almost dawn.*

Her slide-collapse into the driver's seat brought waves of pain bolting through her abdomen, followed by a shrill scream. Tears from pain and fear poured from her eyes as she started her car and flew out of the bare parking lot. She wiped her eyes with the back of her hand, attempting to see the road in front of her through the cracked windshield.

Gala cruised the winding country road, paying no mind to the road itself. An armadillo crossed her path, the tires of her car thumped over the hard shell causing her car to swerve. She jumped and lost control of the vehicle. The steering wheel spun in circles as if possessed causing the car to careen into a large ditch. Her body jolted forwards as the front end smashed into a wall of dirt. For the second time in a few hours her life flashed before her eyes and she knew she would not walk away. Her head continued forward, blasting through the windshield, glass shattering. Her world went black.

Beast of Burden

"Hello," said Detective Alice Burkhalder, waking from the dream arms of a muscled, dark haired hunk.

"Burkhalder, Chloe's stalling in the ocean, upgraded to Cat 2 status. No sayin' where it's headin'. We got a ton of tourists we need to get off the island. I need you workin' crowd control and directin' traffic."

She sighed as her dream man vanished. "Yes, sir, sheriff." She nodded her head. "I know the drill, sir. Got it covered." Burkhalder heaved her body from her inviting bed and headed towards the shower.

☾ ☾ ☾ ☾ ☾

Evan awoke to a stream of light shining through the small sliver where the curtains didn't meet. His bladder about to burst. On his way to the restroom, he passed the TV, snarling over his indiscretion from the previous night. Remembering, he became furious with himself for his loss of control. His bladder wouldn't allow him to dwell on that at the moment. He barely made it to the toilet in time and was sure he'd leave a stream across the carpet. His precious DNA left behind in this forsaken roach motel.

When the stream finally subsided, he noticed a pounding in his head, and his throat begged for water. Turning on the sink, he lapped the water stemming from the faucet knowing it carried multitudes of bacteria swimming into his body. The thought sickened him but his thirst won control.

Not twenty-one yet, he took advantage of his freedom. His curiosity attracted him to the seedy bar where his mother slipped into his thoughts. He scrubbed at the dried puddle on the TV and vowed to never again partake in alcoholic beverages. They clouded his mind and diminished his control.

Evan, get a grip. It's this freedom thing, but you have to get hold of yourself. Practice self-control, isn't that what you learned? Isn't that what got you out? Self-control, and the damn medicine! He avoided his medicine because he wanted to live with clarity and richness of emotion, not the fuzziness the medicine created. His glorious moment of reckoning would soon happen and he didn't want his mind fuzzy.

He allowed the hot water of the shower to cover his body, washing away his sin. He stepped out and wiped the mist from the mirror with a towel, his blue eyes stared back at him. One with a yellow ring around its iris, the other with an amber ring. Dark blond tangles covered his head, springing as he ran his fingers through them. *The hair, mommy's hair. Elfred was lucky he didn't have mommy's hair. Mommy always liked Elfred more. She never touched him. She saved it all for me. At first, it was every once in a while, then every day, several times a day. She touched it and it did things, an innate response. She took it anytime she desired. Her sickness controlled her. Damnit! Get a grip!* His hair needed to go. All of it. He wanted no reminders of his mother or the chance of leaving behind evidence.

Not wanting the burden of luggage, he brought none. With a grunt of disgust he put on his dirty clothes.

He left his room to grab breakfast, so he'd have the energy to fulfill his plans. Two suitcases sitting close to a car on the opposite side of the parking lot caught his attention. He scanned the parking lot, not a person in sight, and opened one of the suitcases. Evan rustled inside until he found what he needed - fresh pants and a shirt.

Bacon, coffee, and pancakes permeated the air from the Flaming Inn's restaurant. He went inside and sat the Formica bar, drank several cups of orange juice with two eggs sunny side up and a rare steak. He buried the teeth of his fork into yoke then squashed it, watching it flow across the plate like blood.

Chloe has sustained wind speeds of 110 mph. The pressure in the center is dropping rapidly. Her

path uncertain as she spins 100 miles off shore...
The TV droned on with evacuation information. Evan finished his breakfast, paid his tab and headed outside into the bright sunlight. A full day of work ahead of him to prepare for the night's events.

He walked past the spot Gala's car occupied and noticed its absence, shrugged his shoulders and continued towards the beach, looking for a store. A trail of cars leaving the area packed every gas station. A smug smile crossed his face.

The large sign of the Everything Mart caught his eye. He purchased a set of clippers for his hair and a toothbrush, toothpaste, and sleeping pills. A row of condoms, everything from ribbed to glow-in-the-dark, hovered above his head. Without hesitating he grabbed a box, style didn't matter to him. Last on his list was a duffle bag. The idea was for him to blend in so he could assert himself onto an unsuspecting family. By the looks of it, there wouldn't be too many families left. His urges strengthening, almost any family would do.

He left the Everything Mart and walked to the closest gas station. Slipping into the men's room, he took out his clippers and shaved his head bald. His one trait like his mother's gone, he turned his head side to side in front of the mirror and admired his new look. He could focus on his work to make mommy disappear forever.

"You're Headin' the Wrong Way"

"**M**orning, Alice," said Deputy Jackson Martin to Burkhalder as he handed her a much needed cup of coffee.

"Black the way ya like."

Burkhalder's mind reminisced on the mornings she awoke in his bed, fresh coffee brewing in the kitchen. "You're a life saver Jax." He didn't allow anyone but her to call him Jax. It was her nickname for him since they met in the third grade.

He loved how the morning light bounced off the red highlights in her auburn hair. "You reckon Tate's stayin' on the island?"

"Jim wouldn't have it any other way. He built a special reinforced closet he keeps stocked with supplies. Thinkin' we should pay him a visit later." Burkhalder, Jim, and Jax grew up together. It was only in the past few months Jax and Alice had started seeing each other.

Through the bumper to bumper cars sunlight glinted off a young man's head from across the street from where Alice and Jax were having their discussion, catching Jax's eye. "What's that kid doin'? We need people off this island not walkin' towards it."

"You stay, I'll take care of it. See you later. What do say to a romantic night at a hurricane shelter?" Joked Burkhalder.

"You got it babe, after we visit Jim."

Burkhalder winked and headed across the street, placing her hand out for cars to let her through.

Evan noted the carrot top cop heading his direction. He ignored her, keeping a steady pace. Neither she nor anyone else would stop his mission.

"Young man!" Evan heard her call. He wanted to continue ignoring her but knew it best to treat her with respect - avoid confrontation. *Control.* Evan halted his pace. "Yes, ma'am." *She's no more than a few years older than me. Where does she get off calling me young man?*

"Help me out. We need you heading off the island not towards it. There's a hurricane headin' our way."

He looked at the peaceful sky above him. "Certainly doesn't appear that way."

A creeping blackness took over his pale blue eyes, causing Burkhalder to look away and avoid being sucked into the dark abyss. She looked back and his normal color returned. *Get hold of yourself. It's your imagination.* "The calm before the storm. Never looks like a hurricane until it hits. These islands get mighty dangerous, so I suggest you head back towards the mainland or to the shelter." She scribbled the address in her cop issue notepad and handed it to him. "Take a right at the light then walk three blocks. Shelter's on the left." He hated their accents and considered Billows Hollow residents as nothing more than undereducated redneck hicks.

Evan resisted the urge to knock her in the head. Instead, he smiled. "Thank you. I guess I'll be headin' that way." He felt her eyes on his back so he followed her directions and made the right, continued on for a block soaking in the dense vegetation then veered through the home-lined streets. Nothing would stop his mission.

Something about the young man, more than his black-pit eyes, didn't sit well with Burkhalder although she couldn't put her finger on it. She made a note to check with the shelter later.

The Tates

Jim Tate piled up the outdoor furniture and carried it to the shed. His deep brown tangles matted and drenched from sweat. His raven-haired wife's liquid blue eyes watched her husband's tanned muscular build work in the morning sun. The sun she knew would soon be replaced by swirling clouds and gale force winds.

"Mommy, can I go outside and help daddy?"

"Evie, how about you help mommy?"

"I'm not a little boy. If Ely can help how come I can't?" He stomped his feet. "I want to help daddy." Lilly looked into her son's eyes. At seven years of age he thought he was a man.

She kneeled and leveled her eyes with his, handing him a stack of plates. "Setting the table will help daddy. He's going to be hungry when he comes inside."

"O... K..." Hesitant, Evie set the plates on the table and silverware beside each plate. When he finished he scrambled to the refrigerator, opened the door, grabbed two bottles of chilly water, and ran towards the front door. "Bringing daddy and Ely water!"

Lilly shook her head, closed the refrigerator door, then watched her youngest son, brown curls flying and bouncy as he ran, hand his father and brother a bottle of water. She read Jim's lips deciphering his words. "Thank you, Evie!" He patted his head and handed him a bucket of beach toys. Jim in the lead, the boys in tow, strutted towards the shed, arms loaded with the last of their outdoor furniture.

Lilly smiled and admired her two year old daughter, Eilida. Her brown curls tied up in a *Pebbles* bow. "Don't grow up too quick, sweetie. Mommy's little girl." Eilida smiled, melting Lilly's heart.

Eilida dropped the last of her toys on the floor. "Oopsie!"

"Oopsie!" Mimicked Lilly, laughing at her daughter's uh-oh expression and widened eyes. She unlatched the highchair and picked up her daughter. "Let's see what daddy and the boys are doing."

"OK, Mommy."

☾ ☾ ☾ ☾ ☾

Telltale hair grass and beach grass jutted upwards from the sandy coastline. Thanks to the meddling Carrot Top Cop he made it to the island quicker than if he'd stayed on the main road. Most of the homes were vacant, so he traipsed through open yards. The sunny sky still gave no sign of Hurricane Chloe's approach. He took his shoes off, rolled the bottoms of his pants up and stepped onto the sandy coast. The calm, peaceful water told the same lie as the sky.

Every house looked the same to him. They all belonged to over-privileged assholes who evacuated at the first hint of a "hurricane". The perfect circumstances for him, he didn't need people around, just one family. The island looked like a ghost town. Huge homes loomed to his left and the coastline to his right.

He followed the curvy coastline looking for signs of life. The sound of hammering caught his attention. At first he wasn't sure if it was phantom sounds his mind conjured or real. The closer he got to the sound he realized it was real. Mingled between hammering he heard voices, one of them sounded like Carrot Top Cop. He stood still, craned his neck and listened. Two men and a woman. Evan strolled towards the voices and stood stock still as Carrot Top's windblown hair shadowed his view of the men.

"Anybody thirsty?" The sound emanated from nowhere. A woman with raven black hair tied into a pony tail walked into Evan's view. To stay hidden, he climbed the steps of a vacant two-story home and sat on the wooden porch he imagined would be all but gone by night's end. The slats of the porch afforded him a view of the group and the wind carried their voices in his direction. Both cops from earlier and a young couple.

"Thanks, honey." Lilly gave her husband a kiss as he grabbed a glass filled with lemonade off the tray.

"Reckon that was the last one," said Jax, lowering the hammer in his hand.

"Jackson, Alice, come inside, sit a spell."

"Jim, we ain't got time. Just wantin' to make sure you, Lilly, and the kids were ready. See if you needed 'nythin'. Try and change your mind. Plenty of room at the shelter."

Burkhalder snapped her fingers and looked towards Jax. "You reminded me. I need to check on that kid we saw earlier. It'll have ta wait, we need to secure the area." The breeze picked up and clouds swam past them. "Be startin' soon," said Burkhalder, peering towards the sky, shading her eyes with her hand.

Two little brown-haired boys chased each other across the sandy beach tossing a football. It landed near the tall, blond cop they called Jackson. He picked up the ball, ran a few yards then hocked it into the air. Both boys ran after it. *Like dogs playing fetch. Two boys - lucky day.*

34

Evan's mother's face appeared on the dark-haired woman as she mouthed to Evan *I love you.* She reached her hand towards him. *I hate you, you rancid bitch!* The dark-haired woman turned back to herself and his mother disappeared. Not sure if he yelled aloud or to himself, he peered through the slats. The group hugged and said their goodbyes. If he shouted out loud nobody noticed.

Evan rested his hands on the wooden flanks in front of him. A loose board bobbled beneath his palm. He pried it upward and reached beneath - a key. Amazed at his unbelievable dumb luck he tried the key in the door. *What dumb-asses.* He marched right into their house and rummaged through their mail piled on a sleek black table beside the door. Every letter addressed to Robert and/or Margaret Plum - he noted their names. He took in the house decorated in a modern theme of high-end black and white furniture. Recessed ceiling lights flicked on and off automatically as he walked into and out of each room. A large, custom designed shower in the upstairs master bedroom caught his attention. A slew of ideas coursed through his head.

He cracked the front door and peered outside. The cops had left. Now was his chance. He closed the door and went out the back, the way he came in, and strolled by the dark-haired family's house. The father and brothers continued to toss the football. It rolled beside Evan's feet. He picked it up and handed it to the littlest boy.

With big blue eyes, the boy looked up at him. "Thanks!" Then he ran to his brother's side.

The father walked towards Evan and extended his hand. "Name's Jim, didn't know anyone else stayed on the island."

Evan, remembering the manners and appropriate behavior he learned at Windy Oaks, shook Jim's hand. Using his real name was out of the question and so was the name Kevin. *The blasted girl may show up again.* "Nyle, nice to meet ya." He hated the southern redneck talk but knew they'd be more welcoming if he used it. He'd almost considered using the name *Bubba* but figured the man might take that as mocking.

"Nyle, you stayin' on the island?"

"Lookin' after my uncle's house. He's payin' me good to keep it up."

"Who's your uncle?"

Nosy bastard aren't you? Evan expected that question and hoped Jim and the Plums weren't real good friends. "Robert Plum."

"The Plums. They just bought that place. Had some remodelin' done."

"It's right nice inside. More luxury than I got at home." Evan drew up his face on one side as he mouthed the words. "What do you mak-a this storm?" The sun beat hot and steady on the men as they talked.

"We go through this every couple-few years. Storm's s'posed to head south. Got a reinforced room, if it gets bad enough you're welcome to join us."

Evan felt the sweat beading on his forehead and bubbling on his chest and legs. "Appreciate the offer. I'll keep it in mind, Jim." The football rolled to Evan's feet.

Hidey Hole

Evan sauntered through the Plums' house, and searched the bedrooms for a fresh pair of pants and shirt. They were void of clothing except the master bedroom which contained *his* and *hers* closets filled with clothes. He figured it was a summer home for a rich, over-privileged couple. Scads of polo shirts and jeans hung in *his* closet, each hanger spaced with an approximate inch and a half width from the next. The tedious nature of the owner amused Evan as something he needed to mimic. *Control, this man is controlled.* He pulled a pair of ironed jeans and a polo off their hangers. *Who irons jeans?* The 38 waist would fit perfect but the inseam was far too long. He'd have to roll them to his ankles. They'd work.

Large square tiles spread across the shower equipped with overhead and side sprayers. He turned them on and slipped inside the oversized shower. A woman's razor and shave cream sat on a shelf. Loofahs and body wash hung on a shower caddy. After washing, he shaved every inch of his body hair. *Best I don't leave evidence.*

Cleaned and fresh, he gathered his dirty clothes, unsure what to do with them. He considered cremating them in the fireplace but smoke would alert the dark-haired family. *His family.* In the end he stuffed them into a trash bag, tied it shut, and pushed them to the bottom of his duffle bag.

Most of the rooms contained furniture and few personal items confirming his *summer home* suspicion. Evan found interest in the kitchen pantry. The room contained a large amount of canned and boxed food, along with bottled water and plenty of room for a comfy chair and radio. The comfy chair he found in the living room and hauled it into the pantry. He reclined it with plenty of room and food within an arm's reach. In the hall closet he found a couple feather pillows and a battery operated TV with an antenna. It wasn't cable but would do. The food-emptied refrigerator contained a stash of batteries of every size. He carried them to the pantry and placed the TV on a shelf.

In the kitchen he fumbled through the cabinets and fixed himself a snack of crackers and processed squeezable cheese. He hated the residents for cleaning the fresh food out of the fridge and leaving him with food that could be put into a time capsule and dug up 100 years later still as fresh as the day they bought it. He parked his butt on a plush couch and clicked on the TV.

C·C·C·C·C

Deputies Martin and Burkhalder did a sweep of the area in their separate patrol cars. He checked along the coastline, weaved in and out of the housing developments. She drove towards the mainland. Her mind focused on Jim and his family. He was a stubborn man. She'd made him promise to get his family into the reinforced room at first sight of strong winds. It wasn't just the winds. The storm surge would be ridiculous. The tide higher than usual already, the water crept close to the road. She knew he'd do anything for Lilly and the kids. They'd be OK. Malice stirred in her gut like snakes in a pit. He'd never once, even as a kid, backed away from a storm. A smile swept across Burkhalder's face as she remembered how stubborn Jim's father was. *He got the stubborn gene honestly.*

Black swirling clouds snaked across the sky moving quick. She flipped the headlights switch. Their reflection glinted off something in the ditch, blinding her. When she regained her vision, she pulled the patrol car over to investigate. As she approached the vehicle, her mouth gaped and she jumped into the ditch, water splashing against her calves.

A car had gone head first. The hood a squashed mess with somebody behind the wheel. Burkhalder trudged through the water and grabbed the door handle but it wouldn't budge. She ran to her trunk and grabbed the jimmy, prying the door open. A few inches of water poured into the front of the car, washing over the girl's feet. Her head embedded in the windshield, dried blood matted her hair and trailed across her forehead and cheek. *Oh my God, Gala!* She'd know her face anywhere. Billows Hollow was a small island town, everyone knew everyone. She pressed two fingers against her neck, checking for a pulse - faint but present. Burkhalder hurried to her car and radioed dispatch.

"I need an ambulance on the mainland road right now! Gala's had a bad accident, her pulse is faint. She's fading. The ditch is filling fast with water."

"Bobby and James are on the way. Let's pray they can get her squared away before the storm really hits. Clouds are startin' to swirl."

"MaddyJo, Bobby and James are the best. If anyone can help her they can."

"I know, I'm thinkin' the worst. Last storm that hit, the hospital lost power, and we lost Old Ray. Remember, he fell off the ladder boardin' up his house?"

"I remember hon, but that won't be Gala's fate. Heck if she can live with her hard ass, lazy father all these years she can survive a car crash."

"You take care a-her. They'll be there in a jiff."

Click... the radio went dead. She walked to Gala's car. The dark swirling clouds gave way to the first bands of rain. She took the girl's hand in hers. The only thoughts running through Burkhalder's head were for the well-being of the young lady lying motionless in her car.

Well Hot Diggety' Slap Me With a Shovel

Evan scanned the channels searching for news about his beloved Hurricane Chloe. The storm that'd release him from his mother's curse. *The mainland road is nearly impassable. Gale force gusts expected within the hour.* The weather forecaster predicted. *The time is here.*

Evan lurched from the couch, took several sleeping pills and a condom out of his bag. Crunching the pills into tiny pieces he wrapped them in a sandwich bag and jammed them into his pocket. Then slid his hand into the duffle bag's inner pocket and slipped his knife out. He forced it under the rim of his pants, nuzzled between Robert Plum's boxer shorts and his butt cheeks. The roads impassable, he knew the nice family would help him. Fast moving black clouds whirled above his head and the tide rushed at his feet.

☾·☾·☾·☾·☾

Water reached Burkhalder's knees by the time the paramedics arrived. She stepped aside to give them room.

"Alice," said Bobby as he walked towards her.

"Found her like this. The water's movin' in quick."

"No time ta waste, more rain bands be comin' soon. We gotta move her now. James ya got that stretcher ready?"

James hauled the stretcher alongside the road. Bobby jumped into the ditch. He checked Gala's pulse. Water rushed past his waist. James jumped in beside him and together they glided Gala's body out of the vehicle. As they climbed the slope, their boots sank into the muddy banks. They coordinated their steps together, masses of muddy water rushed past them. Burkhalder stood on the roadside, cringing with each step they took, praying they all made it up the bank. The second band of rains circled through, pelting Gala's rescuers. "Keep movin' James, gotta get her to the stretcher."

"I can't see," hollered James as he attempted to blink the water out of his eyes.

"One step at a time, almost there."

Burkhalder sighed relief when the threesome reached the bank. Bobby and James laid Gala's body on the stretcher and performed the necessary procedures to secure and load her into the ambulance. The winds and rain blowing and beating against their bodies, threatening to whip them into the air.

She looked on, her fiery hair plastered against her face as the water reached near the top of the ditch, any higher it would spill onto the road. The pressure of the water pushed against the car, dislodging and dragging it.

James closed the back doors of the ambulance. Bobby stepped into the driver's seat. Alice walked towards him. He closed the door and rested his elbow on the window frame. "She's not stable, pulse is real weak. She's lost a lotta blood." Bobby shook his head.

"Right behind ya Bobby," Burkhalder called as she hurried to her patrol car and slammed the door shut. She dialed Jax and put her cell on speaker.

"Hey babe, you ready for our hot date at the shelter?"

The words flew from her mouth. "Gala's been in a bad wreck. I pray she makes it. They're takin' her to the hospital now."

"You follow. I'll meet ya there." His concern for the young girl matched hers.

The ambulance sped off with Burkhalder in pursuit. Within minutes it came to a stop alongside the E.R. They pulled the stretcher out of the back and rushed her inside the hospital, Burkhalder in tow. Jax was already inside waiting for her. She collapsed into his arms. He folded them around her. At six feet, she stood as tall as him.

"She's a fighter," he reassured her.

"When will this day end?" She spoke into his shoulder, muffling her words.

"Look at me." She looked into his amber eyes. "You found her. She has a chance. If she hadn't been…"

"I don't want to think about that. How many people have been across that road today? How many?!" Swells of worry washed over her eyes.

"Nobody was lookin'. They jus' wantin' to git outta town."

"Called her dad. No answer. Can't get there now unless I row." She slumped into a plastic waiting room chair - defeated.

"You can't do anathin' 'bout that." Jax assured her. She took everything to heart. He hoped she'd never lose that part of her.

Burkhalder sighed and leaned her head on Jax's shoulder. "We wait it out." The sturdy walls of the E.R. silenced most of the howling winds. She bolted her head upright. "Her doors were locked! Why would she lock them? She was alone."

"What are you sayin'?" Jax squinted his right eye while lifting his left eyebrow.

"I had to jimmy the door open."

"She'd been there for a while, right? Maybe it was late. She's bein' careful."

"When is Gala ever careful? If she ever had a decent idea, it'd die a loneliness."

Jax cracked a smile. People knew Gala for her physical assets not her intellect. "She gits it honest. Could be one of those snakes in the grass she's always tryin' to pick up."

"Would one of those snakes in the grass try and harm her?" Burkhalder's brain lit up like a southern lawn on Christmas Day. Could be one of those scum suckers chased her down.

"Hon, you gotta change those wet clothes. Sure they have a pair scrubs you can put on."

Her mind half heard Jax's comment. "You take care a that. I'm goin' find a doc." Jax knew her better than anyone alive and recognized she didn't believe Gala's accident was an accident. When it came to investigating crimes, she reminded him of a boa constrictor, sinking her teeth in a death grip on her prey and constricting. She made sure the perps got locked behind bars.

Southern Hospitality

Evan stood on the beach facing the Tates' house. Heavy winds rushed against his bulky frame. He turned to face the ocean, taking in Chloe's magnificence. Her powerful gusts dared to lay him flat. Water sprayed across his body.

He felt a hand against his back. "What are you doin' out here? This storm is comin' in strong."

Evan looked at the dark-haired man the blond cop called Jim. "These winds beatin' against the house and all. Thought I'd take you up on yer offer, gettin' scary."

Jim wasn't sure what to think. He couldn't imagine anyone dumb enough to wander the beach during a hurricane. "Why don't you come inside?" he shouted through the blustering winds.

"Thank ya, sir," said Evan as he followed Jim.

Once inside, a squall blew through, assaulting the house with rain. Jim bolted the door behind them. Evan followed Jim from the entryway into a large room. A few shelves with shells and other knickknacks hung beside an entertainment center to his right. Several family photos clung to the other walls. A hallway was straight across from him and an archway leading to another room stood to his right.

"You never been through one a these have ya?"

"No, sir."

"Like I said, we got plenty a room."

Ely and Evie ran to their daddy. "Who's he?" asked Evie.

Jim picked up his son. "His name is Nyle."

"Hi Nyle," said Evie, unsure of the man. "I wanna play with Ely."

"Fine boys you got," Evan said as Evie ran to his brother's side. *Can't wait till you're all asleep.*

"Take a seat. You thirsty? My wife makes the best homemade lemonade."

"That'd be great."

"Boys why don't you ask mommy to bring us five glasses of lemonade?" Evie narrowed his eyes at the stranger then skipped to the kitchen with his brother.

"Mom, Dad found someone outside…"

"I don't like him," piped Evie.

Lilly laughed inwardly at her youngest son. He always spoke his mind. "Evie, that's rude. Our house is sturdy as it gets. He probably didn't realize how bad storms get around here." She wasn't sure she believed her own words. *Who would comb the beach during a hurricane?*

49

The Calm Before the Storm: Evan's Sins

The boys carried the drinks to the living room. Ely handed one to the stranger. Eilida sobbed from her crib. Hearing her whimper, Lilly went to her daughter and lifted her up, her stuffed monkey dangling from Eilida's tiny hand. Eilida buried her head into her mom's comforting shoulder. It would be a long night, Eilida hated storms and seldom slept through them. With Eilida on her hip, Lilly joined her family in the living room. The weatherman droned on about the storm. *Rain bands now approaching Billows Hollow - expected to head further south… Chloe updated to Category 3.*

"Mighty bad storm out there, glad it's a headin' south," said Evan. Eilida lifted her head off her mother's shoulder, hearing the stranger's voice. She looked at him and screamed loud enough to break a mirror. In his eyes she saw deep pits of blackness, an empty void and a black ring encircling him. Waves of terror needled up the little girl's spine.

What a pleasant surprise, a daughter too. This family is perfect. Evan admired the little girl's brown ringlets and pudgy round face and fingers. Visions of his sister swam into view. *Emily, the one that got away… Stop, stop! Eilida carries around a stupid looking monkey just as Emily always drug around her smelly blanket. Get in control!* He pushed down the beast inside, but not for long.

50

Unable to ignore her daughter's scream of horror. Lilly apologized, "I'm sorry, she just woke from her nap. She hates storms."

"I got her babe." Jim took his daughter in his arms. She buried her head and monkey, Sandy, into his chest unwilling to peek at the stranger. A heavy wind gust pelted the house. The lights flickered then went out. The boards across the windows let in no light. Inside the house was black as a midnight cat. In the darkness, Eilida's fear increased and she clung to her father, grasping his arms as tight as possible.

Using the darkness to his advantage, Evan slipped crushed sleeping pills into Jim and Lilly's lemonade sitting beside his on the oak coffee table. He mushed the baggie into his pocket only seconds before Lilly grabbed a flashlight from the drawer beneath an end table. She flicked the on button and a stream of light illuminated the room. Ely ran to it and made hand gestures. "Look Eilida, a duck."

Eilida lifted her head, holding Sandy up to her face, and peered at her brother. He continued making shadow figures. Her brother's silliness tugged at the corners of her lips, turning into a smile.

Lilly went through the house, lighting the candles she set up earlier. Losing electricity, even from a normal summer thunder storm, was common. She expected to lose electricity and knew it wouldn't be back on for days. Jim

51

invested in a generator but wouldn't use it until after the storm. Lilly walked into the living room as Eilida climbed off her dad's lap and joined Evie on the floor, watching their brother's shadow display.

"I want a turn Ely. Let me try." Ely showed Evie how to make hand shadows and Eilida chuckled. For the moment she forgot the stranger.

"Dinner's ready and we better eat it now while it's hot," voiced Lilly, grabbing her lemonade and taking a sip.

Ely took Eilida's hand, and they ran into the kitchen, Evie and Lilly right behind them.

Jim picked up his lemonade and turned to Evan. "Join us. My wife is a right fine cook and always makes more than enough."

Evan stumbled over his words, attempting to make himself less threatening. "I do… don't wanna upset your daughter again."

"Nonsense. Eilida doesn't like storms and is always wary of new people. She'll be fine."

"Thank you. Do you have a washroom? I'd like to clean up before I eat."

Jim directed Evan to the restroom and walked into the kitchen to join his family for dinner. Evan pretended to use the restroom then walked back to the living room and slipped crushed sleeping pills into Ely and Evie's lemonade.

Ely walked into the living room as Evan dusted the powdery residue off his hands.

"You comin', sir? Mommy made lots to eat," said Ely as he looked up at the stranger and picked up his and Evie's glasses.

"Sure am. Your dad says your mom is a right fine cook." Evan saw glimpses of himself flicker in the boy as he responded. He followed the boy into the kitchen and took the empty seat. His eyes looked through the Tates' envisioning his drunk father slamming another beer, his mother twisting her dishwater blond ringlets while his corny little sister hung onto her germ infested blanket. And his brother - the son they liked... He shook the images from his head. *Not time, not time.*

The family, plus Evan, ate dinner by candlelight. The flames caused shadows to bounce on the walls. Eilida snuggled Sandy close and tried not to glance at the stranger but she couldn't ignore the creeping, disfigured shadow on the wall behind him. Its arms, tendrils of black, unfurled to reveal a shiny object dripping in red. Eilida watched in horror as the shadow moved towards her mother seated beside her. She twisted in her high chair, eyes wide as flying saucers. She wanted to scream, tried to scream, but her vocal chords buckled and no sound escaped her lips.

Washed Away

Burkhalder searched the hospital's skeleton staff for a nurse or available doctor. The normally bustling halls were empty and void of the usual staff. The lights blinked a few times, then blackness coated the hallway. Her wet clothes, hanging on her body, icy against her flesh as if the light masked the chill. She pulled her flashlight off her belt and clicked the on button, nothing. "Jeez, you have to die now," she said as she hit the flashlight against her hand a couple times. Nothing, the flashlight was dead. She dug into her pants for her phone hoping to use its light to guide her back to Jax. No luck. She placed her palm on her forehead remembering she'd thrown it onto the passenger side seat of her cruiser.

She'd been inside the hospital many times and used a mental map and her senses to guide her. Once her outstretched hand felt the wall, she slid her palm against it as she walked. She counted three doors, a waiting room was to her right. She put her foot out and stepped - carpet, the waiting room. Across the hall was a nurses' station. With ginger steps she walked towards it, placed her palm on the smooth wall under the station counter until it turned. She followed it. Now behind the station, she rummaged for a flashlight. She used her sense of touch to distinguish pens, computer, mouse, and medical charts. Ready to give up, she flung her hands towards her sides. The rush movement caused her left hand to push something off the counter that landed with a thud beside her boot.

Wind whistled and cracked outside, beating against the thick hospital doors down the hall and to the right. She leaned and groped on the floor for the object. Something round and smooth, like a rock or paperweight, lay beside her foot. She picked it up to return it to its rightful spot and bumped her head on a shelf beneath the counter. "Shit!" She wrapped her hands around her head, lost her balance and fell backwards. Once the throbbing lessened she reached towards the counter to lift her tall frame off the ground. A rounded object on the shelf skirted her fingertips. She took hold of the slender object - a flashlight. Pushing the switch, a beam of light shone.

With flashlight in hand, Burkhalder padded towards the E.R. waiting room where she left Jax. He sat in a chair, magazine in hand and lights. *The backup generator must only work for certain areas of the hospital.* She clicked off the flashlight. "How did you… " Her sentence trailed as she studied the dry scrubs in the chair beside him. "Who gave you scrubs? I didn't find a soul."

The corner of Jax's mouth turned upwards into a half smile. "They were on that cart." He pointed towards a hospital cart loaded with scrubs and white hospital issue towels and sheets.

She grabbed the scrubs off the seat, plummeted onto it and sighed. His eyes met hers and he touched his hand to her throbbing head. "What's this?"

"I hit my head lookin' for a flashlight. I shoulda waited here with you. This place is 'bout as creepy as a horror movie right now."

Jax leaned in and kissed her bump. "That's gonna be nasty."

Scrubs in hand, she stood. "Maybe you kin find me some ice." She walked towards the restroom to change.

When she returned, Jax held a cold soda in his hand. "Got it outta the machine. Hon, ain't nothin' you can do till they done workin' on the girl."

Burkhalder held the cold drink to the bump on her head. "You got your phone?"

Jax grabbed his sleek, black flip phone from his pocket and handed it to her. He didn't bother to ask why, he heard the wheels turning in her head.

She put the soda down and dialed Harry's number. Owner of Harry's Bar and Grill. The phone rang in Burkhalder's ear.

"Harry here."

"Harry, it's Alice. Gala at your bar last night?"

"Mighty strange time to be askin' that question."

"She was in a wreck. At the hospital with her now."

Burkhalder heard the sorrow in his voice. "That girl. I worry for her. Is she OK?"

"We don't know yet."

"What are you thinkin'?"

"I'm thinkin' she picked up the wrong man. Her car doors were locked."

"It's a different one every night. I'll call Johnny. He worked last night. He'd know."

"Thanks Harry."

She sighed and leaned her head backwards and placed the soda on her now-forming forehead bump.

Twenty minutes later Jax's phone rang and he answered. "Jackson."

"Harry here. You with Alice?"

"Yeah, what you find?"

"Johnny says she left about ten thirty with a dark eyed kid with dirty blond hair. The kid been sittin' at the bar a spell alone before she walked in and sat next to him. She struck conversation with him, then they left but her car was still outside the bar when he left. He meant to check on her but got sidetracked when his wife called sayin' their teen daughter, Julia, hadn't come home."

Burkhalder reached for the phone and Jax held his hand, signaling he'd take care of the call. "Can you tell me more about the kid she left with?"

"Five and a half feet tall, burly build. No noticeable tats. Dark blue shirt, and jeans."

"Thanks Harry. Do you have Johnny's number in case Alice needs to call him?"

Harry rattled off Johnny's number then hung up the phone. Jax repeated their discussion to Burkhalder.

The doctor walked out of the doors and towards the couple. Jax and Burkhalder both stood and met him halfway.

"She's stable. We got all the glass out of her face and stitched her wounds. She's asleep and will be until the drugs wear off. She got lucky, no internal injuries, but we won't know more until she awakens." The doctor scanned both police officers' eyes. "Either of you spoke with her dad?"

Burkhalder responded, anxious to ask her question. "I called, no answer. Did you see any sign of rape?"

"Rape? She has bruising but it's consistent with a bad collision. We didn't check for rape, most of the evidence would have washed away with the rain. She was soaked."

"We need a rape kit done A.S.A.P." Burkhalder pressed.

The heavy E.R. doors slid open, wind and rain rushed into the hospital and the silhouette of a young man and very pregnant woman appeared. The young man shouted with daddy enthusiasm. "Her water broke!" The pregnant woman doubled over in pain, the young man held her. A nurse in ducky scrubs shot out of nowhere and rushed to the woman's side with a wheel chair in hand. The doctor wasted no time in assisting the nurse and getting the pregnant lady to a room, stat.

Sweet Dreams

The rain eased and Lilly lay her daughter, asleep in her arms, inside her crib. She hummed a lullaby as she dropped a gentle kiss on the girl's cheek. Jim, the boys, and Evan played a game of Uno. Large pillar candles on both sides of the coffee table and each end table provided plenty of light. Evan's urges and visions of his mother grew stronger by the minute. He wished for the sleeping pills to do their job so he could get rid of his mother.

"Draw four." Ely giggled as Evan drew four cards from the pile, Reverse, Skip, Draw Four and a yellow two.

Lilly reappeared and took a seat on the floor beside her husband. Evie tugged at his ears. Jim observed his son's signal of tiredness. "When this game is over it's time for bed."

"Daaad," whined Ely.

"Both of you."

Evan used his drawn cards to his advantage and reversed the game on Ely, planning on throwing the Skip and Draw Four his direction. Two rounds later, Evie announced, "Uno!" A huge smile planted between his ears. Evan used his Draw Four on Ely, getting even with him. Evie went out next turn. Evan's mind screamed *Go to sleep!*

"Brush your teeth, boys." The boys scurried down the hallway, reappearing several minutes later in pajamas. "Better run! The bear's gonna get ya," Jim said, puffing out his arms and chasing the giggling boys down the hall.

"Wonderful family." Evan hated them. They were perfect, but not for long.

Lilly smiled at Evan's comment. "Thank you. What about yours?"

"My parents passed when I was a kid, car accident. My grandma raised me."

"Oh, I'm sorry." Lilly's liquid blue eyes darkened at his words, filling with sorrow.

"I was two. I don't remember them." The lies rolled off his tongue just as they did at Windy Oaks. He hated the place but was grateful for the control and proper social interactions he learned while there. *Evan, time for bed* called his mother's sugary voice. His brain shouted *Get Out!* Without his meds she seeped into his thoughts and took over Lilly's body. Her dark, wavy hair becoming a curly, dirty blond.

"Nyle?" The voice coming from his mother wasn't her voice and her form evaporated.

"Are you OK, would you like a drink?"

Evan realized he zoned out on her. "You and Jim have been waiting on me all evening.

61

I'll pour us some of that delicious lemonade you make." He stood before she could object.

"Thank you, Nyle. That's sweet of you to offer."

Evan filled two new glasses, glanced towards the doorway to be sure no one was watching and slipped the rest of the powdery sleeping pills into their drinks. When he returned to the living room, Jim had joined his wife on the couch and turned on the radio. The station purred on about Hurricane Chloe, *Wind speeds of 117 mph, wind gusts recorded at speeds as high as 135 mph... stalled in the Atlantic.* Evan placed their drinks on the table.

☾ ☾ ☾ ☾ ☾

Eilida lay in her crib, afraid of the storm and the stranger. She didn't know which provoked more fear inside her so she lay curled in her crib, cuddling her monkey, Sandy. Shadows danced on the palm trees painted on her walls and the monkeys hanging from the branches came to life. Her parents' and the stranger's voices drifted through the hallway. She recognized her brothers' and father's footsteps when he put them to bed and wanted to cry out, but terror gripped her insides. Eilida didn't want to see the stranger's black marble eyes and the dark shadow that lingered behind him stretching its wispy arms. The memory caused her tiny body to shudder.

Jim, Lilly and Evan's conversation continued for an hour until Lilly stood and walked to the linen closet, returning with a sheet and pillow.

"It's late and we'll be up every couple hours to check on the progress of the storm. Time for us to get some sleep."

"If it gets worse, or the storm moves in closer, we have a reinforced room with plenty of supplies," said Jim, to reassure the strange but amiable young man he would be safe.

The couple walked down the hallway. Jim checked on the boys, both sound asleep. Lilly peeked into Eilida's room, noticing she was awake. Her small body cuddled into a ball, she picked her up and walked towards the master bedroom.

"Those boys are sound asleep and the plywood seems to be holdin' up. I'm gonna set my alarm and check on them in a couple hours."

Eilida gripped her mother's arm with one hand. The other hand latched to Sandy. "This little one here is the insomniac."

Jim leaned towards Eilida and kissed her cheek. "She doesn't like the rain, do you hon?" Eilida let go of her mother's shoulder and attempted to grab her dad's nose.

Jim set his alarm and he, Lilly, and Eilida lay in the large, king-size master bed.

☾ ☾ ☾ ☾ ☾

Irritated, Evan waited for the family to fall asleep. Visions of his mother fluttered around the room. *I couldn't let her come into my bed or drag me to hers anymore! And no more baths! That's how it started. I was eight, my dad beat me with his whip, my mom took me to the bath and cleaned my wounds. It was hard, my beast of burden had never done that before and I thought something was wrong. She laughed and said, 'Look who's becoming a man.' She knelt by the bathtub and touched it. I tried to stop her, but she said, 'It's okay, it's supposed to do that.'*

I whispered, scared my father would overhear and bring his belt, 'I can bathe myself.'

She ruffled my hair with her free hand, 'You look so much like your father.' I never understood that statement. I look nothing like him. That was the day my mother turned into a monster and my father's belt paled in comparison. Every time she touched me from that day forward she reminded me how much like my father I was. I spent hours looking at pictures. My father and I shared no physical resemblances.

The Time is Nigh

The squalls outside came and went. Silence filled the inside of the house. Evan arose, opened the drawer holding the flashlight, clutched it and traipsed down the hallway. His bulky steps alerted Eilida, *clunk, clunk, clunk* then a loud creak. She nudged her parents and whispered, "Mommy, Daddy."

Evan slipped into the boys' room. His mind seeing Elfred, *the son mommy never touched. The brother who followed him like a god.* Gusts beat against the house as Evan pulled his knife from the rim of his pants, flicked it open and brought it to Evie's neck. He wanted Jim first, *his father,* but accepted going back and forth between rooms would cause too much commotion. The years too many, he couldn't risk anyone waking now and ruining it. He closed his eyes, savoring the moment.

Evan opened his eyes and slid the blade across the boy's throat. Evie's eyes looked towards Evan as Elfred's did years ago. Blood trailed from his neck and over his sheets, puddling beneath the boy's little body. He relished the release for a moment and turned to Ely, his eyes wide as he looked at Evan.

He hadn't prepared for one of them to awaken. Evan's mind flashing between reality and the past, a smile crept from the corners of his lips and he whispered, "Mommy will never hurt you, Elfred." Ely shook in fear and peed his pants, soaking the sheets. Evan wrapped his free large hand around Ely's neck and squeezed until the boy stopped jerking and fighting, then let go of it and whipped the blade across his neck.

The clunking steps moving closer to her parents' room. Fear twisted and pulled at Eilida's insides. She pleaded. "Mommy, Daddy." Neither of her parents budged. A loud crash from outside vibrated the house. Dread washed over her tiny body and she scurried to the closet.

Evan pushed the master bedroom door open, shined his flashlight across the sleeping couple. He ambled to their tall bureau and positioned the light shining towards the ceiling. He clunked to Jim's side, looked at his sleeping body and ripped the blade across his neck. Disappointment washed over Evan as Jim's eyes never opened. Desperate for his *release*, he ran to Lilly's side. *Control, get control.* She was it, *Mommy*. He sucked in a deep breath and released, savoring, *not too quick, not like last time.* His mind in the past, reliving slaughtering his mother. He refused to make the same foolish mistakes. He drew the blade to her neck and drug it across, blood seeping into the surrounding pillow. Evan sliced her repeatedly until *Mommy's* soul shot from her body in a black fog. Tendril arms reached for Evan then withered into nothingness. Lilly's eyes fluttered but Evan didn't notice as he ripped off his pants and pushed her nightgown upwards.

Evan pulled the condom from his pocket and slid it over his erection. He raped her dying body. *Release.* A crescendo to Beethoven's Symphony no. 8 vibrated against Evan's cranium walls. Visions of his mother and the past receded from his memory.

A rustling brought him back to the present. *Eilida.* He pulled his pants on, grabbed the flashlight off the dresser and walked towards the sound. "Where are you? I'll find you." He peered into the closet. Eilida hid behind her mommy's dresses. Evan shined the flashlight around the closet but saw no sign of the girl.

He traipsed through the house, checking every small place a child could hide and taunted her. "A little girl can hide many places but you can't hide from me forever."

Eilida stayed still as a statue behind her mommy's dresses, paralyzed with fear.

Hurricane Baby

Jax and Alice snuggled together in a vacant hospital bed. The squalls outside coming and going with increasing intensity. The baby's first cries of life startled Alice awake. She left Jax asleep, grabbed the flashlight and padded down the hallway. She stopped at the E.R. doors and gazed outside. The trees bent close to the ground from wind gusts. She moved away from the sturdy glass doors and walked to the nurses' station. A radio sat in the corner. She flipped the on switch and searched through the static for a station, adjusting the knob when she heard a crackling break through the static. She pulled up the nurses' rolling chair and listened. *Hurricane Chloe upgraded to a Category 4… wind speeds of 131 mph… heading straight for the sleepy island town of Billows Hollow.*

"Holy shit!" Goosebumps crawled across her arms. She jumped off the chair so quick it continued to spin in her absence. Her thoughts drifted to Jim and his family.

"Jax! Wake up!" She pushed his sleeping body until his eyes fluttered open.

When he saw the expression in her eyes he bolted upwards. "What Alice? What is it?"

"Chloe's upgraded to a Cat 4! And headed here!"

It took his mind a moment to process. "Shit. Jim!" He flipped his phone open and dialed the number, nothing. He looked at the screen - roaming.

Burkhalder plucked the phone from his hand and gawked at the *Data Roaming* moving across the phone's screen. She dropped the phone and sank onto the bed. Jax folded her into his arms.

The young man with the pregnant wife walked past their room, catching Burkhalder's attention. She needed good news and remembered the baby's cries had awaken her. Alice jumped off the bed and hurried to the young man's side. "Congratulations!"

Startled, he hadn't noticed her walking towards him. When he saw her he shouted. "It's a boy - Dillon!" He picked her up and spun her in circles. Suddenly aware he was spinning an unknown woman, he set her on her feet. "I'm sorry. I'm just excited. You know? I want to shout it to the world but can't get a call out. Roaming!" He raised the phone to his face.

"You're not gonna get a call out now. Let's see that baby."

Jax walked out of the room, placed his arm around Alice's shoulder and followed the young man to his wife's room. The baby lay sleeping in the plastic hospital style bassinet.

"Isn't he somethin'?" She whispered, not wanting to wake his wife. The young man smiled ear to ear like the proud new father he was.

Siege of the Plums'

After searching every spot a tiny child could fit into, he quit. He had no intention of killing her, yet. *Emily is still alive.* If he changed any more in the pattern he'd have to do it again soon. He needed to keep playing by their rules until he finished school then he'd come back for her. *Come back for Emily.* The monkey, he wanted her monkey as a souvenir or promise to return.

The Tates' door slammed behind him as he sauntered to the Plums'. His mind high on the kills, high on giving back to *Mommy*, high on slashing the life from her worthless body. Almost at the Plums' door, Evan stumbled over a large tree branch, falling forward into the sand, catching the fall with his hands. His gaze fell upon the mass of tree branches, shingles and miscellaneous junk undiscernible to him in the darkness covering the beach. The tide rolling in only inches from where he lay planted in the sand. He realized no winds threatened to take him out, no rain drenched his body. Evan turned his upper body as far as possible, looking at the area. Nothing, calm. Then it hit him, he was in the *eye of the storm.* He tilted his head toward the heavens, blackness and a few stars. No sign of the moon. *A new moon.* Eight years in Windy Oaks in-patient care and two years' out-patient care, Evan was a model patient and provided with many privileges. He used them to study hurricanes and astrology. Evan understood a new moon meant time to set a purpose and plan; the beginning of a new phase of life. A lopsided grin tugged at the corners of his lips. He fulfilled the new moon prophecy without giving it any thought. Dumb luck mixed with the tight leash Windy Oaks Residential Care gave him. They were a yoke around his neck but no longer.

He lifted his body and stood, raising his hands, palms out-stretched above his head which he lifted to the skies. Omnipotence rushed through him, devouring any insecurities. The power of life and death emanated from his fingertips. The stroke of his blade draining the blood from his mother, his family - he held their lives in his hands. He was his siblings' savior and his parents' avenger. Seeker of retribution. In his mind *Emily* and *Eilida* should be grateful to him. *Emily*... he needed to find her...

He stood in the same position until the clouds swirled closer and closer, and wind gusts teased and threatened to push him to the ground. He drew on their raw power, sucking it into his soul, then escaped into the Plums' house. His mood shifting from a death-high to exhaustion. He leaned into the plush recliner, tilted it backwards, pulled the leg lift and lay back, listening to the hurricane. Explosions of wind, throwing objects at the house, merged with torrents of rain. *A hurricane's true strength comes after the eye.*

He grabbed a bag of dried apricots and turned the dial on the TV. Fuzz and snow bubbled across each channel until he found the news. The person's image elongated and bounced from the poor reception, the words interrupted by static. *Hurr... Chlo... 130 plu... miles per... and steady... pressure decreased...* Then the station flat-lined. He turned it off, fluffed the pillow, stuffing it behind his head and fell asleep to the vicious sounds of Chloe's destruction.

☾ ☾ ☾ ☾ ☾

The slamming door alerted Eilida. Her body jumped involuntarily. The tension inside her eased as she realized she no longer heard his heavy footfalls in the house, silence filled the air around her. The pounding from heavy squalls and objects no longer threatened to rip her home apart. Eilida eased out of hiding, leaving Sandy in the closet - safe. On all fours she crawled to her parents' bed, stood and climbed into bed with them. The sticky blood oozed between her fingers and legs. She knew blood and remembered how her parents

73

always bandaged her and her brothers' cuts and scrapes. Eilida jumped off the bed and ran to their bathroom. She flung the cabinet door open and grabbed a handful of bandages. They stuck out from between her pudgy fingers. She returned to her parents' bed and wrapped them around their wounds. *When they wake up they'll be all better*. Death wasn't a concept her young brain understood.

Eilida remembered the stranger also went into her brothers' room. She hopped off her parents' bed and ran to their room. The silence told her the stranger had harmed them too. She stood between their beds and pushed her brothers, trying to awaken them. "Ely, Evie," she whispered, aware she was alone even though her brothers lay on either side of her. Sticky blood covered their sheets and puddled onto the floor. Its gooeyness oozed between her toes. The few bandages left in her hand she used on their wounds thinking *they should all be OK now*.

She returned to her parents' closet, taking one last, longing glance towards her parents, grabbed Sandy and climbed inside the wooden chest her dad built. When she and her brothers played hide and seek it was the place she always hid. Her dad drilled holes in the side he called 'peep holes' and her mom always left small snacks and juice boxes inside it. Eilida snuggled Sandy to her inside the pitch blackness of the chest. She waited for her brothers to wake up and find her like they had many times before. She shut her eyes, her tiny body exhausted, and went to sleep.

Obliteration

C hloe's eye passed over the town of Billows Hollow followed by heavy squalls throwing loose objects hurtling in the air, crashing against the hospital's walls. The staff, Jax, Alice, Gala and the young couple, huddled inside the innermost E.R. room. The only other people in the hospital were in Critical Care; designed to hold through the worst hurricane due to the patients' lack of mobility and around the clock care.

Winds growled in anger and a loud collision sounded above their heads as if the roof had caved. The emergency lights went out leaving the group in darkness. As Alice's eyes adjusted she saw the outline of the new mommy laying against her husband, baby Dillon cradled in her arms.

Jax turned on the flashlight and scanned the ceiling. A crack ran across it. He flashed the light across the room surveying everyone. "Y'all OK?" Wide eyes stared back at him and nodded. "We gotta move." He shone the light across the crack. "Ya see that hairline crack? Another squall like the last and the ceilin'll give."

"Oh no. Oh no," whispered the new mommy over and over, twisting her head side to side in a *no* sweeping motion.

"If we can get to Critical Care it's the safest place in the hospital," announced the doctor.

"What about Gala?" Asked Alice.

Jax took Alice's hand. "She'll have to come with us hon. How do we get there doc?"

The doctor stood, Jax handed him the flashlight, and eased towards the door. He poked his head around the door frame, and surveyed the area. Then motioned for Jax and Alice.

They edged towards the doorway and joined him. Jax twisted his lips in thought. "We can clear that," responded Jax.

A gap in the ceiling caused the crack inside their room. A bed, monitor, and tree limb lay in the hallway. Jax, Alice, and the doctor got to work removing the obstacles. The winds slacked as Jax wielded the tree branch over the bed. Alice grabbed the monitor, and the doctor rolled the bed into a vacant room. Winds howled above them. The heaviness of the branch weighed on Jax's arms as Alice slipped beneath him. His arms gave way, no longer able to bear the load, and the branch crashed to the floor. Alice safe on the other side. With her and the doctor's help they cleared the branch so someone could push Gala through the hall.

The doctor in the lead followed by the young family, Alice, Gala, the nurse, and Jax formed a train. Baby stuff filled the arms of the father and nurse. Both the doctor and Jax had flashlights. The group moved at a slow pace, winds ripped the air above them. Alice looped her purse over her shoulder - her uniform squished inside it. She watched the young mother, concerned for the safety of the baby. His mother held him so tight she feared he'd suffocate.

A shingle plunged through the sky aimed towards the nurse, Jax pushed her out of the way as it skimmed between them slicing Jax's arm. He held in his scream as the pain seared through his bicep. Flames of fiery pain scorched through each muscle. The nurse dropped the baby stuff, yanked the flashlight out of Jax's hand, and wrapped her free arm around him, guiding him through the wreckage. Alice held onto the bed with both hands and plowed backwards. The CCU only a few steps from the doctor. He held the doors open, placing his back against it. The young family went through, Alice, and Gala. He helped push the bed through the doorway. The nurse held tight to Jax's hand as they rushed through the entry. The pain in his arm moving from flaming hot blue fire to red fire. They made it through the cumbersome doors.

Jax and the doctor pushed against the heavy doors, jamming them into place. Tendrils of pain bounced across Jax's arm but fear of losing anyone in the group kept him going. Once they jarred the doors into place the doctor locked them down and fell against them in exhaustion. Jax held his throbbing arm.

"Come with me, all of you, we aren't safe yet," announced the nurse, her voice quivering in fear. The baby cried and Alice let out a whimper of relief hearing him. She guided them into an empty patient room. The sounds of other people reminded them they weren't alone. Alice resisted her instinct to look into each room to check on every persons' safety. If she stopped, she'd endanger Jax further. His bleeding arm leaving a trail of blood drops behind him. He needed medical care right away.

Inside the room, the nurse used the flashlight to seek medical supplies. The baby continued to wail as his mother attempted to breast feed him for the second time. She played the nurses words through her head *cradle the baby across your chest, make sure he opens wide and takes in a mouthful so he can latch*. She swaddled the baby across her chest and teased his tiny mouth with her nipple until he grabbed hold. The father sat beside his wife, watching his family and coaxing breastfeeding.

The Calm Before the Storm: Evan's Sins

Even in the midst of a formidable hurricane there was peace and his beautiful son.

The nurse guided Jax to a table. She placed thick gauze on his wound, guided his arm above his heart and held it until the bleeding stopped then lowered his arm onto the table. She pulled the gauze off his arm not wanting to bring him more pain. Dipping clean gauze into an ointment she dabbed at the slice in his bicep. Alice held his good hand while the nurse cleaned and wrapped his wound. Jax bit down the pain.

Sunshine

Light from the brilliant orb in the sky filtered into the hospital room. Burkhalder blinked her eyes, unaware how she slept with the loud banging and clapping of tree branches and other objects throughout the night. She peered at the happy sun knowing it belied the destruction outside the hospital walls. She clutched and stuffed the pillow beneath her head. The chilly air giving away Jax's absence. The hard floor beneath her body mimicked the stiffness she felt in her muscles. She forced her long, tall frame upwards and padded to Gala's side.

The young girl's breathtaking face swollen and bruised, her forehead covered in bandages. Burkhalder took Gala's hand, brought it to her chest, and whispered, "We'll find the asshole who did this to you." The girl's face would heal but what about her soul? The girl had poor judgment in men but was never assaulted. From that moment forward it became Burkhalder's personal quest to unlock the mystery behind Gala's accident and put the perp behind bars.

The young couple snuggled together, baby Dillon on his mother's chest. Her mouth parted into a smile, amazed how nature could unleash Hurricane Chloe the same night a perfect baby boy entered the world.

"I was nervous, the baby sleeping on his mother but I didn't dare take him and place him in the bassinet. What if we never made it through the storm and it was the only night they had to share? They are a precious family," said the nurse, her eyes smiling at the beautiful family that began during the chaos of the past night.

The voice startled Burkhalder. "Good morning. I didn't hear you walk in." She nodded her head in agreement. "A delicate, tiny soul born during the most ferocious storm to hit Billows Hollow in my lifetime."

"I woke a couple hours ago. My nervous energy. I went room to room checking on everyone. If you're looking, I redid Jackson's dressings, he'll be along in a minute."

"You were a rock last night the way you carried him along and took care of his arm. You never flinched."

The nurse's cheeks flushed. "It's my job, just like you saving that girl's life."

Jax rounded the corner and propped himself against the wall, fresh dressings surrounding his well-defined bicep. "Mornin' ladies!"

Burkhalder grabbed her now dry uniform, wrinkled as a raisin, and swished past Jax, pecking his cheek, then entered the restroom and changed.

Exiting the obstacle course hospital was a tremendous feat for Jax and Burkhalder. Branches, hospital beds and equipment littered the hallways. Nothing looked as it had before the storm. Most of the walls remained but gashes and cracks split the roof and ceiling. They pushed as much aside as possible. Burkhalder's thoughts consumed by her friend Jim and his family. She needed to get to them as soon as possible. Sheer will power gave her the drive and extra human strength to help wounded Jax clear a path.

The closest exit in sight, they heaved equipment aside, Jax temporarily forgetting the pain in his arm. As a team they hauled and carted everything to the nearest rooms. Her heart racing with anxiety, she rushed out the door inhaling the fresh air and soaking in the sun. She kept at a steady pace hoping against all odds her patrol car was drivable.

She rounded the corner to the garage, her heart beating a thousand miles a minute, blood coursing through each vein at a rapid pace. Memories of Jim playing a scene across her mind. Her long legs moving in lengthy strides. Jax ran to keep up with Alice's sudden vampire speed.

The garage was near empty but for a couple cars and ambulances. Jax assumed the cars belonged to the few nurses and doctors inside the hospital. "Slow down. The garage isn't structurally sound." Demanded Jax, his eyes unsmiling, his voice concerned.

"Almost there."

Jax scanned the ceiling, eyeballing the large crack running across it stopping a few feet from Burkhalder's unscathed patrol car. In one swift movement she jetted inside the car and hit the radio. Fuzz blared back at her as she scanned the channels, searching for an open frequency and the welcome kindness in MaddyJo's voice.

Jax placed his large hand over hers and slid the radio out of her hand placing it back on the receiver. "Let's get outta here. I'm driving, you can keep playin' with the radio."

She continued to beep MaddyJo to no avail as Jax dodged debris strewn across the road. Burkhalder dropped the radio. "Look at this! How did my car not get destroyed?!"

"That finally dawned on you?"

"All I could think about was Jim. Now I see these cars dumped on their sides, pushed and thrown aside."

Jax slowed the car to a crawl as they moved through the storm surge tide. Water rose in a wide spray as they cruised through, each crossing their fingers they'd make it to Jim's.

Beep beep squawked the radio. "Alice," sounded a voice over the static on the other end.

"MaddyJo, hon, you're OK. How's everyone else?"

"We're fi… sweet… spent the nigh… in a jai… cell. Get out to J…"

"On our way!" Static vibrated her eardrums. "You there? MaddyJo?"

"Here, the Sheriff… a few… on… the… w… y."

"Maddy! Maddy!" shouted Burkhalder. In response she listened to static - MaddyJo's voice inaudible.

"I thought finding my car untouched was a good thing, the sunshine after the storm, but now I don't know." She buried her head in her hands, tufts of red hair falling across her cheeks.

Keeping one arm on the steering wheel, Jax folded the other around Burkhalder.

C·C·C·C·C·

Evan pushed open the door to his hidey hole in the Plums' pantry. It wouldn't budge more than a few inches - the kitchen table lodged against it. With his back against the door he pushed his stocky bulk with his feet edging the door open inch by inch until he squeezed himself out. He knew enough to cover his tracks and pushed over the round table - glass shattering in every direction. The pantry open, he tossed the items he used for comfort across the three walled house. Convinced it looked as though the hurricane flung the objects, he left the Plums' in search of little Eilida.

The high storm surge and heavy debris made his trek difficult. When he came to the spot where the house was, little of it stood. The high water and homes in shambles made it difficult for Evan to determine the site of the Tates' home. He didn't consider the child surviving the storm. And second guessed his sense of direction. Remembering the previous night, he walked straight along the beach, past three houses which now lay in pieces, strewn everywhere. His mind sure the little child would be found dead and cold beneath something, as he pushed debris out of his way, hunting for their home. He felt as though he spent hours searching when the muffled cry of a child pinged his eardrum. Evan hefted sheet rock, shingles, furniture, and various objects out of his way, desperate to find her. The sound grew louder as he worked until he came to a walled structure with no roof. He tossed debris, uncovering a wooden chest. From the corner of his eye he spotted Lilly's black waves flowing against the side of a bed, rubble covering the bodies. Evan's lips twisted into a satisfied smile.

The sun shone upon the chest like the staircase to heaven and he hummed Clementine. He stood above it, a sinful smirk plastered across his face. He recognized it as belonging in the parents' closet. *Is this where you hid, little one?* His large arms flipped open the lid displaying little Eilida curled inside it. Her nasty monkey nestled in her tiny arms. *Damn Monkey!* "Oh Delilah, Oh Delilah, Oh my darling, Deli-lah you were gone and lost forever, oh my De-Li-i-a-lah," he sang to the tune of *Clementine*. "They named you wrong, you little, devious bitch."

Rescue Crew

As the wooden lid above Eilida's head opened, stunning light blinded her eyes, the melody Evan sang rang through her ears as his looming, dark figure became clear. He leaned downward, distending his arms, and lifted her out of the chest. His eyes black as a starless night. Using a mimicking voice he talked while Eilida screamed loud enough to break glass. His touch sent a wave of fear and panic shivering through her.

"You are clever, little Delilah, hiding in a wooden chest. I looked for you and here you are. I figured I would leave you to the storm. How could a little thing like you live through something so fierce? But yet, here you are. And it looks like you have been busy. You found your Mommy and Daddy. You have their blood all over you." He ran his bulky hand across her blood dried clothing. His piercing black eyes penetrated inside her like a laser beam. "And what is this you are holding onto, a monkey?" Evan heard footsteps behind him. "Well, it looks like I will have to hand you over, but the monkey is mine. It is my souvenir." He grabbed Sandy and slid it under his shirt. *I hadn't planned on killing you anyways, like my sister, I have something else in store for you.*

☾☾☾☾☾

A death scream alerted Burkhalder as she rushed towards the Tates' demolished home. "Eilida! Oh you precious baby," she said, taking the panicking child from Evan's hands. Eilida snuggled her head into Burkhalder's shoulder, quiet sobs and whimpers shaking her little body. The woman meant safety to Eilida.

Evan slipped off as the Carrot Top Cop held and rocked the shaking child. "Wait!" she hollered, recognizing his shiny bald head. "Hold-up," she called.

Evan stopped and turned towards her. "Yes ma'am."

"I sent you to the shelter."

"Yes, you did, but I couldn't sleep when the storm stopped, all I thought about was the people stranded on the beach." Proud of his appropriate, caring lie. "I only meant to help." The blackness in his eyes disappeared, returning to their normal shade.

"You did. You saved this girl's life. We coulda searched all day and never found her. Thank you."

"It's no problem, none at all. Reckon anyone else is buried under the rubble?" His self-absorbed, childish ego accepted the hero role.

"No doubt there is. I just hope they are alive."

"Alice!" called Jax.

"Over here! Found Eilida!" Sidetracked and tired, she forgot about the bald kid. Eilida's weight became too much so she shifted her to the other hip, from the corner of her eye she caught a flowing black mane. She twisted further around, padded towards it, keeping Eilida's head buried in her shoulder. *Lilly's hair – she's under the rubble.*

Jax trotted towards her and she pointed towards the bed buried in debris. He glanced towards the heap she pointed at, then removed the rubble piece by piece. Burkhalder's heart swelled and thumped hard inside her chest as Jax cleared the bed. Jim and Lilly lay side by side, covered in blood. Lilly's nightgown pushed towards her chest. Jax pressed his fingers to Lilly's throat then Jim's - no pulse. He shook his head side to side, his lips in an upside down U. He tossed and heaved everything in his path until he found the boys. Burkhalder held Eilida, pressing her head into her shoulder, steering clear of the bed and followed Jax. He pressed his fingers against their tiny throats - nothing. "I'm sorry, Alice." Both Jax and Alice stared at each other, wide eyed. She blinked several times to hold back the waterfall behind her eyes. Her mind raced with activity, *did the storm do this?*

"I need to get Eilida to safety then we'll come back."

They took Eilida to the rescue shelter at the church where she questioned them about the bald kid. He hadn't been to the shelter, confirming at least one of her suspicions. Delighted to have Eilida, the staff and evacuees waited on her like royalty. Burkhalder and Jax rushed back to the scene to investigate the curious deaths of Jim and his family.

Both stared at their friends' dead bodies. Burkhalder used the camera she kept in her patrol car to take pictures of Jim, Lilly and the boys' bodies. Their blood stemmed from lacerations to their necks. Maybe one could be accepted as a piece of flying glass, but not all four. Someone murdered them.

"The storm couldn't a done this. It's not possible."

She nodded her head. "When I found Eilida, the bald kid was holdin' her and she was screamin' and shakin'. Do you think...?" Her eyes pleaded to Jax for an answer, only he knew less than she.

"You're sayin' he did this?"

"I dunno but he was here. How did he get here? He didn't stay at the shelter last night. Damn it! I wish I'd have checked on him."

Jax bit his upper lip, the wheels in his mind spinning. "Let's not draw conclusions, instead we'll find him and question him and don't be so hard on yourself. How would the night have turned out different if you'd have called the shelter and verified? Gala and those people at the hospital needed you."

She let out a sigh. "I dunno. I couldn't stop this, but I can damn sure find who did this!" Burkhalder made a second vow to find her childhood friend's killer. "If it's the last thing I do," she muttered under her breath.

"I heard that and you're not alone. I'm here, we'll figure this out together." He rested his palms on her upper arms and looked deep into her eyes.

☾☆☾☆☾

At the hospital, Gala lay awake in bed, groggy from drugs. Alice Burkhalder's fiery hair swam into view.

"Gala, honey?" She coaxed the young woman while holding her hand. Gala's eyes shifted, and she attempted to pull herself up to rest against the pillow. A throbbing pain shot through her body and her assailant's face danced through her mind. Burkhalder lifted Gala's back and placed a mound of pillows behind her for support. "Honey, you're OK. I'm here to help."

Tears formed in the corners of Gala's silky, chocolate eyes and she tried to speak. "I... " She choked back a huge breath. "Kevin, his name. He... he... raped me." A flood of tears poured across her cheeks. Burkhalder grabbed the closest thing to her, a blanket, and dabbed Gala's face then wrapped her arms around the weeping girl until her sobs lessened.

"We don't have to do this now. I'm here when you are ready."

To Gala, Burkhalder, even in her disheveled uniform, represented security. "He held a knife to my throat than hit me on the head. When I came to I just wanted to get home, you know. My car hit something in the road and I lost control. That's all I remember."

"If I brought someone in would you be able to give them a description, something that can be drawn?"

Evan's block shaped face, wild blond curls, and black eyes spun across Gala's memories. "Yes, I think so. I'm sure."

"OK." She held her until Gala fell asleep, then rushed to the shelter. She busted through the door. "Any artists in here? I need someone who can sketch."

A teenager with caramel brown hair, freckles covering her cheeks and nose, and large, round, amber eyes raised her hand. "I'll do it. I can sketch."

93

The Calm Before the Storm: Evan's Sins

"Come with me. I have a job for you."
She dragged the girl to the hospital where they
waited for Gala to awaken.

Sketch Extraordinaire

Burkhalder and her fourteen-year-old sketch artist, Lacey, sat by Gala's bed. Lacey pressed her back against the chair and propped her feet on the edge of the bed. The sketch pad resting against her legs. Alice, opposite Lacey, wrapped her hands around Gala's and gave her a gentle squeeze whenever her eyes teared and her throat choked. After about thirty minutes, Lacey finished a rough sketch.

"Are you ready, Gala?" asked Burkhalder.

Gala clucked her tongue, then through barred teeth said, "Yeah, OK."

"I need you to confirm whether this man looks like him. You don't have to speak. You can nod yes or no." She squeezed Gala's hand one more time. "Lacey, please turn the picture around so Gala can see it."

Lacey flipped the picture. Gala's arm went stiff as a marble tile, her hand clutched Burkhalder's, causing her knuckles to turn bleached white. Nails like knives dug into Alice's hand. Gala's head bobbed in a *yes* gesture. The square jaw and ball tipped nose unmistakable identifiers. And she'd let him slip through her hands. Spheres of anger ascended inside her causing a quickening of her heartbeat.

"Lacey, thank you. Please wait for me outside the door. I need to talk to Gala alone."

Lacey bolted from her seat then looked towards Gala – her pasty face drained of its natural dark beauty. "I'm sorry." She hung her head and slipped out the door. The sketchpad against her chest.

Gala eased her grip and Burkhalder slipped her hand from beneath Gala's. She glimpsed the aching hand, splotches of blood gathered around nail dents. She shook it and buried it beneath her other arm attempting to rid the pain.

"You're OK. You did it. Now I have something to go on." She smoothed Gala's hair with her good hand. "I have to ask, are you sure? Did you see his face while he did this?"

"You don't believe me?"

"I do, hon, but I have to ask."

Gala blinked back her tears. "I fell into the car face first then he assaulted me so I didn't watch, but it was him. I know it!"

"I'll find him or damn sure do my best."

Gala turned her head, forlorn brown eyes met Burkhalder's. "Promise?"

"I promise." She understood the stupidity in making promises as a police officer. Many perps got away. Small town, not far for this guy to run. Her mind shifted to the bald kid. He was out of place, didn't belong in Billows Hollow.

She stood, padded to the door, then slipped into the hall. Lacey sat on the floor Indian style, the sketch pad still plastered against her chest. She slipped down the wall and sat beside her. "Lacey, I know it's hard but what you have given the police is invaluable. Now we can identify him and stop him from harmin' other people."

Lacey shoved the pad onto Burkhalder's lap. "I get what you're sayin' but I don't ever wanna look at this again."

The couple sat side by side for several minutes, Burkhalder deep in meditation.

"I'm ready to go back to the shelter if you don't mind."

"Of course. The little girl I brought in earlier could probably use a friend like you right now."

Lacey's face brightened and a short chuckle escaped her lips. "She's cute."

"Yeah, she is. Let's go."

Burkhalder dropped Lacey at the shelter. Lacey stayed by Eilida's side until her aunt and uncle made it to town and took her home with them. They adopted Eilida, legally changing her last name to Riley. Over time, her young mind forgot the experience, but remnants lingered manifesting in night terrors.

Vanish

The governor called a state of emergency. Billows Hollow swarmed in activity. Workers got the backup power on at the hospital and the shelter. As the lights blinked into action, an exhausted Burkhalder melted into a pillowy waiting room hospital chair. She propped her legs over the side onto the seat beside her and took a minute to relax in a position that would be uncomfortable any other day.

Heavy, fast moving footsteps pounded the floor, getting closer with each stride. Her wearied mind ignored them, seeking a few minutes of sleep.

A deep male voice boomed. "He's nowhere. Nowhere, just vanished. The road's flooded out, impassable. I don't get it." Tension mixed with confusion evident in Jax's tone. He planted himself in the seat beside her, grabbing her ankles.

Burkhalder's right eye slid open a crack followed by her left. She rubbed them with her fists then met Jax's gaze. "We'll get back to it tomorrow. We need rest. Let the…" His words and their implications sank into her gut.

While she cared for Gala and had her perp sketched he went after the bald kid. She

98

jolted upwards, swinging her legs in front of her. "He's somewhere. There is no way off the island! We'll find him tomorrow. I have somethin' you need to see."

The sketch pad lay closed on the floor beneath her chair. Reaching down, she swung the pad onto her lap and flipped it open to the sketch. She cupped her hands around the man's head in a semi-circle covering his curls. "Who does that look like?"

Jax didn't need to study the picture. "That's him!"

The following day, Burkhalder and Jax presented their evidence and hypothesis to the sheriff who gave them little attention. "I have an entire town wiped out and you're chasing a possible killer. We don't know if this boy did anything."

"Lilly's thighs and vaginal area are bruised, consistent with rape. And Gala was raped!" Burkhalder insisted.

"The doc said that about Gala?"

Burkhalder twisted her face. "Not exactly. She's bruised everywhere."

"She didn't actually see him do it, did she?"

"No, but that doesn't mean he didn't. It happened fast."

The sheriff swiped the sweat from his brow and sighed. "Gala's always in trouble with a boy. She picks up anything she finds. What makes you think it wasn't consensual sex turned rough? Or maybe she passed out and someone else came along. It's not always the best crowd hangs out late nights at Harry's." Burkhalder let out a heavy sigh, frustrated with his lack of concern. She folded her arms against her chest, tapping her fingers with nervous, angry energy.

The entire town was in disarray and she wanted to pursue a possible murder/rape taking man hours he couldn't spare. Before she could boast a fight he laid down his law. "I loved that family as much as anyone but I can't have you both pursuing this right now!"

Burkhalder's stance and steam ascended off her at an alarming rate causing the temperature in the room to change from warm to sweltering in seconds. Jax knew her well and this wouldn't end well if the sheriff didn't give her a carrot. "Can we at least send Lilly's body for an autopsy?"

The sheriff clucked his tongue and swished his lips sideways. "OK, I'll see that Lilly's body gets sent to the mainland for an autopsy and I'll have his sketch faxed to the surrounding areas. That's the best I can do."

Relief swarmed the room and the temperature dropped to lukewarm. Burkhalder accepted his bargain.

Lilly's autopsy came back consistent with rape. The coroner's report confirmed her neck lacerations were deliberate and made with a sharp blade. Little to no chance of a random flying piece of glass or metal. Evan's sketch yielded no results. Her toxicology report showed a high level of sleeping aid. *He subdued them first.* This made sense to Burkhalder, as Jim's large, muscular build made him a formidable match, especially for a kid. The bald kid stood several inches shorter than Jim. His physique solid but no match for Jim's strength.

He vanished. Burkhalder, stubborn as a screw stuck in a too small bolt didn't quit. In her free time she faxed and hand delivered the sketch across the state.

A rape kit performed on Gala due to Burkhalder's insistence came back positive for rape. The lack of physical evidence, her disappearing suspect, and the sheriff's insisting he 'couldn't spare man hours' made persuing her rape a slow go.

Gala's physical injuries healed but her soul remained severed. For six months, Burkhalder transported her back and forth to a therapist on the mainland. She helped her find a job as a clerk in Wilson's Grocery and find an apartment in Hatter's Park.

Guilt and the need for justice drove Burkhalder's internal drive to find "Kevin". She searched for similar crimes, finding a cold case murder in Horn City ten years prior. Both parents killed with neck lacerations and one son murdered. A two-year-old daughter and ten-year-old son found alive. To her

101

further interest, the night of the murders a heavy summer storm cell blasted through, moving as far inland as Horn City. The murder weapon never recovered. She took a few days off work, packed her overnight bag and headed to Horn City.

Mommy's Gift

1994

On June twenty-third, almost two years after Hurricane Chloe, Evan received a call from his mother's lawyer. Evan had no clue either of his parents had a lawyer or the money to afford one. They lived in a crackerjack home in suburbia Horn City.

"There is a plane ticket to Albuquerque waiting at the airport for you. The flight leaves at seven thirteen Thursday evening. A driver will pick you up at the airport, deposit you at the hotel, and pick you up in the morning and escort you to my office." The lawyer ordered. Evan's ears listened in shock and curiosity.

"Mr. Fritz I think you have the wrong Evan."

"No, Mr. O'Conner you are the Evan I seek. There is much to tell you. It seems your mother's *untimely,*" he cleared his throat, "death didn't provide her the opportunity to tell you the truth."

"The truth I know is my father was a lousy drunk who whipped my ass daily with his leather belt and my mother…" Evan sucked in a deep breath, purging his mind of the ugly memories his mother left scarred on his brain. "I will be on the flight."

The Calm Before the Storm: Evan's Sins

"There is much to tell you. Until Friday, Mr. O'Conner."

Evan dropped the phone on the receiver, leaned his back against the door and propped his foot on the wall behind him. He couldn't imagine what he needed to know and what secrets lurked in *Mommy's* past life. He sucked in a deep breath and released.

Thursday evening, Evan waited at Charlotte Douglas International Airport waiting for his flight. The attendant called for first-class boarding. He looked at his ticket and boarded the plane. His body sank into the large padded seat. His mind reeled with the implications of money - flying first class, a driver escorting him. Were his parents secretly rich?

When the plane touched down at Albuquerque International at eight fifty-seven p.m. New Mexico time, he gathered his one bag of luggage and made his way to the doors Mr. Fritz instructed. A tall man with a receding hairline waited and held up a sign *Evan O'Conner*. As he walked towards the man he greeted him by taking his luggage and stowing it in the trunk then opened the back door to the car pointing for Evan to sit. Evan took the seat. His eyes mystified over the plushness surrounding him. *How could his parents afford this?*

The driver said nothing until they arrived at the hotel. He opened Evan's door, walked around the car to the trunk, took out Evan's bag and handed it to him. "I'll be here nine o'clock sharp to escort you to Mr. Fritz's office, don't be late." He tipped his hat, got into the driver's seat and sped off, leaving Evan to wonder.

The dry, cool desert air felt refreshing to Evan's lungs and skin. Back home on the eastern seacoast the air was hot and humid. The night allowed little reprieve from the morning sun as regular rainfall soaked into the ground retaining the moisture and heat.

The following morning, like clockwork, the driver pulled the limo under the car port, jumped out and held Evan's door open for him. The driver remained quiet and Evan soaked in the sprawling city. Not confined like eastern cities. Sparse vegetation dotted a few patched strips between towering buildings. The limo pulled under a car port outside one of the towering buildings. The driver stated, "Elevator is inside the glass double doors to your right. Mr. Fritz's office is on the third floor, number 317."

Evan followed the driver's instructions, tension and curiosity building inside him. He opened the door to Mr. Fritz's office. A young, blond secretary poised in a lavish black chair, greeted him. "Mr. O'Conner. Mr. Fritz is waiting for you." She stood, her long, tan legs enough to drive any man but Evan wild.

The Calm Before the Storm: Evan's Sins

She opened a large bulky oak door. "Mr. O'Conner is here."

"Thank you, Angelica." He gave her a wink. She flashed a smile at him. Evan caught their coy, flirting gestures.

He walked into the office. A large window covered the wall behind Mr. Fritz's desk, displaying the city's skyline. He imagined it lit up at night. Posh leather chairs sat on either side of his bulky oak desk. A leather couch with gold buttons sewed into the pillow cushions sat against the wall to his right and a glass bar took up the opposite wall.

A plump man of medium stature, wearing gold rimmed round glasses and curly light brown hair streaked with gray, stood. "Take a seat Evan. Angelica please close the doors." Mr. Fritz was aware of Evan's past sins. As the lawyer of record and through his multitude of connections he'd read the police report of Evan's family's murders. He knew Evan was guilty. The police never proved it or found the murder weapon. Mr. Fritz sent his own investigator into the house. He found it in the parents' room, wedged between the floor and baseboard under a heavy wood chest. Once they learned Evan's mother sexually abused him, sympathy and healing were in order, not conviction of a minor.

Mr. Fritz looked Evan over, no doubt he was the man he sought. His short, stocky stature, broad shoulders, even the fleshy ball on the end of his nose were identical to his father. He sat in his posh leather chair and cleared his throat. "Evan, your twenty-first birthday on June twenty-third marked the day you can now receive the funds your father left you. Not the father you grew up with but your biological father. Many years ago, your mom worked at a club as a stripper, she met your father there. He loved to watch her dance. She aroused him and brought life to body parts he loved and thought were dead. After weeks of watching her, he had to have her. She made his sex drive alive. You see, he was an eighty-seven year old nymphomaniac. I understand this is a lot to absorb but I see no look of shock or surprise on your face."

Evan held a poker face, unsure what emotions he should feel at the moment. Windy Oaks taught him appropriate emotional responses but they didn't prepare him for this. He knew his evil mother, nothing Mr. Fritz said so far shocked him, except the part about his father not being the asshole he killed. "Please continue Mr. Fritz."

Mr. Fritz found Evan amiable but couldn't decide if it was his friendship with his father that provoked his feelings. He knew what Evan did, and was capable of, yet he liked the young man. Mr. Fritz placed his folded hands beneath his chin and continued the story. "Your mother fulfilled his wildest sexual fantasies, and he married her. He refused to have me write a prenuptial, but agreed to have me write financial precautions into his will. She would receive forty thousand a year, doled out in equal monthly amounts until the day of her death. If the marriage produced children, a DNA test must be done to prove paternity, the child or children would receive the rest of his estate."

Evan's mind stopped at DNA test. "DNA test?"

"Yes, to receive the estate you have to take one. It was a stipulation I wrote in the will to protect the estate so it would go to valid heirs. Your mother loved sex, and I didn't see an eighty-seven year old man subduing her sex drive, nympho or not. His body was too old to keep up with her. She was nineteen. However, even bald, you are an exact replica of your father." Mr. Fritz scooted his chair closer to his desk and opened a folder. He pulled out a picture, placing it in front of Evan. "This is your father, Evan O'Conner Senior."

Evan held a straight face as he studied the picture on the desk - his own face looking back at him in black and white film. The only difference, thick, dark hair covered his head. He gazed at the picture then realized Mr. Fritz called the picture-man Mr. Evan O'Conner Senior. "Mr. Fritz, if this man is my father, why did my dad and siblings carry the name O'Conner?"

Mr. Fritz smiled, "If your mother ever remarried she would lose her inheritance and every dime would go to you. As a widow, she retained the name O'Conner and signed it to your siblings' birth certificates. The father you grew up with changed his name legally. Her forty thousand a year meant he didn't need to work." Flashbacks of the lazy man reclined with a beer in hand flew through his head. "When your father died, your mother was distraught and stuck at home with a three-month-old baby. She met Sheldon when a water pipe broke. Hungry and desperate for sex, she seduced him. He continued to stop by and see her. Neighbors looked and talked. The two packed up and moved to the east coast, he changed his name and they introduced themselves as a married couple. Soon after the move, Elfred was born."

Evan stared at the picture of his biological father unphased by Mr. Fritz's words. He placed his fat pointer finger on the picture. "How did he die?"

Evan's lack of emotion alarmed Mr. Fritz. He understood the young man suffered psychiatric problems but didn't expect a sociopath. "Heart attack."

Evan looked into Mr. Fritz's cool blue eyes and asked, "Did my mother do it?"

The Calm Before the Storm: Evan's Sins

The air behind Mr. Fritz swirled in motion and Evan's mother's form coalesced. She rolled her tongue over her lips and propped her elbow on Mr. Fritz's head. *Darling, this man knows nothing. He is an idiot.* She gazed at her son. *Evan, you understand why you are my special son?*

Black bubbled from Evan's pupils and diffused through his irises until his eyes were black as coal. *I hate you! You incestuous pedophilic whore!* Unsure if he said it aloud, he caught eye contact with Mr. Fritz who pulled his body forward and edged closer to his desk. His behavior suggesting fear but his blue eyes gave away no recollection of Evan's words. They stayed inside his head. *Go away! Go away!* The mantra inside his head. Under everyday circumstances, the medicine kept her away, but on this day and extraordinary circumstances she weaseled her form into the office, running her fingers through Mr. Fritz's curly locks. Evan ignored his mother's coaxing and focused on Mr. Fritz.

☪ ☪ ☪ ☪ ☪

Mr. Fritz felt a strong sense of brooding and hate inside Evan. The hair on his body stood at attention and he feared what he had to say next. "In a manner of speaking she did." He held his finger just beneath the emergency buzzer under his desk. Sweat dimpled his forehead. He hoped Evan didn't notice his sudden nervous behavior.

"They were having sex when his ticker stopped." He didn't mention she had him bound to the bed and his father held a leather whip in his hand.

C C C C C

That's part true Evan. He's not telling you the truth. His mother coaxed.

Shut up! Evan shouted inside his head and his mother's form vanished.

The blackness left Evan's eyes, returning to their normal shade of blue except a yellow ring surrounding one iris and amber the other. Mr. Fritz relaxed a little. He kept his hand close to the emergency button.

"How much was my father worth?"

"3.8 million and his mansion. His will allowed servants to live in and maintain the home upon his death."

Evan's mind considered how he could spend 3.8 million. The money he needed to find *Emily,* and the crusty lawyer seemed the man to hire for the job. He imagined he must have a few rule-bending private investigators in his pocket. How else would he know such detail about his parents? "Take me to the house." He demanded.

Happiness is... My Own Estate

The limo turned right onto a long road. The sign read *Poppy Hills*. At the end of the road stood a black metal fence connected by a double gate. The driver hit a button and both sides slid open. Lush, thin bladed grass surrounded the driveway leading towards a massive two story salmon colored adobe home with two separate adobe structures on either side. A calliope of colors surrounded the home stemming from the vast array of poppies and various wildflowers.

The driver parked the car and opened the doors for Evan and Mr. Fritz. Evan stepped onto the driveway and asked, "This is it? My home?" His eyes scanned the vast area. The driveway connected to a sidewalk separating the flowers from the lawn and meandered around the entire house.

"Yes, all of this. Follow me and I'll give you the tour." Mr. Fritz's nerves calmed during the long drive. He and Evan shared conversation. He learned not to mention Evan's mother, as her name triggered the darkness in Evan who was otherwise a polite and enjoyable young man.

Inside the home, Evan scanned the open floor plan. To the right, a staircase wound upstairs to a walkway leading to five doors. Light from the skylight above him glinted off the staircase's glass railing, illuminating the entire area. Handmade Aztec area rugs lay between a fluffy sectional, Evan and glass doors leading to the pool patio.

"This is the living room. To the right, under the stairs, is the kitchen and dining room. That area was your father's library. Do you like to read?"

Without answering, Evan walked towards the library, running his hands along the many books. Shelves and shelves of books high as the second floor ceiling lined the walls. Each book placed in alphabetical order, according to subject; fiction, nonfiction, medical texts. "Was my father a doctor?"

Mr. Fritz cleared his throat. "One might think so by the amount of medical journals and texts on the shelves. But no, he made his fortune selling medical supplies. When he died the company was sold."

Evan compared his father's career to that of his choice, pharmaceuticals, and wondered what secrets his father hid.

"There is more to see." Evan followed Mr. Fritz up the staircase. "Bedrooms and your father's office are up here. The room on the far left is the master suite…" Evan strolled towards the room, pushed the door open and gawked at the contents of the room.

Sweat on Mr. Fritz's head bubbled, and he held his breath as he took one nervous step after the other to see what caught Evan's attention. He'd asked Mr. and Mrs. Kurl to rid the house of pictures and sex toys and wondered if they'd missed something. He stepped to the side of Evan and let out a sigh. The room appeared void of paraphernalia and memories. Aware of Evan's past, he decided taking the memories of his parents out of the house was a safe choice. Witnessing Evan's mommy-behavior he'd made a wise choice.

"This room is bigger than my entire apartment," Evan whispered as his eyes took in every square inch of the room. A bed big enough for a family straddled the wall to the left, complimented by built in nightstands. More Aztec rugs covered the tiled floor. In the middle of the room, a lime green loveseat faced a built in entertainment center. Bulky curtains covered a glass door. Evan glided to the curtains and drew them back, a balcony with stairs leading to the pool area. Another adobe building sat on the other side of the Olympic size swimming pool. On the far end of the property he spied a small adobe structure. "What's that building at the end of the property?"

"Mr. and Mrs. Kurl stay there, the couple who keep up the house and grounds. Let us continue and I'll introduce you."

Evan took one last gawk at *his* room then followed Mr. Fritz. The room to the farthest right caught Evan's attention. He pushed the door and it swung open revealing a room with blue diaper pins painted midway across the wall. Below the diaper pins the walls were light blue, above them white. A white cradle and matching rocking chair the only furniture in the room. Sheer, matching blue curtains fell across the window. He walked into the room, ran his hand along the cradle, then he noticed a closet. He slid the door open. Several baby outfits of varying sizes hung on blue hangers with silk bows. Below the clothes were shelves with baskets filled with blankets, bibs, toys, and undershirts.

"Your room," said Mr. Fritz.

Evan looked towards him, water puddled in the corners of his eyes. He blinked it away. "Everything is here. What did she take?" Speaking of his vile mother.

"I think everything you hadn't grown out of. Mrs. Kurl has done an excellent job preserving all of it. Let me show you the rest."

Evan left the room, closing the door behind him, and followed Mr. Fritz through the rest of the tour of the house and grounds. Evan remained almost speechless, his eyes wide as they passed the pool area, guest house, and entered the garage filled with classic sports cars. "Your father loved cars."

The wall near the door held several keys, each labeled *Vette, Mercedes, Ferrari*... "These are mine too?"

Mr. Fritz smiled wide. "All of it."

Evan ran his finger across the dust-free shiny hood of the '63 Vette. He opened the wide door and slipped inside, grasping the shifter, placing his foot on the clutch, he went through the gears. *Smooth as snakeskin*, he thought.

A tall man with a gray rim of hair surrounding a shimmering bald patch walked through the door followed by a thin woman. Her long, grayish-brown hair swept into a loose bun, wisps plastered her cheeks from sweat. "You must be the Kurls?" asked Evan.

Mr. Kurl extended his hand, patches of darkened skin covered his hands and arms. A sign he was no stranger to hard labor in the sun. "Haldon Kurl, a pleasure to meet you."

Evan shook his hand then turned to Mrs. Kurl. He raised her hand to his mouth and kissed her wrinkled skin. Inside, his stomach wrenched, outside he was cool as an icicle. Her face turned flush. No one had kissed her hand in many years. "Amelia Kurl."

"Did you both work for my father?" The more Evan learned about his father the more he liked him and connected with the house, his belongings, and the elderly couple in front of him.

Mr. Kurl wiped the sweat off his brow and neck. "Your father hired me as a young man. My wife and I were starting out, had a young' un" and I needed a job. He was a kind man."

Evan imagined them as a young hippy couple who realized living a "free" life meant supporting their "young' un". "You must share stories with me sometime. I'm curious to learn more about him." Evan flashed them a smile. At first, the thought of the couple staying on his property disturbed him but after meeting them he knew they'd be perfect, filled with tidbits about his father and *mommy*.

"Kevin" Has a Name

"Possibly the most gruesome crime scene in my career and durin' a nasty summer storm cell," said Horn City Sheriff Jones as he swished the toothpick in his mouth from the left to the right.

A young lady with caramel colored hair hanging past her breasts swished past Burkhalder with a file in hand - heels clicking on the tile floor. "Thanks, Sue." He took the file from her.

Sheriff Jones's large paws passed the file to Burkhalder. "This is it, everything we got. If you have questions I'll be in my office." He pointed towards a dark wood door bearing a metal placard with his name.

"Thanks." She snatched the folder, turned to the blue fabric chair with a rip across the seat and sat. Burkhalder flipped through the folder, disheartened by the amount of bloodshed evident in each picture. Her eyes shifted to the dust and dark splotches lingering on the wall and baseboard of the station. She sucked in her breath and flipped to the report, pushing the other pictures aside. The oldest son, Evan, found on his mother. Her brows pulled together, the skin wrinkling between them, as she read the

118

details. The two-year-old daughter, Emily, found beneath her dresser. Her eyes studied the pictures again, too many similarities to the Tates'. *Is it possible Evan is Kevin?* Her mind lingered on the similarities and wondered if Evan killed his family or if he was emulating the murders of his family?

The attacker sliced the mother several times. Her lacerations not clean and neat like Lilly's but jagged. Fleshy meat hung from her neck. The knife used was never found. She wrote the address on her notepad then laid the pictures on the particle board table and compared both crime scenes. Flipping through the file, she found the toxicology report. Drugs consistent with over the counter sleeping aids were found in the mother and son, the mother raped. *A sloppier, less experienced assailant?*

Nowhere in the report did it mention the fate of the two surviving children. She rapped on the Sheriff's door.

"Come in!"

She placed the file on his desk then sat down across from him. "What happened to the surviving children?"

He took the toothpick out of his mouth and threw it into the trashcan beside his desk, leaned forward and nodded. "No family, Emily went into foster care and a family adopted her right away. She was a cute little girl with bouncy blond curls. A real doll.

Evan, they sent him for evaluation and then to Windy Oaks Mental Facility - a little unusual. Most kids are sent to a local facility. Windy Oaks is an upstate facility for children with severe disorders."

"Doctor patient confidentiality and all that prohibits any information, but did you ever check on him?"

He punched his bottom lip over his top lip and shook his head. "Nope. You saw the scene. I always thought he did it but had no evidence. The front door locked, no signs of forced entry. A neighbor called it in after she saw the father's body, a bloody mess, dead in the recliner. They put him away, and I prayed they'd keep him there and transfer him to an adult facility when he turned eighteen."

She dipped her hand into her purse and pulled out the sketch, unfolded it, and placed it on the metal desk in front of him. "Did Evan look anything like this sketch?"

He reached in his drawer and pulled out reading glasses, scooting them over his nose until they rested square in front of his eyes. "That could be him. It was ten years ago. He's a grown man now."

"I believe this man raped a woman in Billows Hollow a year ago. During Hurricane Chloe this family," she laid her crime scene photos on the desk before him, "we found them, their necks slit."

Sheriff Jones slid a new toothpick into his mouth. "Tell you what, I got an intern in our forensics department, he's been talking about some facial aging software he's designing. He may can help you out."

She followed the Sheriff through a dingy blue corridor, the overhead fluorescents blinking- begging to be changed out. And into a sterile white room. "Welcome to our forensics department."

Burkhalder was in awe of the cleanliness surrounding her. So far the station looked like most - half-ass clean and shitty lighting.

"I leave you with Jeremy." Sheriff Jones turned on his heels and disappeared out the door.

A thin man near twenty-five walked up to her offering his hand. "I'm Jeremy. What can I help you with?"

She accepted his hand and gave it a quick shake. "I have a sketch and need to know if you can take it and age the face in the picture back ten years. The Sheriff says you have software you're developing for facial recognition and such."

His thin lips parted into a wide smile. "He did? I... I'd... be pleased to help you. So this is a real case." A twinkle blinked in the corners of his eyes.

"Yes it is." She handed him the sketch.

"Why not go to the FBI?" he asked, while studying the hand sketched picture.

"I have no real evidence, no leads. Only a sketch and a hunch."

"I can work with this. It may take time since this isn't an actual photo." He handed the sketch to her. "The software's not here. It's at my house. Can you meet me there when my shift is over?"

"Write me directions." Her heart smiled at his anticipation of using his software in an actual police case.

He ran to a counter, grabbed a pen and paper out of the drawer then scribbled a crude map. "See ya tonight."

"Thanks, Jeremy." She opened the door, surprised at the heaviness of it, and traipsed through the corridor and out of the police station.

Windy Oaks

Fewer homes on larger plots of land and thicker groups of trees dotted the landscape as Burkhalder headed north-west. Her car crept towards the mountains. She unrolled the window to allow the fresh mountain scents to fill her car.

Lush trees swallowed the road as her car climbed into the mountains and deposited her in Rocky Mount. She continued through the city, taking in the views surrounding her. She spent her entire life on the islands, since Chloe she longed to move away. A breeze swept through the trees calling her, feeding her desire for change.

Rocky Mount disappeared behind her. To her right she spotted a white sign with bold blue lettering *Windy Oaks Mental Facility*. She eased the car onto the winding road lined with oak trees and pulled her car into the guest parking area. A three story brick structure hidden amongst the trees emerged as she followed the sidewalk.

Inside, a large waiting room filled with couches and tables gave the facility a homey, relaxing feel. Nothing like what she imagined. Two aqua colored doors on each side of the waiting room separated patients from visitors.

A white haired woman sat behind the typical doctor's office plexi-glass.

"Can I help you?" said the older woman in a soft gentle voice.

"Detective Burkhalder. I'm here to see Dr. Ratzlove."

"Yes, honey, she'll be with you in a minute. Please take a seat."

Several minutes later, one of the aqua doors opened. A thin woman with salt and pepper hair tied back in a tight bun motioned for Burkhalder.

The woman's suit designed in mixed shades of grays. Beneath her jacket an antique white blouse with ruffles. She introduced herself. "I'm Dr. Ratzlove, let's talk in my office." Her slacks swished as she walked. The halls painted a sky blue.

Dr. Ratzlove carried her curveless thin frame with ease, opening the door with her frail arm. "Please take a seat," she requested, pointing towards a plush tan chair across from a heavy wooden desk. The enormity of Dr. Ratzlove's chair swallowed her bony body as she sat and scooted towards the desk. She peered at Burkhalder through round John Lennon style glasses. The lens thickness bulged her eyes out similar to looking at a fly beneath a microscope. Dr. Ratzlove folded her hands under her pointed chin. "You know I can't give you any specifics due to his age and confidentiality."

Burkhalder nodded her head without getting a word out before Dr. Ratzlove spoke again. "During Evan's stay he was a model patient, completing inpatient, group, one on one and outpatient care. He always followed the rules, never stepped out line, and was always polite. He reacted well to our treatment plan for him."

Sure he did. Aren't sociopaths intelligent and manipulative? Dr. Ratzlove's icy demeanor told Burkhalder she wouldn't get much information, so she wasted no time. "I understand this facility is for those who have severe disorders, such as Antisocial Personality Disorder?"

"In some cases, yes, but not all." Over the eight years Evan spent at Windy Oaks, Dr. Ratzlove had grown to adore the boy. Unable to bear children of her own after suffering several years of molestation from her uncle, Evan and her patients filled the motherhood void inside her. She would protect him at all costs. At ten, hatred and anxiety filled him inside, outside he stayed calm and cool. The only time she feared him was the moments she brought up his sexually abusive mother. His pupils grew so large they took over his iris and a cold chill settled upon the room. Thinking about it sent chills down her spine. She learned never to bring up his mother.

"The local facility first diagnosed Evan, but their diagnoses are always less than acceptable. Too many patients and not enough staff. I re-diagnosed him upon his arrival at Windy Oaks." She cleared her throat.

Burkhalder, aware of all the recent budget cuts to mental health care couldn't imagine him staying at Windy Oaks unless paid for privately. *Who is his benefactor?* "Is Windy Oaks a private facility?"

"It is."

"Does the state finance any patients?" she questioned, hoping to at least get a lead. *Who financed his stay if not the state?*

"Not often and only under special circumstances."

Annoyed by Dr. Ratzlove side-stepping her questions she tried another avenue. "When did Evan leave Windy Oaks?"

"Three years ago, at age eighteen. We had no reason to continue inpatient treatment with him. We placed him in one of our group homes and I continued to treat him on an outpatient basis until a year ago. He's continued to do well."

Relieved she received a straight answer and a carrot to prolong the conversation, hoping she'd drop her guard and a morsel. She rolled her tongue across the inside of her bottom lip as she chose her words. "In my line of work I don't see many success stories. I imagine you don't either. Can you elaborate?"

"Evan left here and went to college. He took more than the required courses each semester and graduated this past May. I went to his graduation." Her lips curved upwards into a smile. "That type of success we don't see every day. I'm proud of him. He carried a lot of baggage when he arrived here."

Burkhalder's nervous tension eased, she got her to smile. "I read the police report. I imagine witnessing his parents' and brother's brutal murders and his mother's rape would do severe psychological damage to anyone."

"Yes it can. Is there anything more?"

"I have a sketch, a young man who found a child during our clean-up efforts after Hurricane Chloe. I never got to thank him. Could you take a look at it and tell me if it's Evan?"

"You must excuse my bluntness today. We don't often get visits from police officers because our patients might be heroes. Yes, please, let me see the sketch." She reached out her boney arm.

Burkhalder slipped it from her notepad, unfolded it and placed it on the desk between them.

Dr. Ratzlove picked it up, adjusted her coke bottle glasses, and cocked her head as she studied the picture. "That looks like Evan."

"I know it's against rules but I'd appreciate an address on him so I can thank him proper."

Dr. Ratzlove wanted to believe her ears, wanted to trust that somebody wanted to do something good for one of her patients. Her own inside voice sided with caution. "I don't have a current address on him but you can get the address of the group home he stayed at from Matilda at the front desk. Maybe they have a forwarding address."

"Thank you." Burkhalder rose from her chair and let herself out. *The doctor went to his graduation yet has no address? Bullshit!* She sucked up what she couldn't force out of the doctor and accepted the address of the group home. A crumb, not quite a morsel, but enough to continue her search.

Dr. Ratzlove shifted in her chair. "Detective Burkhalder, I hope your intentions are honest. Evan doesn't need more nightmares in his life."

Burkhalder, one foot out the door, froze, turned and nodded, acknowledging Dr. Ratzlove's words. She wanted to imagine Evan, as a ten-year-old, was innocent but the cards were against him and the Tates' murders were near identical. It's not often a serial killer is "born" as a child but it happens. Her curiosity about his mother and father heightened. *Did they trigger the "gene"?*

We Got a Winner

Burkhalder, following Jeremy's crude map to his apartment, pulled onto the private road that curved through the complex. Brick two story buildings surrounded by a variety of trees, she swung her car into a parking space.

Slender Jeremy opened the door, a wide smile displaying his ruler straight white teeth. "Come in. I am so pleased to use my software in a real case." Excitement filled his voice. He held the door open for her and closed and locked it behind her. "This neighborhood isn't always so good, so I keep it locked."

"I lock my doors at home, too," voiced Burkhalder.

"Would you like a beer?"

"Sounds good."

The apartment was so small it took him just a few long strides to reach the refrigerator. The fizz-pop of a fresh can of beer filled her ears. The bubbly liquid slid down her throat too easily after the day she'd had.

Jeremy dragged a kitchen chair to his computer and took a seat in a black rolling chair. "Take a seat." The computer swooshed and clacked as he turned it on and started up the software.

Burkhalder pulled the sketch from her purse, handing it to Jeremy.

"That's great sketch work! Billows Hollow's so tiny, didn't think you had a sketch artist?"

"We don't. I hijacked a willing teen with incredible talent the day after the hurricane."

Jeremy's thin lips pulled across his face. "Guess you need to be resourceful."

She nodded.

He scanned the picture, which loaded to his screen. In full black and white in front of her eyes. He guided his mouse over the picture and clicked on specific points, making the image appear as if someone had performed acupuncture on its face.

"How many years backwards are we going?"

"Eleven."

He typed in the parameters then waited. "Would you like another beer while we wait? It may take thirty minutes."

"I could use another."

He tossed her one and Jeremy picked her brain about police work. A beeping interrupted their conversation. He leaned his torso backwards and viewed the computer.

"It's ready." He jumped off the couch and swung around it to the computer.

Burkhalder walked behind Jeremy seated in his chair, leaned against his couch and peered at the computer. "Can you print that out?"

"Already sent, give it a minute to warm up." The machine's tapping and clunking shadowed his words. Within a few minutes, he laid a wet color picture beside the computer.

She hovered above it, dumbfounded by the ability of his software. "All those questions earlier about being a cop. You really don't plan to. This is your calling."

His face turned a light shade of red. He shrugged his shoulders and swished his wispy lips to the side causing his cheek to puff. "You got me. It's still got a few bugs but once it's ready I'll patent it and search for a buyer."

"You let me know if'n I can return the favor?"

The following day, she swung back by the police station so the sheriff could look at the photo.

"That's a good likeness to him." Sheriff Jones confirmed. "I reckon he'll make a pretty penny off that software."

"Reckon he will." She took a sip of steaming coffee. "You said the neighbor called in the murders. What's the address? I'd like to ask her questions."

He cleared his throat. "Doubt she forgot. She cleared out of there after the murders, scared I guess." He scribbled on a notepad, ripped off the paper and handed it to her.

"Since she was the closest thing we had to a witness I couldn't let her off the hook. This is the family's last known address, but that was ten years ago."

She parked her car alongside the road and rechecked the address then strode to the door and rang the bell. A barking from the other side grew louder as a large dog scratched at the door. "Beast, down!" She heard from the other side. "Who is it?" came a woman's voice.

Detective Burkhalder lifted her badge in front of the peephole. "I'm here to ask you questions about a murder scene you witnessed eleven years ago."

Burkhalder listened to the clank of several locks. After a few clanks the door slid open. A small, ebony skinned woman with short curly hair opened the door in slow motion. She signaled inside the door at her dog then finished opening the door. "Mrs. Zander." She held out her hand.

"Detective Burkhalder."

"Can I see that badge again?"

Taking note of her precautionary nature, Burkhalder flipped out her badge. Mrs. Zander studied it then welcomed her inside the house. From the entryway a garlic aroma teased her nose. The modern motif with square leather couches and tables reminded Burkhalder of the '70s furnishings her parents had in black and shades of white instead of orange and puke green.

Mrs. Zander ran her palms down the sides of her jeans. "This isn't easy for me. I hoped the day would never come. I know that sounds wrong but I want no part of any of it." She lowered herself onto a cream colored loveseat and motioned for Burkhalder to take the matching chair across from her. A large sable Rottweiler followed the woman, sitting on the floor by her feet, eyes glued to Burkhalder.

"Mrs. Zander, we don't have to go back to the scene. I've seen the crime scene photos. I'm more interested in the family dynamics."

With a dramatic sweeping motion Mrs. Zander swiped her hand across her forehead. "We moved after the... after the family... not because of what happened. We talked with a realtor before that. They had problems, and we lived across the street."

"What type of problems?"

"Mr. O'Conner had a terrible drinking problem. He'd drive home drunk - his Ford truck always sideways in the driveway. On a couple occasions he side swiped vehicles. The damage never discovered until the morning. Insurance reports would be filed, the police called, but too late to arrest him for a DUI. Oh, and he treated the oldest son, my, just so badly. I never heard him say a kind word to him ever. I felt horrible for him. A few times we invited him over to do odd jobs, something to get the child away from his father. Such a polite young man, always yes ma'am, no ma'am. He wasn't a bad kid."

"How did he treat the other children?"

"I didn't see him with the baby much. The boys would be outside playing and he'd come running out swinging his belt cussing up a storm at Evan. He wouldn't say a word to Elfred." Her hands flailed through the air as she reminisced. "Nothing," she said while nodding her head.

Burkhalder thought on that. An abused child many times becomes the abuser, but a murderer? *And why did the father pick on him and not the other children?* "Mrs. Zander."

"Call me Tina."

"Tina, how did the mother treat the children?"

"One second, I need to tend my vegetable soup."

Beast, the well trained Rottweiler, stayed put, Burkhalder in his sights. Mrs. Zander entered the room, two steaming bowls in her hands. "I hope you are hungry." She handed a bowl to Burkhalder.

"Thank you," she said, taking the bowl of soup.

Mrs. Zander returned to her seat. Beast eased his head onto her feet, one eye on Burkhalder. "The mother, I never saw her treat any of the children wrong. It seemed she was extra affectionate to Evan. Always tousling his blond curls, her hand on his shoulder, that kind of thing."

"You think the father was jealous?"

"I don't think Mr. O'Conner cared or noticed who she paid attention to. Only thing mattered to him was the bottle."

Burkhalder dwelt on her words while she sipped her soup. The flavors mingling together on her tongue creating a tasty sensation. "This is the best vegetable soup I've ever ate!"

Tina smiled. "It won first prize in the Horn City cook off last year."

"How about the boys, did they get along?" Remembering her own dueling sibling rivalry she imagined Evan disliked his brother.

"Elfred followed Evan everywhere, even when Evan was in trouble. Instead of staying outside playing, he'd go inside, like a puppy dog he was towards Evan."

None of it made sense. *If Evan is guilty and killed his family, why not just the father? Why all of them?* "What school did the children in that neighborhood attend?"

Tina wrote the name and address on a tablet and ripped off the page, handing it to Burkhalder. "Thank you, detective."

"Thank you?" she questioned, eyebrows burrowing into the crevice above her nose.

"That was the scariest sight I've seen. You're the only officer I've spoken to who hasn't made me relive it."

"Thank you for the soup."

"You have a goodnight." Tina closed the door behind Burkhalder.

Outside, the humidity in the evening air hung in suspended water droplets clouding the street light giving it a fuzzy appearance.

Her pocket buzzed from the vibration of her cell phone. "Hello."

"Hon, where are ya?" asked Jax.

"I took a few personal days to research the suspect in Gala's rape. Since I'm not allowed to do it on the clock."

The swish of his phone against his cheek as he nodded sounded on the other line. "Maybe you can talk to the sheriff again. It's been two years and the town's healin' and back together."

"A day when he's in a good mood. I learned someone murdered my perp's family near twelve years ago, eerily similar to the Tates' murders down to the youngest, a girl, surviving. It's been a long day, I'm heading back to my room. I'll share everything with you when I get back to town."

"You be careful. If this guy is a rapist/serial killer you don't want to be on his list. And don't go leavin' town without sayin' somethin' to me. Had me worried."

"We're cops, it's what we do and I don't go anywhere without my gun."

"I'll see you when you get back."

"Good night, Jax." She knew he wanted and deserved far more than she offered such as a wife, children, and white picket fence. But that would never be her.

One Thing

Evan's DNA test came back with a forty-nine percent match to Evan O'Conner Senior. What Mr. Fritz didn't tell him is his DNA was only a twenty-three percent match to his mother. He left that crumb out. As Mr. O'Conner senior's lawyer, all that mattered was a match to his father and the estate was his. Fear also dictated Mr. Fritz's actions. He dreaded the blackness that controlled Evan at the mention of his mother.

☾ ☾ ☾ ☾ ☾

Evan packed his belongings and settled into his father's home in New Mexico. His first order of business was setting up rules for his staff. He liked his privacy, therefore only allowed Mrs. Kurl to clean once a week, every room except his parents'. He changed the locks and kept that room locked. It was his "special room". Eilida's monkey, Sandy, lay propped in the center of the pillows resting against the headboard and a map of the southeast U.S. hung on the wall with a thumbtack pinned to Billows Hollow and Horn City. His next order of business was having the room sealed off from the hallway and having a single entrance to the room. A private, secret entrance from the office next door.

As an unemployed millionaire he used his time to study his interests. Hurricanes, astrology, and developing serums. He installed an astrology program on his computer. Hitting the new moon during Hurricane Chloe had been a lucky accident. To him, the stars were on his side. He wanted to understand to what extent so he ran his natal chart, running his fat pointer finger across the connecting lines and reading the text as if was a fictional cliffhanger.

Scorpio Rising:

You are very strong-willed and proud, but intensely private and not easy to know well. Behind your quiet exterior lies a great deal of emotional depth, sensitivity, complexity, and also fierce determination. When you want something you go after it rather quietly but insistently and wholeheartedly - and you usually get it.

You want to live passionately and intensely and are not averse to challenge, danger, or to facing the darker side of life - human pain and struggle.

The edges of his thin lips curled into a smile at the accuracy of the words. It wasn't luck. The stars dictated his cunning success.

The Calm Before the Storm: Evan's Sins

His need to challenge nature and the ability to hold life in his fingertips. He continued reading, proud to be a Cancer on the Gemini Cusp. He accepted all that was him, until he read...

Moon in 4th house:

You have strong attachments to your past, the place where you grew up, your heritage, and family traditions. In fact, you may be unable to step out of the habits and roles you learned as a child. Your tie to your mother is very strong.

Sun in Cancer:

You have powerful emotional attachments to the past, your family, your childhood, those places you associate with safety and security and your beginnings. Maintaining a connection with your roots and heritage and keeping family bonds strong are very important to you.

Visions of his mother taunting him, touching him, flooded the words. He clutched the report and scrunched it, balling it into a paper-wad and threw it across the room. From across the room the paper-wad spoke to him.

You are primarily emotional and your views are often dominated by your feelings and by your own personal, subjective experiences, rather than reason, logic, or abstract principles.

His eyes glued to the paper, steam rising inside him. How dare the stars dictate his mother's sickness towards him and his inability to rid her from his life permanently! Another idea ploughed through the anger in his head. He rolled his plush leather chair towards his computer and punched in his birth digits and determined his life number. A four. The website explained a person with a life number of four tended towards organization, methodical planning, and deep commitment. Sinking back into the chair he considered the years he spent in Windy Oaks preparing for his return to society to rid his life of his *mother*. The map on his wall with two thumbtacks and a string between them, the girls' names labeled beside each, and the folders in his desk labeled with possible *families*. Four fit him well, too well.

He rolled his chair backwards and propped his feet on his desk. Mars retrograde occurs a little over every two years. A bad time to start something new, an even worse time to use his metal blade to slice the breath out of his victims. Metal, a toxic tool during Mars retrograde, it's sure to backfire. A life number of four, Mars retrograde every two years, he chose every three years. A midpoint to use as the day of his mother's reckoning, skating by sure doom.

☾ ☾ ☾ ☾ ☾

Burkhalder made a stop at Evan's elementary school. None of his teachers remained but the new principal was nice enough to provide her with the retired principal's phone number after she fed him the "hero" story.

They met at Bean and Bear It, a coffeehouse. Civil war guns and artifacts hung from the tan walls alongside black and white pictures in tin frames. They sat in a private corner on aged cypress chairs. "Evan was a good kid. A model student." Burkhalder sucked in her thoughts as Principal Webber continued with the same drip and garble everyone else had to say. "There was this one time… " She sipped her coffee, placing her mug onto the wooden barrel between them. "I hesitate. It wasn't anything wrong, more a strange reaction. His closest school friend, Jason, fell off a swing in the school yard. The children gathered around oohing and aahing but Evan found the teacher on duty and told her Tyler, the school bully, pushed Jason off the swing and hurt his arm. That's how Evan was, always the good kid." She opened her mouth as if to continue, then stopped.

"Sounds like he was a hero as a child too," piped Burkhalder, hoping to keep her talking.

She heaved her chunky leg over the other and twisted in her seat. "Yes and no. I thought so then. One other child backed Evan's story about Tyler pushing Jason off the swing. It was enough to suspend him for a few days. Tyler rode his bike to school every day. After his suspension, on his way home, his bicycle veered into a tree while heading downhill. The result, a severed spinal cord. Accidents happen, Tyler wasn't a nice kid - anybody could have sabotaged his bike or maybe nobody did. The boys were all about nine. Evan showed no expression through either accident. He went on as if nothing happened. Tyler's cronies were sad, their leader reduced to a wheel chair. Tyler's victims were elated while many of the students were scared and sad. My point, Detective Burkhalder, is all the children but Evan displayed emotion through both accidents."

Burkhalder sighed relief, somebody who thought maybe Evan wasn't so perfect.

Lack of emotion the sure sign of a sociopath. Was it possible to diagnose children that age with such a debilitating mental illness?

"Were you aware his father was an abusive alcoholic?"

"I wasn't. Evan showed no source of discomfort or pain. He was a private child yet got along well with the other children."

Burkhalder checked her watch. "I have an appointment and need to get going, but thank you for your time, Ms. Webber."

Principal Webber leaned her back against the hard wooden chair. "You are most welcome." She took another sip of her coffee and pulled a book to her nose.

Burkhalder rushed off to make her appointment at the group home Evan stayed in until a year ago. He moved out a few weeks prior to the hurricane.

The cozy A-frame log cabin crested Mount Wilde in Chesterville. It sat back off the main road on a private dirt drive. A breeze whipped the thick curl of hair dangling from her ponytail across her face. She wiped the auburn mass of tangles from her face and welcomed the less muggy windy air.

A fortyish man with a thick brown halo of hair surrounding a bald center answered the door and welcomed her inside the house. "Detective Burkhalder, right on schedule. Take a seat in my office and I'll be right with you." A thick brown mustache covered his upper lip and moved as he spoke. He motioned for her to take a seat in a side room with a floor to ceiling window exposing the colorful dips and peaks of the mountain.

Deer antlers clung to each side of the wall surrounding the window. Pictures hung in various sized, non-matching frames, covering the wall to the left of the window. She studied the pictures, searching for anything she could learn about Evan that Mr. Cantor might withhold. A single group picture with the year 1991 written in the corner. In the picture he looked identical to the sketch, wild blond ringlets sprang at every angle from his head and pale blue eyes stared back at her. Her body shuddered. His photo gave her the sense of being followed.

She peeked around the door and saw no one, then studied the walls for hidden cameras. Nothing caught her eye, so she walked past the tall metal file cabinet beside the thrift store variety particle board desk and gave it a yank - locked.

"Thank you for waiting," said Mr. Cantor.

She jumped and flipped her body towards the voice. "You gave me a fright."

"I didn't mean to. Take a seat." He slid into a seat behind the desk.

She looked towards the vacant chair covered in a flowery fabric and sat.

"What can I help you with?"

"Two years ago, Hurricane Chloe devastated my community and I believe Evan O'Conner saved a young child's life. Somehow she got trapped in a chest. He found her and lifted her out of a chest. I didn't get a chance to thank him. Now the town is settling back into our usual rhythm and I want to thank him proper."

"As part of our program, residents are required to leave a forwarding address when they move out." He lifted his tall frame from his seat and took two steps to the file cabinet, unlocked it, flipped through a few files then pulled out a note card. He took another step to the printer and made a copy then slipped the note card back into the file cabinet and locked it. His willingness to hand over Evan's address surprised her.

"Detective Burkhalder, I can't guarantee he's still at this address but it's all I have. Is there anything else I can help you with?"

"My moment with him was brief. Can you tell me about his personality? I would like to buy him a gift of some type. Does he have interests?"

Mr. Cantor picked up a pencil, tapped it on the desk then swirled it in the air and laid it in front of him. "Evan's a decent kid, graduated with a bachelors in Pharmaceutical Science." *Surprise, surprise, he likes and knows drugs,* thought Burkhalder. "A pharmacy offered him job right out of college but I can't remember where." He swirled the pencil again. "He used to watch the stars through the telescope in the loft. Had a few books on Astrology. Oh yeah! He was damn good at predicting weather." *Well that explains a lot,* her mind jested.

"And he chose pharmaceuticals, huh? With all those interests and talents he chose drugs." She chuckled.

"He was smart enough for med school. I encouraged him to go, but he said blood made him queasy. He wanted to help people feel better without having to operate or see blood." Burkhalder nearly choked on her own spit. "Heck, it didn't matter, having one of these young' uns" go to college then graduate is a huge achievement. Most of them end up working a blue collar job and a few of them end up back in mental health facilities and sometimes jail. We do our darned best to keep them on the straight and narrow."

He'd given her a plethora of information. Her next stop was to stop by the address Mr. Cantor provided.

Houdini

The address led to a brick ranch style apartment building in Horn City. She traipsed around it, opened the back door and slipped inside it. The hall smelled of fresh paint. One of the doors was open, number 3. She looked at the card - Evan's apartment. Humming from the inside caught her attention. She knocked on the open door and a young, gangly man looked her direction. He slipped earphones off his ears. "Apartment won't be ready to look at for another day or so. The paint's gotta dry."

"I'm not lookin' to rent. I'm lookin' for this apartment's last tenant."

"Well ma'am I can't help you there. He's left and no forwarding address."

"Aren't most tenants required to leave forwarding addresses?"

"He vacated without telling us anythin'"

"He talk much with the neighbors?"

"I wouldn't know ma'am."

"Thank you." She turned and walked towards the exit. A young woman leaned against the exterior of the building. The sun catching blond highlights in her hair. She blew a smoke ring. A cigarette between her thumb and forefinger. Bootie shorts crawling into her camel toe. "You lookin' for Evan?"

"I am."

"He done something?"

"Not exactly, why do you ask?"

She dropped her cigarette and ground it into the cement with her flip-flop. "The walls here are thin. I used to hear him talking to his mom but nobody else was in his apartment, if you get what I'm sayin'."

"Anything else?"

"Yeah, overheard him on the phone, couple weeks before he disappeared. Something about the airport and some place called Albakerkee." She struggled to pronounce the name. "Then he vanished for a couple days. Came back and left again."

Burkhalder offered her hand. "Thank you."

"Don't thank me. I'm jus' glad he's gone. He gave me the creeps. At first I thought he was a nice guy then I started overhearin' him talkin', home alone. One day I got curious and knocked on his door. He answered and his eyes were dark as tar. But they were usually a light blue. But sometimes he'd have these weird rings around the colored part. One ring would be yellow the other amber. I also noticed from the corner of my eye, I'm real observant, a pair of men's underwear with a wet spot right in the crotch area. So I automatic looked downward, and he had a bulge behind the zipper of his pants. So I know men like porn and beat off and all, but he'd been talkin' to his mom. How many guys beat off to thoughts of their mom?"

Chills spiked the hair on Burkhalder's arms. She remembered Mrs. Zander's words, 'Always tousling his blond curls, her hand on his shoulder, that kind of thing'. *Did she sexually abuse him?* The idea made sense. It explained why he raped the mothers and mutilated their necks. A crime of passion and hate.

This young lady was the first person she'd met that found Evan disturbing. "Are you hungry?"

"If you're payin'. By the way, name is Misty."

Misty turned out to have a surplus of information about Evan, including his place of employment.

He worked at a popular pharmacy on the other end of town as a tech. His boss didn't tell her much different than anybody else - nice guy, hard worker, smart, blah, blah. He quit over the phone. Told her his father was ill, in the hospital, and he needed to help take care of him upon release. She asked for the address where he sent his final paycheck and he gave her an address in Albuquerque New Mexico!

Burkhalder drove home that night, with a renewed devotion and vigor to find him. She

had something beyond a dead end and
another person who didn't buy his "nice guy"
act. And he had a CNPR license. She could
track that!

72 Hours

Less than seventy-two hours later, Burkhalder found a huge list of Evan O'Conners across the country but only one in Albuquerque. Evan O'Conner Senior, deceased November 22, 1973. Ten years to the day of President Kennedy's mysterious assassination. To her, this struck bells. A senior, a possible relation to the Evan she sought? If Evan loved astrology it wouldn't be a far reach for him to be superstitious. His name didn't come up alone, but synonymous with a lawyer named Fritz.

Her lips spread across her face in the largest smile of her life. She picked up the phone receiver and dialed the lawyer's number.

"Fritz Legal Services. How can I help you?" Spoken in business ease sailed through the earpiece into Burkhalder's ear.

Attempting to erase the southern from her voice as non-southerner's generally disliked the accent she answered, "Can I speak with Mr. Fritz please?"

"He's with a client. What is your name and number? He'll return your call."

Burkhalder left her private number and name, telling the receptionist she was seeking legal assistance. She figured she had a better chance of him calling her back if it meant money.

Three hours later, as she stepped over the threshold of her house, the phone rang. She snatched it out of her pocket and walked towards her back deck as she had the best cell reception there.

"Hello?"

"Ms. Burkhalder, this is Mr. Fritz."

Again masking her southern accent she answered, "Mr. Fritz, thank you for returning my call so quickly."

"You're seeking legal advice but your number is out of state. Are you aware each state has their own laws?"

"Yes I am. I'm seeking advice for me. I work for the Billows Hollow Register and I'm trying to locate a young man who was instrumental in saving a girl's life. I think you can help me."

"How's that?"

"I think he, or a relation of his, is a client of yours."

His line went silent for a few seconds longer than it should have. "Who is the client?"

"He's deceased, but the name is Evan O'Conner."

"And how can I help you?"

"Does he have any living relatives?"

"He does. I'm not at liberty to give you information on them but I can answer questions pertaining to the deceased as confidentiality no longer applies."

"The young man I seek carries the same name and recently moved to Albuquerque. Of course, I put two and two together which led me to you. He carries the same name and believe he's an heir." She touched the cushion on her lawn chair to determine if it had dried since the previous day's rain. She sat down when her finger tips didn't squish any water.

"Ms. Burkhalder, if you have no further questions pertaining to the deceased our phone call is over."

"My information says he lived on an estate called Poppy Hills."

"That's true. His estate is large and belongs to his heirs."

She had to pry out everything she could. If Evan was his heir than the estate was his, making him a very wealthy man and giving him the financial security and freedom to continue his killing sprees. It would also explain his stay in Windy Oaks. Why, when the country was experiencing huge cut backs to mental health care, he was comfortable in a high class mental health facility getting the best care and treatment. It would also explain why Dr. Ratzlove wouldn't give her any info about how his stay was financed. "Did he have a child, a son?"

"He does, but I'm not at liberty to tell any more about him."

Bingo! "Can you give him a message?"

She heard him sigh. "What is the message?"

"That he's a hero and Billows Hollow would like to thank him with a piece in the local paper and a small reward." She banked on Evan having a large self-centered ego that accepted and fed off the hero role.

"If my client is the man you seek and if he's willing, who should he call?"

"He can call me. I'll be the one to interview him and write the article," she lied, hoping to persuade Evan's huge ego into returning the call.

"I will relay this information. Have a good day, Ms. Burkhalder."

"Thank you." She clicked her phone off and admired the golden violet hues sinking into the horizon.

He never returned the *call* and she wondered if Mr. Fritz even relayed the message. Disgusted and determined, she bought a plane ticket to Albuquerque.

I Am the Estate

Months went by, Evan gave the Kurls time to tell his parents' secrets yet they remained tight lipped. Their silence cost them. They would tell him everything he wanted to know over dinner.

He lifted the baked salmon from the oven, moved the steaming asparagus and tossed the salad. Covering the hot dishes, he set them on the table and arranged the plates, silverware, bowls and accessories. The doorbell rang as he grabbed the bottle of Pinot Noir, setting it on the table he shuffled to the door.

"Come in."

"Thank you, Mr. O'Conner."

Evan curled his lips into an amiable smile. "We don't do this often enough." He led them into the dining room. The sleek chandelier offered enough light to set a relaxed mood. He pulled out Mrs. Kurl's chair and pushed it in after she sat. After pouring wine into each glass, Evan scooted into his seat. The large table offered plenty of room but he placed the Kurls on either side of him while he sat at the head. Soft jazz music played in the background.

"The meal looks and smells delicious. I didn't know you cooked," said Mr. Kurl, as he cut into his salmon.

"It's a hobby. I'm sure there is a lot we don't know about each other." He glanced towards Mrs. Kurl. "Amelia, is it to your liking?"

"Oh yes, quite good." Her thin cheeks puffed beneath her eyes. The group made small talk while Evan waited for the *wine* to take effect.

"I'm going to haul these dishes to the kitchen, why don't you move into the living room?"

"You're very generous Mr. O'Conner, but we should be getting back. I don't want to take advantage."

"Don't be silly, you are my guests for the evening. I want you comfortable here with me and we're miles from town and further than shouting distance to our closest neighbors."

Evan loaded several dishes in his hands, watching the Kurls from the corner of his eye. Their gait told him the wine did the trick. He swirled the untouched liquid in his glass then poured it down the drain.

Mrs. Kurl was perched on the edge of the sectional and Mr. Kurl swayed as he gazed out the glass doors at the picturesque sunset. Evan clasped his hands in front of him and took a seat. "Now that I passed the *DNA test.*" He chuckled. All four eyes looked towards him, attempting to focus.

Mr. Kurl, on unsteady feet, tumbled onto the sectional beside his wife.

"In other words, I am the estate. I pay your checks. Mr. Fritz works for me and there's no other way to say this but both of you have been quiet too long. I want to know more about my parents, namely my father."

The couple glanced at each other. Mrs. Kurl blinked her eyes in rapid movement and Evan wondered if he added too large a dose of drugs to the wine. Relief washed over him when she spoke. "What is it you want to know?"

"Was he happy?"

"Yes, he was. He hired us sixteen years before he married your mother. I'd never seen him happier than after they married. He adored her and, well, he was not only a lover to her but in many ways a father figure. Sometimes we'd see them dancing here is this room, the setting sun behind them."

Visions of his mother waltzing across the floor in front of him made Evan's skin crawl. "They did? What else? Why aren't there any pictures or personal stuff besides his medical library?"

Mr. Kurl scratched his wobbly, balding head. "Mr. Fritz asked us to gather everything and get rid of it."

"Get rid of it where?"

"It's on the property. There's a secret room above the garage. We put it all there."

Evan liked the drug's results and the direction of the conversation. "You'll have to show me tonight. Is there a key?"

His mother draped her arms around his shoulders, *Of course there's a key.*

"Yes, it's on his key chain."

Evan looked towards Mr. Kurl. "I need you to give me that key."

Mr. Kurl nodded his head in agreement, slid a plain silver house key off his key ring and placed it in Evan's waiting palm.

"What else. What did they do out here alone?"

"Oh, they had parties. Couples parties, if you know what I mean." Mrs. Kurl winked her left eye. "A young woman, looked like your mom, once spent a couple weeks here. They didn't say, and we never asked, but she looked like a sister."

A sister. Evan rolled the idea through his head. His mother propped her head on his left shoulder and stroked his face. Annoyed, he put his hand in her translucent face breaking her image. She swirled and reappeared on Mr. Kurl. She sat in his lap and sucked his chin. Her tongue lashed across his bottom lip.

Go, get out! he shouted in his head. Evan stood. "It's late, why don't I take you home?" *Control, stay in control.*

"Got the golf cart, Mr. O'Conner, no need for you to trouble with taking us home." Mr. Kurl stood and Evan's mother fell off his lap, her form eddying towards the ceiling.

Visions of Mr. Kurl weaving the golf cart around his property and headlong into the pool, their drugged bodies sinking like rocks, flooded his head.

"Allow me. Please, it's my pleasure." Evan held the front door open for them. Mrs. Kurl climbed into the passenger seat of the golf cart while Mr. Kurl took a seat in the back.

"I once saw your dad eating something, it looked like celery, right out of her…"

Evan cut him off, attempting to change the subject. "What a clear night."

Mrs. Kurl looked towards her husband. "And the things they did with whipped cream and fruit."

Evan felt his dinner bubbling in his belly. He forced the accelerator down, pushing the limits of the golf cart's engine.

"The worst was the stuff they did inside." She leaned towards Evan's ear and whispered, "I never saw it." Then sat back, hands clutched in her lap. "The house was a mess, dildos, handcuffs, feather dusters…"

"Oh look, we're here." Evan couldn't hear any more. His dinner rose into his throat. He swallowed, pushing it down his esophagus.

"Tonight was a pleasure. We'll have to do this again," voiced Mrs. Kurl, stepping and tripping out of the golf cart. Evan ran to her side, helping her towards the house.

I hope not! The serum worked too well.

"I second that, our place next time."

Evan waved and pulled the golf cart away from their house. *I might have gone too heavy on the drugs?*

Hallucinations of his mother twirled through his head. He'd find the secret room another day, tonight his food was about to force its way out!

Courage

1995

O ver a year later, Evan built up the nerve and dragged himself to the private room above the garage. He waited till evening and still the heat sweltered. Wiping his brow, he sifted through each box, random sex toys and negligees filled the first several he opened. He refused to touch anything, images of his mother filtered through his mind. Sickened, he pushed those boxes aside. Underneath were heavier ones containing photos, lots of photos. Most of them framed, of his father at various ages. He'd never get over the similarities between him and his father. It was like looking at himself, except his hair, the same as *her hair*. Pictures of his parents, he picked one up, studied it then threw the picture against the wall.

The force caused the glass to break into several large pieces and countless tiny shards. He grabbed a larger piece and carved over his mother's face, mutilating the picture. Blood dribbled over her hacked up face, opening his palm, he dropped the glass and studied red droplets trickling from it. Images of his mother on her death bed, streams of crimson flowing, soaking into the sheets, engulfed his mind. A drop of sweat trickled into his eye causing a burning sensation, waking him from his trance. He ripped off his shirt and wrapped his hand.

He shoved the box to the side, out of his vision, and opened the next - photo albums. Taking a deep breath he flipped the cover. The first picture, a blond lady. At first glance he thought it was his mother and slammed the album closed, but the woman stared into his soul. He reopened the album and studied her bizarre eyes. One of them green, the other an amber-yellow color. His eyes changed depending on his mood, usually to the same color, except in his youth. They sometimes changed into separate colors, one yellow the other amber. He slid the photo out of its sleeve and turned it over. The only word *Scarlett*.

He placed the picture aside and flipped through the rest of the album and the next. The final album stared at him from the bottom of the box. He picked it up and gazed at an innocent baby, *himself*. The baby in front of him smiled. As he flipped through the photos his smile disappeared and his eyes changed from blue to one yellow, one amber. He compared the woman's picture to that of his baby picture. Both had different colored eyes but his changed over time, no longer did he have two eye colors, instead they changed color according to his mood. Something that set him apart from the monster-parents he grew up with and his siblings.

Somehow he and *Scarlett* were related, an aunt, a cousin. Mrs. Kurl's insight echoed in the air surrounding him, 'A young woman, looked like your mom, once spent a couple weeks here. They didn't say, and we never asked, but she looked like a sister'. Mr. Fritz never turned down his money no matter what he asked of him. Evan wanted to understand the connection. *Who is she?*

In his good hand he clutched the photos and left the attic room, locking the door behind him. Curious what other *secrets* were hidden upstairs, he sauntered to the other side, wiping his sweat with the backside of his wrapped hand. The attic space was the entire length of the garage. He walked the distance to the opposite end where he found an operating table, syringes, scalpels and other medical supplies. His father being a medical equipment supplier, he dismissed the equipment as supplies on hand when he passed away.

In the garage, the cool air brushed past Evan's skin, drying the sweat rolling across his head and chest. Mr. Kurl stood with his back towards Evan as he fumbled with something at his work bench. Evan strolled towards him and leaned against the bench, his wrapped hand to his side, out of Mr. Kurl's vision, "Good afternoon."

Mr. Kurl jumped. "I didn't hear or see you walk up."

He handed him the picture. "Who is this woman?"

"Got me. She visited and stayed for a while. First time I saw her, I thought she was your mom with a new do."

"Thanks." Evan turned on his heel to leave, allowing his injured hand to hang loose by his side. The shirt around his wound bearing crimson streaks.

"What's wrong with your hand?"

"Sliced it on the loose edge of the golf cart. It's nothing."

"Mrs. Kurl might recognize her. She spent more time inside the house. Bet she can wrap that hand too, doesn't look good." He hesitated then asked, "I know it's not my business but where did you find that photo?"

Evan smiled, pleased his drug concoction worked so well. "My father's old office."

Mr. Kurl nodded his head. "I'll repair the cart first thing tomorrow."

Evan saluted with his injured hand and hopped into his golf cart to track down Mrs. Kurl. He found her tending a garden. He pulled up alongside the garden and joined her. "You have a green thumb," he said, while leaning towards the flowers to sniff their fragrance.

"Well, thank you, Mr. O'Conner. It's a hobby, relaxes me."

"I won't lie, I'm not here to sniff the flowers. I have a question about my parents."

She looked him in the eye and placed her trimmers in her gardening cart. Then she noticed his hand. "Oh my. We need to tend to that now." She reached for his hand.

He pulled it behind him. "It's nothing, sliced it on the loose edge of the cart."

"Let's go inside. You can ask me anything as I bandage your wound."

Inside, she led him to the table, got a few first-aid supplies, unwrapped his hand and cleaned his wound. He winced but sucked in the pain, almost enjoying it.

He placed the picture on the table. "Tell me about her."

She paused for a moment and glanced at the photo. "A friend of your parents."

"What kind of friend?" His mother drifted towards Mrs. Kurl, slipped her hands inside her shirt and fondled the old woman's breasts. Evan diverted his eyes towards the window.

Mrs. Kurl saw flashes of darkness pass over his irises. "She spent time here. Her name is Scarlett."

"Is she family?"

"Mr. O'Conner, they didn't tell me much."

She was back to her evasive self, pissing off Evan. He wanted to scream but remained

166

calm and shifted his eyes back to hers. His mother eddied towards him. "Is she related?"

She licked her lips. "I'm not sure. At first I thought maybe she was a sister. I remember your mom became pregnant shortly after her visit and she never visited again."

The woman in the picture was the woman the Kurls thought was his mom's sister. He mulled the thought over in his head. His mother drifted to his ear and whispered *observant, nosy woman. Don't listen to her.* Evan closed his eyes and took a deep breath. *Go away, go away, go away!* When he reopened them, she had disappeared. "Did she visit alone or was she with others?"

"Alone, Mr. O'Conner. They didn't let me inside the house much during her visit - very hush hush."

"Thank you, Mrs.Kurl."

"You're all done but you may need a professional. That cut is deep." He stood, grabbed his picture off the table and walked towards the door. He lifted his wounded hand. "Thanks."

Mrs. Kurl let out a deep breath as soon as he left.

And the World Went Blank

1998

Burkhalder drummed her fingers on the steering wheel of her Ford Explorer. She gazed at the embossed invitation. Its gold lettering a blur as tears swelled behind her eyelids. She ached for Jax to snake his arms around her again and blinked several times to fight the onslaught of tears. He'd wanted to marry her, asked her and she'd almost said yes. In '94 she made a whirlwind trip to Albuquerque, learning nothing except Poppy Hills was a huge estate surrounded by a heavy gate, no doubt meant to keep people out. For twenty-four hours she monitored it and nothing. No sign of movement but she only saw the front of the estate, no saying what activity happened behind it. Then in 1995 another family in the Florida Panhandle, slaughtered during Hurricane Darlene. The youngest a girl, three years old, left alive. Her older brother, Derek, and her parents killed in the same fashion as the Tates, the mother raped as she bled out. She caught the next flight and arrived at the scene, leaving Jax in a quandary. That was the deal breaker for him. He deserved better than she offered. He chose the nurse who mended his arm during the fateful night of Hurricane Chloe. Sucking it up and ending her pity party, she twirled Jax's wedding invitation across the dashboard then tucked it into the glove box. She wouldn't be making his wedding.

Her mind sped through Evan's pattern. So far he struck at three year intervals and always the first hurricane of the season to hit North America. His family, each child's name started with *E,* the Tate children's names started with *E.* The Florida family, every child had a *D* name. She banked on the name pattern now as she staked out the family she presumed would be his next victims.

Movement from the bushes beside the house caught her eye. An orange tabby leaped from the bush onto the front porch and meowed at the door. A boy, eleven-year-old Darrin she *assumed,* slid the door open. The tabby sauntered inside, rubbing Darrin's legs, tail cocked high, twitching at the tip.

Her mind back on Evan. She'd traced his address in New Mexico. It was phony - a real address but not his. She traced his CNPR license but couldn't find a work place for him. Dead ends. Darlene renewed her search. The murders didn't go unnoticed yet no evidence turned up - no DNA on the bodies, no fingerprints, no semen on or inside the mother. And not a single witness!

With success she dug up dirt on his mom, Philmonia. Her father a convicted rapist, sentenced to twenty-five years, none of his victims over the age of fifteen. Her mother committed suicide via an over dose of sleeping pills. Philmonia, at sixteen, ran away from foster care and made a living stripping at various clubs. She married a wealthy, elderly man, Mr. O'Conner, who died several months later during intercourse, his arms tied to the bedposts. No evidence of anything other than a heart attack during his climax.

She twisted uncomfortably, her full bladder about to explode. Her eyes scanned the quiet street for a place no one could see her squat, finding a grouping of trees she climbed out of her SUV.

☾ ☾ ☾ ☾ ☾

Evan entered a wooden shed filled with yard equipment, tools and deck furniture the owners wanted locked away when the winds kicked and howled. He edged against the wall, sliding his body through a narrow gap between folded lawn chairs and cushions. Evan leaned his bulky torso against the slats, turned sideways and peered through the dirt caked window with binoculars at the surrounding neighborhood. A Ford Explorer parked several paces up the road caught his

attention, someone sat inside it. He adjusted
the binoculars and the driver's auburn mane
flooded his vision. When she reached towards
something in the back seat he recognized her
oval face and slender nose. "Carrot Top
Cop," he whispered. His first thought, she'd
traded in her Billows Hollow badge for
Fradenton but her casual T-shirt said
otherwise. For the next couple hours he
observed and waited. His mind curious, *why is
she here?*

When she crept out of the vehicle he
used the opportunity to sneak towards it,
pulling a black baseball cap over his head. The
passenger side door unlocked, he opened it,
studying the contents laying across the seat. A
map, the street marked with a red X, and his
family's address scribbled next to the X.
Beneath the map lay a sketch and a red pen.
Without picking up the sketch he stared into
the familiar face, his face. His mind zoomed
backwards in time, attempting to piece
together what evidence she might have. He
shaved his body, used a condom, and kept
hold of his knife. He left the girl alive. *Did she
talk? Impossible. She was too young.* Then he
remembered the girl from the bar. He left her
alive too. He cringed at his immature
mistakes. Impressed with Carrot Top Cop's
skills, he needed a good adversary.

Burkhalder's open soda filled the space
of the driver's seat cup holder. Evan dipped

his hand into his front pocket, pulling out a small bottle. He squeezed three drops from the bottle into her drink. The crunching of footsteps walking towards the car startled him out of his thoughts. He eased the door closed and slid downward against the side of the SUV as Burkhalder hopped back into the driver's seat. Then he edged his way around the vehicle, stopping by the passenger side back tire. His blade nestled between the waistband of his pants and his back. Evan needed to be sure she couldn't follow him, his sleeping serum wouldn't work fast enough. He jammed the tip of his blade into her tire and twisted. His heart threatening to jump out of his chest. Sweat beaded on his forehead as anger roiled inside him. He crouch-walked towards the closest bushes and used the oleanders for cover. Parting the pink flowers, he peered towards her vehicle, and regained control of his anger. His plans for the family ruined. He ran through the ungated yards until he came upon his nondescript silver CRV.

Evan's mother waited in the passenger seat, dirty blond curls dangling just above her dark, quarter sized nipples. She stuck her pointer finger into her vagina then pulled it out, running her glistening finger across her tongue.

"Get out!" Her form vanished on his command.

He pulled his hat off and tossed it into the back seat as he drove, glimpsing a flash of red in his rear-view. Evan sniggered, knowing the more energy she exerted the faster her heart pumped forcing the drugs to circulate through her body at a quicker rate.

☪ ☪ ☪ ☪ ☪

The bushes behind her SUV rustled, catching her attention. She grabbed her soda, gulping it down, her eyes fixated on the bush. Something glistened behind it, then a burst of black cloth. She readied her gun. Whoever it was ran through the yard. She cocked the door open, pushed her back against the vehicle, holding her gun with both hands towards the sky and slid alongside it. Her eyes darting from side to side. She jumped around the bush - empty. The cranking of an engine resonated inside her eardrums.

A squall passed overhead, blowing tree branches and leaves, obscuring her vision. A small silver car pulled away from the road. At the sight, her legs pounded the earth, trying to get the plate number. Blinking through the heavy downpour, she attempted to read the license plate *CL* or *CI*, her vision blurred before she could read it. She bent forward, rested her hands on her knees, attempting to catch her breath. She lifted her head, still panting, her head dizzy. The trees and houses swirled through her mind and she collapsed to the ground. Rain pounding her body, small tree limbs whipping through the air.

Plan B

Evan never planned on any cop stalking him and ruining his kills. He never left behind any DNA or evidence. His methods were methodical - any possible evidence that might be left destroyed with the impact of the storm. However, he worked with hurricanes and always took into consideration that family A may evacuate so he designed back-up plans B, C and D. Plan B included the Mora family further north along the coastline. The daughter, Chelsea, three and a half, he wished for younger. The son, Carter, thirteen - not ideal either. No third child but that was simply a bonus when he found those families. His mother's abuse caused Evan to die, symbolically, at eight. His urges didn't include killing himself again. Instead, he wanted to feel alive. Energy running through his veins, his heart beating strong and energetic inside his chest.

His good fortune, the family didn't evacuate. They were further inland - not ideal either unless the storm turned stronger than his predicted category two. At this point he wasn't being choosy. The Mora's home was located outside of town. A definite plus - no nosy or scared neighbors. The Florida family,

175

he thought, he'd have to drug and kill two families or try plan B. His luck prevailed and the man he presumed was the husband of the extra family returned and took them home.

Cycles of rain and wind followed Evan up the coastline, threatening to toss his little CRV across the road. He turned onto the dirt road leading to their home, pulled the car over, popped the hood and pulled a couple plugs rendering it unstartable. He didn't need a *hero* dad helping him *fix* his car. Evan patted his own back for using his cunning nature to his benefit.

Westward wind gusts pushed trees sideways, forcing their limbs to brush against the ground. Buckets of water fell from the sky. Water charged in rivulets down his smooth, shaven head and across his face. He didn't bother to swipe them away. His sneakers sinking into the soggy ground as he trudged to his *family's* home. By the time he reached the house not a dry area existed on his body.

The wooden log cabin style home looked warm and inviting. He slogged up their front steps under the shelter of their porch, knocked on the door. Water puddled beneath his feet. The squall disappeared, and the rain eased. A small man, dark, thin hair framing his head, opened the door a sliver. With his pointer finger he pushed his wire rimmed glasses further up his nose towards his eyes. "Can I help you?"

Easy pickings. "My car stalled out. I called to get a tow but ain't no one comin' until after the storm. I hate to put you out but I could use a dry place to wait the storm out."

The man dropped his eyes to Evan's muddy sneakers, scanning his appearance upwards and resting on his face.

"Who is at the..." A woman no taller than five feet with a muffin top apparent under her T-shirt appeared at the door. She looked to the man, their eyes talking a silent language. Then she turned to Evan. "Let me get dry clothes for you."

The man shut the door, leaving Evan on the porch. He turned towards the desolate woods and took in the fallen branches covering the forest floor. A few minutes later the man reappeared. In a meek voice he said, "Follow me." They trekked through the muddy ground, stepping over mangled tree branches. "I'm Sullivan." He stopped, turned towards Evan and offered his hand.

"Nyle." The alias he used with the Tates stuck and he used it every time. He hated shaking his hand, as he disliked human contact, but refusing would make him stand out so he clutched the man's tiny hand and shook once, bile rising in his throat.

"I apologize. My wife doesn't like strangers in the house. You'll be safe enough

177

in our garage. There is a studio apartment above it. My mother stays in it when she visits." He chuckled.

Evan's mind rerouted knowing now he'd have to break into their home unless he could come up with a clever plan to allow him inside the house. Sullivan opened a side door attached to the garage. "Here you are, Nyle." He handed him the dry clothes. "I hope these'll fit OK. There's food in the pantry and water in the fridge. Oh, and take this flashlight."

Evan thanked him. His mind occupied with how he would get inside the house.

C·C·C·C·C

Burkhalder lay flush with the ground. A large, chocolate colored dog with white feet and tip on her tail nuzzled and sniffed Burkhalder's face. "Lady!" called a teen with straight blond hair and freckles covering her face and extremities. Blue eyes bulged when she saw her dog, Lady, sniffing at someone on the ground. Her first thought, a dead body. She ran up the porch to her home and called her uncle for help.

He placed his hand against Burkhalder's neck checking her pulse. "She's alive. Help me get her into the house." He cradled her body in his arms like a father carrying a child to bed. The blond girl opened the door, Lady trailed behind them. Inside, he laid her on the couch and checked her body for injuries. He found nothing and her steady pulse and breathing told him she was OK, just knocked out. He assumed a branch fell on her head or she tripped in the mud. Not recognizing her as a neighbor, he couldn't imagine why a stranger wandered around the neighborhood with the likes of a hurricane coming on shore. By candlelight, the power out for a good hour, they cleaned her up, put fresh clothes on her and waited for her to wake.

☾ ☾ ☾ ☾ ☾

Evan wrapped latex gloves over his hands and scavenged through each drawer and nook in the apartment searching for a house key. Frustrated, he plopped onto the bed, exhaling a large stream of air. In the silence he heard a scratch followed by another. He followed the sound to the living room window. A large, loose tree branch swayed against the apartment, swiping the glass.

He slid the window open, jimmied the screen loose, letting it fall to the ground. The branch sturdy in his grip, it would take a hell of a squall to knock it loose unless he helped it. Downstairs in the garage he scanned the yard equipment hung on the walls in level, organized rows, weed eater, trimmer, chainsaw, a couple of gas cans. He considered the chain saw for a second but decided against it. The noise would alert the family. Then he spotted a set of bungee cords and the wheels in his mind began to spin.

He wrapped a bungee cord around the loose branch and slid the window down above the bungee cord. Using his upper body strength, he planted his feet against the wall for leverage and pulled at the branch until it gave. A crack, followed by another. He waited, bungee in hand, for a good wind gust then tugged, jumping backwards as the limb crashed against the window with a thud and shattering of glass. His body falling backwards, landing sideways on his left arm.

The bungee didn't budge as he yanked. He stepped towards the window, careful not to squash the glass and fiddled with the cord. His peripheral vision caught sight of the blast of sudden light from the porch. The metal end of the bungee got caught beneath the window. He popped it out with his knife then closed and slid the blade into the waist of his pants, dropped the window the rest of the way and slid the curtains into place.

Evan raced down the stairs, strung the bungee back on its hook and bounded up the stairs, slipped off his gloves, smashing them into the front pocket of his wet pants. Blood trickled down his arm. A sliver of glass stuck out of his left bicep and several gashes dotted his right bicep. He took a seat on the edge of a mauve recliner and grasped his arm, moaning for extra effect as Sullivan bounded the stairs.

Breathless, he took a moment to catch his breath, then rushed to Evan. "Hold still, I need to see your arm."

Evan tilted his arm towards Sullivan. "A branch came right through the window with that last gust."

"I don't care about the window. I'm a Nurse Practitioner and we need to get this glass out of you. There are supplies in the house, come with me."

The Weight of the World

Quiet moans escaped Burkhalder's lips as she wakened. Her eyes opening to a cloud of fuzz that cleared to reveal slats of wood. Lights blinked and shadows on the walls bounced. A deep voice called to her. "Take it easy."

She looked towards the voice, fuzzy light illuminated thick, dark hair surrounded by a triangular face. Crow's feet tugged at his kind, dark eyes and a Tom Selleck mustache covered the skin between his nose and upper lip. Muscles exploded beneath his T-shirt, accentuated by his broad shoulders. For a second she thought she died and went to eye candy heaven.

She pulled her torso upwards, leaning it against the back of the couch. "Where am I?" The last thing she remembered was sitting in her truck reminiscing about Jax.

"Lady, our dog, found you lying in the dirt behind our house. Lucky thing. The storms getting hairy."

She rolled her head backwards resting it on the couch, placing her hands over her eyes and pulling them downwards across her cheeks, she sifted through the grogginess of her mind.

"You thirsty? Hungry? My niece made a mean beef stew and the best cornbread you ever ate." He patted his solid, defined belly. Even through his shirt she admired his build.

"Food sounds good. Thank you."

Snug fitting jeans revealed a beefy round ass and legs. She watched him move across the room with long, powerful strides, imagining him in bed. He disappeared around the corner then reappeared with a bottled water. Screwing the cap off, he handed it to her and took his former seat.

"The stew will be ready in a few minutes." He raked his fingers through his thick waves, tousling them. "I thought maybe you tripped and hit your head but found notta one injury. Are you prone to seizures, black-outs?"

"No, never. My mind is groggy like I'm siftin' through cobwebs." She propped her elbows on her legs, resting her chin in her cupped hands. Long, loose auburn curls fell across her shoulders.

"What did you last eat or drink? What do you remember?"

She remembered staking out the house, waiting for Evan, and her Jax pity party. She had a water bottle and a soda in her truck, then she'd left to pee. *What else? What happened after?* "I don't know. I drank water and part of a soda in my truck."

He leaned forward, resting his palms on his thighs. Heat rose and shot through her. *Why am I so attracted to this guy?* She chalked it up to sex deprivation. Her pussy had seen no action since Jax and that'd been a couple years ago. She recalled his strong arms around her waist, his soft lips teasing hers. He spoke, bringing her mind front and center to the present. "I'm gonna get personal. Why are you here?"

"I'm a police officer and I believe a man, a killer, may be here."

He sucked in the bottom corner of his lip. "Hmm… A killer during a hurricane? There was that Florida family I read about."

"Yes! Exactly. The Florida family wasn't his first victims. They were the first to hit national news. There have been others." Memories of Jim and little Eilida - the only survivor - flooded her mind.

"Hold that thought. Your stew should be warm. When I get back we'll continue our discussion." He disappeared again and returned carrying a steaming bowl with a slice of thick cornbread on the side. He slid onto the couch beside her. Chunks of meat, potatoes and carrots looked delicious to Burkhalder's eyes, and the aroma filled the air around her taking her back to winters as a child.

"We haven't yet introduced ourselves. Retired Lieutenant Commander Frank Roy."

Retired Navy, that explained the mouthwatering body. "Detective Burkhalder, Billows Hollow." Comfort radiated from Frank's warm eyes as she peered into them.

"Open up," he ordered, bringing the spoon towards her mouth. "I was an investigator, Jag. When my sister and brother were killed in a car crash I took in my niece, Talla, and retired. The Navy life and raising a distraught teenager didn't work. She needed me more. Bought this place and been here since. I can help you. I want to help you," he stressed while scooping spoonfuls of stew and bringing them to her mouth.

She'd never had anyone feed her and was very capable of doing it. But she liked his take command and control attitude and enjoyed being pampered. To her he looked more like a Navy SEAL than Jag. He continued talking until the bowl was empty then laid it on the thick walnut coffee table. Up till now the only cooperation she'd gotten was from the police in Florida. They were curious and listened, but had nothing to corroborate that her guy was their guy. Happy to have someone willing to assist her, she filled him in on the details she'd gathered over the past six years. Tears gathered in the corners of her eyes. As a cop working with men, growing up with brothers, she kept her feminine side under wraps. The existence of this man, his willingness to listen and help, brought her feelings into the open and streaming from her eyes. He folded her into his arms and she wept.

Her head against his broad chest, she smelled the tantalizing scent of his aftershave. They sat in silence for a few minutes before he spoke.

"Why every three years?"

"It's barely a pattern, more like a hunch, but I don't know. My guess, there were three children in his family."

Frank sat quiet for a minute. "That's almost too simple. This guy is smart, calculating. What are his interests?"

"Ha! Weather and astrology. Hitler was into astrology too and there's always the Zodiac killer."

"Huh… astrology… In numerology the number three is usually associated with creativity. Could he be using it to *paint his canvas*? His victims, knife, their blood, part of his masterpiece?"

"I'd never thought of that. Anythin' is possible. I think his mind is twisted enough you may have hit the nail on the head."

"I'm good at what I do and I have connections you don't. We'll find him. Right now, I need you to go in the bathroom. I have Dixie cups in there. I need you to pee in one so we can determine if you've been drugged and with what type of drug. Can you walk?"

She sniffled and sucked in her emotions, pulling away she said, "I think so. The grogginess is wearing off. The food helped."

Shattered Glass

Mr. Mora reached the back steps of the house and eased the door open. He peered inside, then ushered Evan inside the house, pulling his finger to his lips for Evan to remain quiet he took gentle steps down the hall. Evan sensed Sullivan's fear and nervousness, but it wasn't towards him. The man dreaded something inside his house. Sullivan guided him to a restroom at the end of the hall and closed the door without a creak or moan. In a low voice he said, "Put your arms out." He opened a cabinet filled with medical supplies, including syringes still wrapped in plastic. Short pinches of pain stabbed at Evan's arms as Mr. Mora tweezed out the glass slivers and dabbed medicine on the cuts.

Footsteps pounded the floor and Sullivan's arms shook as he finished placing bandages on Evan's wounds. The door opened and Mrs. Mora stood in the doorway, bathed in the light from a lantern she held firm in her grasp. Sullivan's eyes grew twice their size. He stammered, "The s... s... sound we... we heard was the, uh... the glass shattered on Nyle."

Her lips pulled into a smile but her eyes drove daggers into Mr. Mora and Evan. She turned to Evan. "Nyle, I apologize for my actions earlier. A person can never be too careful with strangers. Please, join us." She turned her back to the door and waited for Mr. Mora and Evan to follow. Evan listened to her footsteps behind him and mentally mapped the layout of the house and the restroom with the syringes. He felt the tiny bottle of his personal sleeping serum in his right front pocket and his closed blade rubbing the skin between his T-shirt and jeans.

They entered a large room with a huge lime green sectional. Two children, a boy and a girl, sat on one end of the sectional. He assumed, Chelsea and Carter. The children sat with their backs straight and their mouths closed. The way Evan thought children should act instead of running around like wild monkeys.

"Nyle, why don't you take a seat. Are you thirsty?" asked Mr. Mora.

Something about the Mora's didn't set well with Evan. He sensed they had their own agenda and kept his hand ready to pull and flip his blade any second. "No, thank you." A crash sounded against his skull and sharp pain sliced his head. Everything went black as his head collapsed forward.

The Calm Before the Storm: Evan's Sins

Hours later, Evan's eyes fluttered open. His head burst with pain as he took in the darkness surrounding him. He blinked a few times, orienting himself to his surroundings. After a few minutes his eyes adjusted enough for him to see the outline out of a dresser or desk on the other side of the room. Shelves clung to the walls. His head throbbed, jolts of pain sheared down his back and tingled his toes. He lifted his hand to his head but found it tied to his other hand behind his back. His legs tied in front of him. *What the...* He wiggled and scooted his butt on the floor. No longer did he feel the comfort of his blade in his waistband. His small bottle of sleeping serum, still in his front pocket, eased his mind, but he needed to get the ropes off his extremities.

A mocking laugh emanated from a corner of the room and his mother floated to him. *Tsk, tsk, tsk.* She wagged her finger at him. *What were you thinking? This family is more fucked up than ours.* She laughed, her floating body bent towards him. *Oh Evan. You need to stop this craziness. Can't you see I'll always be with you, my little man?*

Her presence and voice drove all his rage and anger through his arms and legs as the ropes binding him burst under his force. He shouted *Get out Bitch!* And she vanished, but not for long. She'd be back. The pain in his head subsided as his rage took control. He stood and felt his way around the room. A quiet whimpering caught his attention. He placed his ear against the wall and listened. A child's whimper. He continued feeling his way around the room until he found a frame jutting from the wall - a door. Groping the door, he found the knob and attempted to twist, but it wouldn't budge.

In the darkness, using gentle steps, he found the desk or dresser and patted the sides. There were drawers, and they were unlocked, luck was on his side. His hands shuffled inside each drawer until he found something with a pointy tip. The thin handle told him it was a letter opener. Tracing his path towards the door he toyed with the flimsy lock until it opened. He pushed along the wall, listening for the whimpering, found the room, tried the knob - also locked. He continued sliding along the wall until he found steps.

Mrs. Mora was a threat he needed to subdue as soon as possible. With ginger footing he padded down the stairs, a dim light shone at the bottom and voices stemmed from the large room. Remembering his mental map, he made a right and followed the corridor to the bathroom where Mr. Mora bandaged his arm. He slipped inside, opened the cabinet, pulled out two syringes, dipping each into his serum and pulling. The liquid bubbled into each syringe.

"Shut up! Just follow my instructions and stop blabbering, you idiot," Mrs. Mora shouted at her husband. "I'm checking on him and the kid. Can you handle waiting here?" Her tone filled with sarcasm.

Evan slipped into the kitchen. A closed door across the hall from him. He pushed the door open, a candle provided low light - enough. Evan saw a bed and dressers. Careful not to make a sound, he closed the door and crossed the hall to the kitchen.

Her heavy footsteps pounded the floor as she entered the walkway and crunched up the stairs. When she reached the top he went into the large room. Mr. Mora's saucer eyes pleaded with Evan. "I'm sorry, so sorry. Go, please," he whispered as Evan moved towards him.

Arms to his sides, Evan held the syringe steady between his fingers. "Your wife is crazy. She hit me on the head, knocked me out. I think you're innocent, you tried to help me, but she's insane." Evan inched closer, placed his hand with the syringe on Mr. Mora's shoulder then slid the needle into his neck. His body went limp. Evan caught it and laid it on one side of the lime sectional. Seconds later he heard Mrs. Mora clamor down the stairs. He slid behind a display case full of knickknacks.

She halted at the bottom of the stairs as if not sure which direction to move. He heard rustling, then the cock of a gun. He steadied the next syringe in his hand. She moved towards the kitchen. He closed his eyes, listening for each of her footsteps. After several minutes the crunching of her shoes on the carpet grew closer than froze. "You dumbass," she whispered, then slunk into the room, her back towards Evan. She held the gun in front of her chest, making a slow circle of the room while planted in one spot. Evan edged closer to her and plunged the force of his thick body into her. She dropped to the floor, palms splayed in front of her. A loud thud hit the floor as the gun landed and spun, stopping when it hit the wall beneath a small lamp table. "What the…" she called out.

He straddled her ass, placing his large hand on her back, "Where is my knife?"

"Get off me." She squirmed.

He pressed harder on her back, forcing her chest to the floor. "Tell me where my knife is or I will drain the life from you with my bare hands!"

She gasped. "Above the refrigerator." He drove the syringe into her neck. She soon stopped kicking and went limp.

He grabbed her flashlight, refilled his syringes, found his knife and crept up the stairs. He hated when circumstances made him deviate from his plan. When he reached the top of the stairs, he shone his flashlight. Four doors, all of them closed except the room where he awoke. Taking long strides, Evan tried all the doors - each locked. His mother floated between him and the door, he swiped her out of the way and unlocked the door, peering inside the room. Quiet snores sounded from the tiny child. He closed and locked the door behind him.

In the room next door lay a larger frame. Evan stalked to the bed. Quiet filled the room and he wondered if the child was alive. Touching his neck, he checked for a pulse. A steady rhythm thumped against his fingers. Downstairs he'd made a ruckus taking down the mother. The woman he couldn't wait to destroy. She would be extra special, so much like destroying his own mother. *How were the children still sleeping?* The evil he saw in Mrs. Mora he wondered if she drugged them already. He remembered the children sitting calm on the couch. The way he and his siblings did. His father's belt flashed through his mind, whipping the air and anger burning inside him. His mother's hand rested on his shoulder, he looked into her blue eyes, memories of her fondling hands flickered through his muddled brain.

It wasn't Elfred's time, he allowed the boy to sleep for now. Silence came from Whimpering Kid's room. He turned the lock, a creak sounded as he pushed the door open. The beam from the flashlight illuminated a small form in the corner. The child's knees towards his chest, arms folded around them. His dark skin told Evan he wasn't a Mora. Unsure what to do with the small child, he closed and locked the door and ran downstairs to finish his work.

He propped Mr. Mora into a recliner. "You dumb bastard. I'm making your life so much better." He didn't follow the rules of when each should die with the Tates, but refused to make that mistake again. Dad first, then brother, and last mother. The same as his family. With precision, he carved a line across Mr. Mora's neck with the point of his blade. Blood gurgled and trailed down his shirt, onto the recliner. He leaned in and whispered into the dying man's ear, "I saved your stupid ass."

Mrs. Mora lay on the floor, knocked out from drugs. He picked her up and carried her like a sleeping child. In his head he saw his mother. Her blond curls bouncing with each of his steps. Evan dropped her body on the master bed, stripped her clothes – naked, *mommy was naked.* She coaxed him to join her. *Control, not yet!*

He turned on his heels and strolled upstairs to his *brother's* room. Small shuffling noises sounded from Whimpering Kid's room. His mind considered whether he should kill him too. He wasn't a Mora, maybe he'd allow him to live.

Elfred lay in a peaceful state, the covers tucked at his waist. Evan flipped open his blade, sliding it along the boy's soft skin. Blood poured around his head, soaking into the sheets. The child's eyes flickered for a second. "Now you're free." He stepped outside the boy's room, a stoic expression and eyes black as tar. *What a bunch of stiffs. They don't even fight it.* He sniggered at his own morbid joke.

Above Mrs. Mora's sleeping form, he caressed her hair, slipping it behind her ear, seeing only his mother. The candle's light created a glint on his knife as he placed it against the skin on her neck. The blade twirled in his hand, creating a tiny puncture. Drops of crimson dribbled from the wound, trickled down her neck and disappeared underneath her hair. He dragged the blade along her neck, slow and deliberate. His urges consumed him, replaying the night of his mother's death. He slashed using the strength in his arm. Again and again he slashed. The area below her head a mangled mess. Pieces of flesh clung to vertebrae, a scarlet river soaked the bed, already puddling on the floor. He pulled at the zipper of his pants, pushing them off his legs, his release begging to happen. He slipped on a condom and mounted her, screaming obscenities towards his mother. Her arms extended towards him then evaporated into a black cloud. His rage disappearing with his discharge.

Upstairs he opened Whimpering Kid's door. The boy dropped and huddled. Fear filling his large round eyes. "Where do you come from?" Evan demanded.

The boy gulped and sucked in his lips.

"Do you know where you live?"

The boy nodded his head, yes.

"I'm going to get you out of here. OK?"

The boy nodded yes again.

"Follow me."

The boy picked himself off the floor and followed Evan out of the house. The worst of the storm over, swirling clouds filled the sky. No rain and only light winds circled around them. "I have a silver car at the end of the road. Run to it and wait for me." He saw no need to kill the boy, he wasn't a Mora.

The boy, no more than seven, took off in the direction Evan pointed.

Evan remembered seeing a couple gas cans in the garage. His DNA all over the house. He couldn't have that, so he sprinkled gas through the garage starting with the upstairs and continued throughout the house. Once both cans were empty, he went back for the girl.

A coffee-colored bear lay wrapped in her arms. He pulled it out and inhaled the girl's baby powder scent. "I'm taking this for now but I'll return it one day." He injected a small amount of serum into the girl's arm, wanting her to sleep until her rescue. Cradling her in his arms he carried her outside and laid her small, sleeping body several yards from the house.

Inside the garage he took a match to a sheer curtain. The glowing flame flourished. He dropped it on the floor next to his gas trail and smiled as the flames shot through the room.

He grabbed a newspaper, lit the end on fire and released it inside the house. It sailed to the floor. Instant flames enveloped it. He strolled outside, watching with pride until flames encased the house. He strolled to the car whistling "Oh my Darlin' Clementine". The darkness in his eyes receded as a large explosion sounded behind him.

Hold Me Tonight

Burkhalder and Frank talked for a couple hours, falling asleep together on his pillowy couch. Her head slumped on his broad shoulder. His arm wrapped around her.

Talla's lips curved into a smile as she took in the sight of her uncle and Burkhalder on the couch. She padded into the kitchen, Lady at her side, and started the camp stove. She opened the door and let Lady out to do her business. Her uncle stuffed their cold food into a couple coolers. She reached inside one, pulling out half a dozen eggs, cracked them into a bowl and whipped in milk and chives. She grabbed the pancake mix out of the pantry and made batter, humming to herself while she cooked.

Twenty minutes later, the coffee and breakfast was ready. She waltzed into the living room, cleared her throat and watched as they buzzed to life. Lady walked up to Frank and licked his available hand slung over the side of the couch. He twitched from the dog's wet tongue. The smell of coffee reached Burkhalder's nose as she stretched, only to hit Frank in the forehead. Startled, she pulled her hand back. "I'm so sorry." She rubbed his forehead.

"Talla, honey. This is Alice Burkhalder."

Up till then, Burkhalder hadn't noticed the teenager staring at them, arms crossed.

"Really? I find a woman in the woods and the two of you are already bed buddies." An authoritative tap to her foot.

"Talla, no we... I'm the adult in this house."

Talla burst out laughing. "Precarious situation. Coffee and breakfast is ready. Nice to meet you Alice." She turned and waltzed into the kitchen. Her plate was already on the table.

Burkhalder turned to Frank. "She's charming."

"She'll be more charming if we don't get in there and eat." His smile gave away his adoration of Talla.

After breakfast, the three plus Lady traced Burkhalder's steps to her SUV. A large branch had fallen on her hood and squashed it. "Great!" Alice yanked the driver's door open and pulled out the soda can.

"Look at this," called Talla.

Burkhalder and Frank walked around the car to the passenger side. He leaned down and felt along the tire. "This wasn't the storm. Feel here, someone didn't want you going anywhere."

Burkhalder thought for a minute. The cobwebs inside her head gone. "From my rear-view I saw someone behind those bushes." She pointed to the leafy clump of oleanders. "I eased out of my truck and moved towards them." She walked past the bush towards the spot Lady found her. "A silver vehicle pulled out from the curb there." She pointed towards the curb.

Lady sniffed the ground where she found Burkhalder and barked twice. Talla rushed to the dog's side. "Hey, Alice. Is that yours?"

Burkhlader jogged to Talla's side, skipping over tree branches, and leaned down, picking up her gun. A wave of relief coursed through her being. A mind full of cobwebs, she'd forgotten about her gun. "Oh my. I can't imagine if a small child found this. Thank you!" She checked the magazine and the safety then tucked it into the waistband of her pants.

Talla shrugged. "Lady found it, and you."

"Did you get the plates?" asked Frank as he walked towards the spot Alice identified as where the silver car was sitting.

She joined him and rolled her eyes in thought. "It was raining. I think it was a Cl. It was a silver compact, a Honda, I believe. The drugs took effect, and that's everything I remember until I woke up on your couch."

"I can work with that. Let's see if your car starts."

Burkhalder turned to Talla. "Thank you."

She shrugged. "It was Lady. I just got my uncle."

Burkhalder pet Lady's head and tickled her behind the ears. "Thank you, Lady." Lady gave her hand a slobbery lick.

Talla smiled. "Let's go, Lady." They walked towards the house. Burkhalder joined Frank at her car. He'd already removed the tree branch from her hood. She smoothed her palm over the dent and leaned sideways, determining the scope of damage.

"I guess it's not too bad."

"Start her up."

The key still in the ignition, Burkhalder turned the key, and the SUV's engine rumbled. Frank came around the driver's side open door and leaned his back against it. "Guess we need to change that tire. You have a spare?"

"You've already done enough," said Burkhalder, as Frank walked around her vehicle.

"Pop the hatch. Once we change it out I have a friend in town who will replace the tire for you and get that hood fixed."

She twisted her lips. "If I knew you better I might say you're just tryin' to keep me here a few days."

His chocolate eyes shot a glance at her and his lips curled into a smile, showing off a dimple on his left cheek. She hadn't noticed it earlier. "I don't often get attractive redheaded detectives passing out in my back yard." The heat radiated off his statement.

"His shop won't be open today but I'll call him when the phone lines are up. He owes me a few favors."

That evening the electricity came on and Frank turned the news on, the three curled up on the couch and watched. A pit of doom swarmed in Burkhalder's stomach as she waited for the inevitable. A family somewhere, devastated by Hurricane *Evan*. Instead, a house fire taking a family, except the daughter found outside the home, asleep. And a few areas that looked rough after the storm. No devastation.

The wheel inside Burkhalder's head rotated at high speed. He didn't burn families, but the similarity of the youngest, a daughter found alive, untouched, made it investigation worthy. Maybe something went wrong. She looked to Frank. "After we drop my car off let's take a drive?"

His eyes narrowed. "You think he did that. You never mentioned fires. Serial killers don't generally change their M.O."

Burkhalder lifted up, stuffing one foot under her rear and propped her arm across the back of the couch. "They found the little girl outside asleep. How did she get there when the rest of the family burned? Look at the house. There's nothing left."

"Gotcha, we'll investigate."

"An eight-year-old missing child turns up, the two of you say nothing. A house burns to the ground and you're all over it," Talla said, shaking her head back and forth for emphasis. "Jeez something worse coulda happened to this kid, but it didn't. This is good news!"

Frank's dimple pressed into his cheek as he grinned at his niece's comment.

Home

The boy waited beside the car as Evan ordered. "Thank you, Mister."

"You speak. Get in." A smile tarried on his lips while he hit the door unlock button. The boy climbed into the passenger seat, pulled his seatbelt around him and clicked it while Evan popped the hood and reconnected everything.

He liked the kid, but hesitated at getting personal. The child did as he asked, didn't ask questions he shouldn't, and treated him with respect. The boy clicking his seatbelt impressed Evan the most. Someone taught him well. "What's your name?"

"Tyrus."

"Tyrus, I'm Nyle. Where do you live?"

He rattled the address to Evan.

"Do your parents treat you well?"

"Yes."

"Have they ever hurt you?"

"No, sir. My parents love me."

"That's why today is a lucky day for you.

"You're at least an hour from home." He started the car and backed out between the trees, the tires clunking over fallen branches. The storm hadn't been bad yet debris lay across the road and trees lay fallen in his path.

A few trees fell on the tops of homes or lay across driveways and yards. When they reached the outskirts of the storm's devastation, he pulled the car into a vacant gas station and parked beside a pay phone. "Can you read?"

"Yes, sir. Best in my class," Tyrus said with pride.

"Good." He scribbled on a piece of paper, then turned to Tyrus. "Call 9-1-1. Tell them you see flames." He handed the paper to Tyrus. "Hang up and don't mention me or who you are. Only tell them what I said, got it?"

"Yes, sir." Tyrus took the paper and hopped out of the car, running to the pay phone. He did as Evan commanded then hopped back in the car. "I did as you asked."

Evan had eavesdropped on the conversation and the boy did as requested. "Good job." He started the car, and the two rode in silence until they arrived a few blocks from Tyrus's house.

"When I drop you off don't mention me to anyone, including your parents. Understood? Tell them you got free on your own and ran through the woods until a stranger found you and brought you home. Don't give them my description. Make one up. Can you do that?"

The boy shook his head. "Yes, sir." Tyrus trusted Evan even though his shirt bore splotches of blood. He knew he harmed the family but looked at him as a savior.

"Those people are bad."

"They were." Evan agreed.

"They were going to hurt me."

Annoyed by the boy's insistence of telling him about his experience he said, "Yes, they planned on hurting you, but they can't hurt you or anyone else again. Got it?"

"Yes, sir."

"No more about it."

Tyrus shook his head in agreement.

The waxing crescent moon was a sliver in the sky. To Evan it meant a time of new beginnings, a time for planting. His lunar return report warned him of the potential for violence, even murder, of a violent nature. Good ol' Pluto. Power, control and hidden corruption. But it cut both ways. A double edged sword. He got away with destroying the Moras who were planning on harming, or even murdering, young Tyrus. His surprise at this unexpected turn of events was also seen in the lunar chart with Uranus conjuncting Jupiter. The biggest surprise was Carrot Top Cop forcing him to abandon plan A and go to plan B. Neptune sextile Mars, an opportunity for the secret act of aggression - Mrs. Mora. He hated his natal chart and challenged it, yet believed in Astrology. The Sun and Planets guided his path in life. The Universe knew who he really was even if no one else did.

The Calm Before the Storm: Evan's Sins

Evan pulled onto Tyrus's street and stopped a couple houses from his home. "When you can't see my car anymore walk to your house."

Tyrus jumped out of the car and watched Evan pull away. He continued standing in the same spot until Evan's car left his sight, then ran home and rang the doorbell several times. His mother opened the door, squealed, and wrapped her arms around him, smothering his face in kisses. His father and older sister soon joined in as they brought him inside, closing the door behind them.

Evan drove to the closest, highest peak he knew of and pushed his CRV off it. He watched as it rushed through trees, landing in the ravine below bursting into flames. In case Tyrus squealed or Carrot Top Cop remembered his plates, he figured it was better to destroy the evidence than allow the possibility of its existence.

Five and a half hours later, he leaned against a tree, his left calf crossed over his right foot. His black baseball cap covering his bald head. A teen with bouncy blond curls fell into the seat of a blue convertible, kissed the teenage driver - a dark, wavy haired boy. She fastened her seat belt while the convertible pulled away from the curb. Mr. Fritz's services were well worth the price. Expensive as hell, but he supplied Emily's address.

Drugged

Burkhalder and Frank dropped her SUV at his friend's shop for repairs then headed towards the scene of the house fire. The roads cleared of debris, but destruction still visible as they headed north along the coast.

"I'll never get used to looking at this."

"How's that?" asked Frank.

"Water and wind enough to crush the roof of a house, flooded yards and drainage ditches turned into raging rivers."

"And the next day the sun shines. It's deceiving. Chloe was one of the worst. I remember the highlights on the news. Your town suffered few casualties, excellent job detective." His dimple popped with his smile.

Burkhalder shuddered at the thought.

One hand on the wheel, he smoothed his mustache with the other. "You want to tell me about it?"

She looked towards him and couldn't help but admire his profile. A straight, masculine nose with a small flare at the nostril, triangular chin, and his hair skirted the outer edge of his ear. She wanted to take him to bed, not talk about Chloe. "Not really. I lost one of my best childhood friends. I miss him every day."

"Losing loved ones is the worst. My niece, she's had it rough, just now coming around. We don't always see it coming."

His words echoed in her head. Most of the time we never see death coming. She turned towards the window and watched the trees whip past them as the truck cruised forward.

"First we're stopping at the college so I can drop off your samples. One of the chemistry professors is a good friend."

"You have friends everywhere. Do they all owe you favors?"

"Not all of them." He chuckled.

"We were roommates in college, then I joined the navy and he got a PHD."

Brick buildings dotted the campus. Large trees, sidewalks, and grass filled the landscape. It reminded Burkhalder of old money and respect. They left his truck and walked towards a campus lake. A salt and pepper headed man with a matching beard stood beside it dressed in a collared shirt and khakis. He turned towards them. "Morning, Frank."

"Alice Burkhalder." She held out her hand.

He gave her hand a quick shake. "Dr. Telp. Pleasure to meet you."

Frank handed him her urine sample and the soda can. "If we had more time today I'd invite you to lunch."

"The misses has me on a diet. My tofu lunch is waiting." His beard curved with his smile. "I'll call you when I get this done."

"Thank you, Dr. Telp."

"It's no problem, Alice."

"I owe you," said Frank, as they walked away.

"You owe me nothing but you need to take her out. She's a looker."

Frank gave him a thumbs up.

Her face grew flush. "I can't believe he just said that."

"Chemistry professors don't get out much, but he's right. You are a beautiful woman and I'd like to take you for dinner."

Her cheeks flushed more. She kept walking to avoid him noticing. "I'll consider it." She reached the truck before him and waited alongside it.

He stopped in front of her and leaned his right hand against the windshield. She took in the outline of his body.

"There's this place, candlelight dinners, violin…"

His aftershave lingered in the air between them and the gentle curve of his lips drove her wild. She imagined him thrusting his tongue deep inside her mouth. "Another friend?"

He leaned closer. "It's a small town."

She arched her back and grabbed the door handle behind her and pulled. "Dinner sounds nice." He stepped backwards, allowing her to hop inside the truck, then closed the door behind her. Walking around the hood of his truck, he took his place in the driver's seat and turned the key. The engine roared to life. "Shall we get a glimpse of the bodies?"

The moment over, Burkhalder's cheeks returned to their normal pale coloring. "I reckon so."

Frank's truck purred out of the parking lot and onto the road, slowing thirty minutes later when he turned into the police station - a simple, brick, ranch style structure. It reminded Burkhalder of Billows Hollow.

"You ready."

She smiled. "Let's go."

Inside a dark haired lady stood behind a cage. Brown hair rested on her shoulders, the ends swooping upwards. The cage separated people walking into the station from the police. They walked towards her.

"Can I help you?" she asked. Her double chin thickening when she spoke.

"Is it possible to speak with the sheriff or officer that was at the scene of the house fire?"

"Oh, such a horrible thing. It's usually quiet around here. I never met the family, but I feel so horrible." She clutched her chest. "I'll direct you to officer Sugda. Hold on a second." She picked up the phone and dialed.

Burkhalder and Frank took a seat on the brown metal bench. Within a few minutes a young, dark skinned man opened the door. "I'm officer Sugda. What can I do ya for?"

"Frank Roy retired Lieutenant Commander."

"Detective Alice Burkhalder." She held out her badge.

His eyes widened. "A detective and a retired naval officer. This case isn't a simple house fire is it?"

Frank smiled. "We aren't sure. Det. Burkhalder's been investigating a murder that happened during Hurricane Chloe. The house fire caught our attention. There are similarities."

"Similarities, huh? What are we talkin'?"

"Other than the daughter found unharmed, we don't know. That's the reason we're here. If it's the same sicko he needs to be stopped. Did your forensics department or coroner find anything resembling foul play?" The urgency in her voice evident as the words tumbled from her mouth, clear and concise.

Officer Sugda grimaced. "Always willin' to help another officer. We fight the same fight. The bodies are charred. Not much left. If you'd like to take a look I can take ya to the morgue."

"Please," Frank and Burkhalder said in sync. They looked at each other and grinned.

The Calm Before the Storm: Evan's Sins

They filled Officer Sugda in on their suspicions while he escorted them to a brick building housed behind the police station labeled *Morgue* in white letters. Inside it smelled of heady chemicals and burned flesh. Heavy metal music hummed in the background. "Guy, this here is Detective Burkhalder and…"

"Frank Roy," he interjected.

Guy held up his hands, encased in latex gloves. "I'd shake but uh… another time. What's the pleasure?"

Burkhalder got straight to the point. "We think your burn victims may be due to foul play."

Guy lifted his pointer finger. "Come with me."

He uncovered the bodies of each charred victim. Disgust and hate flooded Burkhalder. *He's a monster.*

"Look at the necks of father and son. Now look at the mother."

"Looks like his handy work, half her neck is missing." Flashbacks of Lilly and the other female victims crawled through her mind. Their necks maimed, vaginal contusions…

"The fire didn't do this… I have more work to do, but initially I'd say this is more than an unfortunate house fire."

Burkhalder barely heard the coroner's words when she blurted, "Have you checked her for rape?"

"A real sickopath. He's got mommy issues." He peeled her legs apart. "Her burns are extensive but I'll see what I can do."

"I have a few connections, would you be willing to let a team do forensic testing you're not equipped for?" asked Frank.

Guy pushed a flop of white hair out of his eyes using his arm. "That's up to the sheriff but we need all the help we can get."

The Sheriff listened to Burkhalder's story and what little the coroner had on the dead family. He pulled at his pointed chin and swished his lips. "Alright, before I allow government folks into my sleepy town, how convinced are you?"

"This is the third crime scene I've witnessed the day after. It fits. The wife's neck is missing. He also rapes the mothers. That's what he does. He slices the children and husband once, lets them bleed out, then mangles the mother's neck with his knife until it's hanging off the bone. The daughter found safe outside the house, sleeping. How did she get there? The fire is the only piece that doesn't fit."

The sheriff's eyes met Frank's. "Bring them in. If it's the same guy than he's a national threat. I'm not gonna ignore that. "

Frank and Burkhalder swung by the Mora's house. They walked as far as the tape but didn't go inside the home. Frank made his phone calls and a forensics team would arrive in the morning to assess the situation.

The tires of Frank's truck crunched the gravel as it purred along the dirt road. Burkhalder peered out her window, watching the trees pass. Something in the dirt caught her eye. "Stop!"

He pressed the brake, shifted the truck into park and left it running. They stepped out of the vehicle. She pointed towards the ground, an area pushed downward with grooves at distinct locations. "Tire tracks?"

"Not only tire tracks. Looks like shoe prints. A small set." He followed, careful to step alongside them. "In some places the shoe prints were visible, in others they stopped, starting back up a yard or so away. "These prints are leading from the house and stop by the tire grooves. Doesn't make sense."

"It doesn't make any sense. He took a kid with him?"

"Another piece that doesn't fit."

She ran her tongue across her lips, considering his words. At the moment she was overjoyed she met Frank. Even more so that he believed her and was helping. She no longer felt alone in her search. "A team will be here tomorrow. We'll let them do their job and wait for their results."

The ring of Frank's phone sang through the air. He looked at the I.D. then answered.

"Did you find anything? Like we suspected. Thanks." He tapped the *end call* button.

Frank looked into Burkhalder's expectant green eyes. "Dr. Telp. He found traces of a combination of common sleeping meds in your urine sample and the soda."

"Did I tell you the psycho has a degree in pharmaceuticals and a license?"

He raised his eyebrows. "You did. Here's my theory. In the other murders the storms were far stronger than yesterday's, destroying evidence. He burned the house because the storm didn't destroy it. He also burned the garage. Why? This family challenged him. They didn't let him inside so he found another way."

The puzzle pieces came together for Burkhalder. "He drugged me and slashed my tire but didn't kill me. He raped Gala but let her live. He only wants the families, like he's reliving his family's murder. The small foot prints were made by a child who isn't part of the family. He couldn't kill him."

"At age ten, when his family was murdered, he didn't have the body strength to kill anyone unless they were subdued. He's got mommy issues. What do you know about her?"

"Not much, I spoke with the neighbor. According to her, the mom was extra affectionate. I couldn't get anything out of the psychiatrist. After his release, his neighbor filled me in on some weird shit. My guess is she sexually abused him."

They stepped into the truck and headed towards Frank's home, discussing the facts and leads.

The forensics team found traces of the same sleeping intoxicants in the burned bodies found in Burkhalder - except the child. They found a different combination of drugs built up in his system. The team connected the dots between Florida and the Billows Hollow murders. The media dubbed him the Hurricane Killer 'He blows in with the storm and out with the storm'. It spread across the news to every part of the U.S.

The police linked Tyrus's abduction to the Mora family. He kept tight lipped about Evan, telling the police someone threw a bag over his head while he walked home from school. He kicked and screamed, then they shot a needle in his arm. Several hours later he woke up in a dark room, scared. He heard a struggle then someone unlocked his door. When the house went silent he snuck out of the room and ran until a car stopped on the main road. He saw the house in flames. So he asked the old man with white hair and a wrinkly face if he could use his phone. He didn't have one so he pulled into a gas station and Tyrus used the payphone. The police didn't press the eight-year-old boy. They looked for the man and the car, but found neither.

Frank took Burkhalder to a candle lit, violin dinner. Six months later she moved in with him and they opened a consulting firm. No direct evidence pointed to Evan. She never doubted his guilt and continued digging into his life. Bit by bit, Burkhalder and Frank pieced together the life of a man who fit the Hurricane Killer profile.

Find Her!

Evan barged into Mr. Fritz's office without an appointment. "Mr. O'Conner, please take a seat."

"No thanks. What did you find? I don't want any excuses this time."

Mr. Fritz edged towards his desk. "Not much."

"'Not much' better be more than last time."

Wiping his bushy brow, Mr. Fritz picked up a skinny file and flipped through it. He'd been avoiding telling Evan the news, scared of his dark side. "Please take a seat. I'll share with you the information on the woman in question."

Evan perched on the edge of the seat across from Mr. Fritz's desk.

He swallowed, the emergency buzzer below his desk just above his knee. "The woman's name is Scarlett Jones. She is your mother's sister."

Evan leaned back. "My aunt?"

"Yes. I haven't been able to locate her, she disappeared and was reported as a missing person in August 1972."

"Mr. Fritz, look into my eyes. What do you see?"

"Light blue."

Evan scooted closer. "Get closer and look again."

Mr. Fritz scooted closer with caution. He gazed into his eyes, hoping the blackness didn't envelop them.

"Colored rings around your iris."

"Each eye is different."

"Yes, a yellow and an amber ring."

Evan picked up Mr. Fritz's file. "My mother had solid blue eyes." The festering darkness lingered at the edge of his pupil. "This woman has two different colored eyes. That's not common. Find her!" He slammed the folder onto Mr. Fritz's desk and left his office.

Mr. Fritz let out a deep breath. He hadn't lied, yet he hadn't quite told the truth. There was far more to the story. Scarlett was a product of rape. A half-sister to Evan's mother, less than a year apart in age. Her mother, a fourteen-year-old victim of Philmonia's father. Mr. Fritz took a handkerchief to his forehead, wiping the sweat bubbling above his brows. He wanted to find her too, alive rather than dead. He believed Scarlett to be Evan's biological mother, but couldn't figure out how they did it. His birth certificate listed Philmonia as his mother and the doctor and nurses confirmed his mother giving birth saying, 'I'd have remembered her eyes. That's not something I see every day'.

Philmonia's father died in jail, shanked. Even hardened prisoners don't like child abusers. He opened the file and flipped to the man's picture and spoke to it. "How could you do it, including your own daughter, Philmonia? It's no wonder she turned out wrong." The man's eyes, Evan's eyes, stared at him. Their irises growing darker the longer he stared at the picture. He flipped it over and shoved it into the folder.

At home that evening he slid a stone from the bottom of his fireplace and placed Scarlett's file beside a sealed bag containing a blood crusted knife. He replaced the stone then poured himself a brandy.

Secrets

2000

The tall, balding custodian whistled while he clutched his caddy of cleaners and headed into Mr. Fritz's office. Fritz hadn't been forthcoming with Burkhalder so Frank took the matter into his own hands. Side-stepping Burkhalder. She'd be upset but would get over it. He slipped around the corner. Keeping one eye on the custodian, he wrapped his gloved hand around his keys, careful not to make noise, then slipped around the corner. He made an imprint and temporary key. With his back to the wall, Frank peered around the corner. The custodian's whistling stopped as he rummaged through his cart looking for his keys. Scratching his head, he darted into Mr. Fritz's office. Frank slunk towards the cart and placed the keys on a towel, then crept around the corner.

The custodian returned to his cart, picked up the keys and chuckled. "How did I miss this?" he said to the air then whistled while he moved onto the next office. When he moved far enough away, Frank dashed from his hiding spot, slipped his generic, homemade key into the lock and entered the office.

Inside, he shone his flashlight, found a file cabinet and pulled a drawer - locked. He jarred the lock open with his Swiss army knife and flipped through the files, finding two, one labeled *Evan O'Conner Senior* the other *Evan O'Conner Junior.* Frank snapped photos of several pages of interest with his digital camera. The name Philmonia O'Conner jumped off a page as his eyes scanned the print. *Evan's mother.*

He placed the folders in the file drawer and picked through the remaining files in the drawer, not one labeled with her name. A stack of files lay on the edge of Mr. Fritz's thick wooden desk. He thumbed through, finding Philmonia's, snapped more pictures, then placed it back. Careful nothing appeared disturbed.

Footfalls in the hallway caught his attention. He scooted towards the door and edged against the wall so when the door opened he'd be behind it. The lock clicked and the doorknob twisted. A light shone around the room. Frank stood motionless, sucking in steady, slow breaths of air, ready to drop his flashlight on the head of whoever stood on the other side of the door. The door closed and his phone buzzed in his back pocket. He stayed still, hoping the person didn't hear. The door reopened, illumination from a flashlight beamed towards the desk, the person walked towards it. The door ajar, but not closed against him, Frank noted black shoes and a dark blue security uniform. Frank eased his head behind the door. The guard turned off his flashlight and exited the room. His footfalls continued down the hallway. Frank breathed normally and lowered his flashlight. When he no longer heard the footfalls, Frank edged into the hallway, looking each direction he slipped out, locking the door behind him.

Once downstairs, he snuck through the halls, ninja-like, and found the security room. He listened behind the door. Hearing no sound, he tried the knob. To his surprise it was unlocked. Frank slipped inside, went to the computer and tweaked with the times, erasing the past hour from every camera's memory, and turning off the outside cameras and alarm for fifteen minutes.

He slipped out the back door and ran-walked to his vehicle. Wasting no time, he pulled away and headed towards the airport. Once inside the terminal, he pulled his phone out of his pocket. A call from Alice. No need to listen to her voicemail, he knew her well. He dialed her as he scanned through his camera photos.

"What the hell, Frank?! Where are you?"

"I'm on my way home. I'm in New Mexico."

"New… You went to the lawyer's without mentioning it to me."

He sighed. "I did and found great stuff."

"Should I kick your ass when you get home or beat and torture you during sex?!"

"Torture me during sex anytime, baby."

"I'll be waiting." She hung up, and the line went dead in his ear.

He loved her fire.

Eight hours later, at home, Burkhalder breathed over his shoulder as he uploaded the pictures to his computer. They scanned each photo, reading the details of Evan O'Conner Senior's will. "Evan collected the whole shit and caboodle! No wonder I couldn't track him through his license or otherwise. He's the stinkin' rich heir." She drug a chair to the computer and planted herself beside him. "According to this, daddy's estate sent large donations to Windy Oaks during his stay." She'd known this but had no evidence legally, or illegally, obtained.

"Yeah."

Burkhalder jumped out of her seat. "We're both going to New Mexico."

"Hold up." Frank pointed to the screen. "Philmonia isn't his mom. They only share twenty-three percent of the same DNA!"

"They are related, halves."

"Her father is a convicted rapist..." Burkhalder dropped in the chair beside Frank, "and Philmonia has no siblings. After her father went to prison her mom committed suicide."

"He's a convicted rapist. A victim he impregnated?"

"Where, what prison?" She leaned over his shoulder, speed reading.

He nodded his head. "He's dead. Killed in prison."

Frank picked up his phone, holding his hand over the mouthpiece, he flashed his eyes to Burkhalder. "I have a friend."

What Are Friends For

Frank's friend discovered Scarlett's mother gave birth to her at fifteen. A victim of Philmonia's father. The baby given up and bounced from foster home to foster home until she turned eighteen and disappeared.

Burkhalder knocked on Scarlett's last foster parent's door. The woman who filed the missing person's report. An elderly woman, slouched in a walker, opened the door. "Ms. Burkhalder, come in. Please take a seat."

The house smelled of a distinct combination of menthol and lavender. Afghans draped over the couch and a chair. A doily lay on the table covered in knickknacks.

The woman shuffled to the couch, waving her arm. "Forget the formalities, everyone has been here asking about Scarlett, but not for many years. She went out one afternoon and never returned. She was a real secretive girl, but sweet. And she loved to cook and had quite the knack for it."

"How long did she stay with you?"

"Gosh, my husband was alive then and we had her for, I guess, about four years. She came to us at the start of high school and graduated just before she disappeared."

"Did she have any friends?"

"Nah, not close ones. She was a loner."

"Anything else you remember about her?"

"It's been a long time. Like I said, she was a sweet girl. I knew the story. She was a product of rape. She never talked about her past or asked about her mother."

"If you think of anything more, please call me." Burkhalder handed her one of her and Frank's business cards.

"I'm not sure why the renewed interest, but another investigator visited just a few weeks ago."

"Do you have his name?"

"Better." She reached onto the table, moving aside an owl, and picked up a card. "Take this."

"Thank you for your time." Burkhalder slipped the card inside the front pocket of her jeans.

A text from Frank popped up on the screen of her phone. *Meet me in the hotel lobby.* Anxious to share notes, she rushed to the hotel.

Frank waited for her seated in a posh leather booth inside the hotel bar. "Ordered you a gin and tonic," he said, standing and kissing her cheek.

His touch caused an automatic reaction and heat rose inside her. She refocused her mind. "What did you find?" She eased into the booth. He slid in across from her.

"Scarlett didn't have a lot of friends, so when her English teacher saw her getting into a car with another blond she found it odd. This happened only weeks before she disappeared. At first, she did a double take, thinking the young blond in the car was Scarlett. Then she saw Scarlett run towards the car and hop into the passenger seat."

"She knew Philmonia. Did she give this information to the police?"

"She did, but all she had was a description of the driver and a possible make of the car. Not enough for them to find the driver. What did you find, babe?"

"Quiet girl, loner, loved to cook. Not much."

"And her mother?"

"Dead end. She wouldn't even let me in the door," said Burkhalder with a sigh.

"Where are we with Evan's address?"

"Nowhere. Just the P.O. Box we have from Fritz's files and the estate surrounded by a heavy metal fence, might as well be a moat with alligators." She hooked her fingers into her front pocket. A card poked the tip of her pointer finger and she remembered a P.I. had visited Scarlett's foster mother. She pulled it out of her pocket and handed it to Frank. "He visited Scarlett's foster mom."

Frank pulled his phone out of his pocket and walked outside. Burkhalder waited in anticipation. Within a few minutes he returned. "Noon tomorrow at Hidden Park. He'll be wearing a Red Cardinals Cap."

☾ ☾ ☾ ☾ ☾

The next day, Frank and Burkhalder headed towards Hidden Park for their meeting. Lush grass and large trees shaded their walk from the blistering sun. They scanned the park on the look-out for a red cap.

"Over there, your two o'clock," said Burkhalder, leaning towards Frank.

"See him."

As they approached, Burkhalder noted the detective's slender frame, dressed in casual shorts and a tank.

"Mr. Dawson."

"Yup. Mr. Roy and..." He tipped his hat, a spider web of lines ebbed from the corners of his eyes displaying his age. At least fifty, guessed Burkhalder.

"Alice."

"As I mentioned on the phone, we have a consulting business and a client who is interested in finding Scarlett." Frank's no nonsense tone apparent in his voice.

"I'd like to find her myself. My client is breathing down my neck but every lead dead-ends."

They strolled through the park, careful to stay in the shade of the trees. As they passed under some places the leaves parted, allowing the sun to filter through, Burkhalder's hair, shining bright red.

An hour later they knew little more about Scarlett's whereabouts. They did learn Mr. Dawson found Scarlett years ago and the blond in the car was Philmonia. That came as no shock to them or that Mr. Fritz hired him for a client, most likely Philmonia or Mr. O'Conner Senior. They were back to square one.

With no information about Evan or Scarlett, they went home to North Carolina. Over the next several years Hurricane Evan struck every three years, making slight changes to his pattern, enough that he remained elusive.

The police questioned Gala, who got married to a wonderful young man who treated her like an angel from heaven. She didn't want to relive or go back to the day of the rape, and told the police she left with Kevin but never saw her attacker's face. She couldn't confirm the rapist's identity.

Witness

2007

July thirteenth, ten days had passed since his grandparents yanked him from Tech camp. His parents' faces flew around him as he followed the familiar trail to his best friend, Mark's, house. He saw his young self, collecting shells on the beach, his mother smiling with his elation over finding a large shark's tooth. The necklace with the tooth on it bobbed against his chest as he walked. At fifteen, he wasn't ready to let go of his parents who were killed in a plane crash on their way home from vacationing in San Diego.

Dillon swiped the pelting rain mixed with tears from his eyes. The winds surrounded him, whipping clumps of leaves and small branches. Oblivious to them, his heart filled with sorrow, he continued on his path toward the beach. Mark's mother dead and his father shacked up with a new girlfriend, he'd understand Dillon's sorrow and offered him an alternate reality as they squashed *The Flood in Halo*.

He marched up the back steps to his friend's house. The heavy winds and rains pelted his back. He twisted the knob and shut the door behind him. He and Mark had known each other so long they were like brothers. His home, usually a bustle of noise caused by his father's girlfriend's two children, now filled with an eerie silence. Dillon halted, perking his ear to a muffled noise on the far side of the beach home.

Nervous energy simmered inside him as he strolled towards the noise. The closer he got, the louder the noise. Side-stepping the living room he jaunted faster now, cornering the hallway. His mind focused on the sound emanating from the master bedroom. The door open, he peered inside and gasped, covering his hands over his mouth. His eyes wide as flying saucers. A man thrust himself into the girlfriend, blood curled over the sheets and puddled on the floor beside the bed. The man intent on raping the dying woman didn't notice Dillon, so he eased toward the dresser where a heavy paperweight lay, grabbed it and lunged toward the back of the man's head, hitting him with it. The man fell face first on top of the girlfriend. Unsure what to do next, Dillon rushed out of the house.

Halfway home he realized he still carried the paperweight. He let it drop. Tears streaked across his cheeks. *Is he dead? Did I kill him? Is Mark still alive?* Lost in the thoughts circling his brain, he didn't notice her until he heard a voice ask, "Are you alright?"

He turned towards the voice and looked upon her angelic face for the first time, blond ringlets blowing across it. "I… No. Do you have a phone?" Reality sunk in, he needed to call the police.

"I've already called. I saw it too."

He narrowed his eyes. "Called what in?"

"You're being coy. I watched you run out of the house and drop the paperweight." She pulled her arm from behind her back and uncurled her fingers. The bloody paperweight lying in her palm. "He's not dead and he'll find you if we stand here any longer and talk. Come with me."

She darted across the rain laden sand, her feet sinking into the sand, splashing water as they rose again. He chased after the mystery woman. Curiosity consumed him.

In a Pinch

Evan stirred. A throbbing pain thumped from the back of his head. He blinked his eyes, orienting himself. A Victorian style dresser to his right, a peach wall behind it. Shifting his eyes downward, he lay on a bed. A dead woman beneath him. Blood dripped from his arm as he lifted it towards his head. Freezing mid movement. A deluge of memories flooded his mind. He killed her and the entire family, even an older teen boy who shouldn't have been there. He was finishing the job, watching his mother's form rise from the dead woman when, behind, something crashed against his skull. *Did somebody witness the event? How much did they see?* A siren wailed in the distance and his pulse quickened. The pain in his head seared as he lifted his body off the woman. His gloves slid in the oozing blood surrounding him. He grabbed hold of the sheets squeezing them in his fist and jolted upright. He leapt from the bed and grabbed his pants and knife. Stumbling as he yanked them on, slipping his knife into his waist band. A steady hammering beat against his cranium as he ambled towards the master bath. The siren's call getting closer with each second.

Stay in control! Stay in control! He threw
open the cabinet doors beneath the sink and
rifled through the contents. Smudges of blood
covered everything he touched. He grabbed a
bottle of hydrogen peroxide and twisted the
top. His glove caught on the lid ripping a
sliver sized hole. He didn't notice. His heart
drummed against his chest. The siren's roar
grew louder. He splashed the peroxide over
the area he laid. The blood bubbled from the
chemical reaction. Screeching tires rounded
the corner. He threw the empty bottle to the
ground.

Evan ran into the living room and
grasped his bag. Two brown eyes blinked at
him from the little girl curled beneath an end
table, cuddling a baby doll. She sucked at her
thumb as Evan sprinted through the house.
From his bag he pulled out his baseball hat
and slipped it on his head. Then he pulled out
a sandwich bag containing an arrowhead on a
leather rope. He dipped the point in the
father's blood then rushed to the door.
Almost forgetting to grab the girl's favorite
toy. He spied her underneath the table and
yanked the doll out of her hand. Opening the
door he peered both directions then slipped
out, tossing the bloody arrowhead towards a
bush of tall ornamental grass. *Take control!* He
sucked in the layout of the area determining
the quickest route to his car. Police sirens
shrieked as the cars halted in front of the

house. The squawking of police radios told him they were in the house. The pounding in his head increasing with the quickening of his pulse. He spotted a shed and raced through the vacant yards. Stuffing his bloody gloves into his pockets he threw open the door. Tools and yard equipment filled the shed. A thin work-suit hung on a peg behind him. He yanked it off and slipped into it.

Stay calm Evan. You're just a neighbor. You're no one unless you draw attention to yourself. A small gathering of people collected in front of the house. He steady-walked through the yards, everyone's eyes on the house. Heavy footsteps clogged the earth behind him. Evan veered towards the side of a house and peered around the corner as a cop ran past him. He slid along the house. His car in sight. Just then a heavy band of rain burst from the sky and pelted against him. He used it as cover and ran to his car, sliding into the driver's seat. A police car rounded the corner. He ducked, pushing his torso over the gear shift and rested his head on the passenger seat. The car cruised by at a slug's pace. He waited several minutes then lifted his head and started the engine. He knew more cops would invade the area. He watched the news. People feared the Hurricane Killer. It was a risk he took. A risk he enjoyed. The suspense added to his omnipotence. He couldn't be caught. Not now, not ever!

Careful to keep to the speed limit, he drove through the streets, staying to the roads less traveled. A police car wailed past him. The best way to evade them was to blend in, not draw attention to himself. He turned the radio on and scanned the stations. He didn't take the freeway but stayed on the quiet roads, rain and winds pushing against his car.

Blue lights from two police cars flashed at the county line. Stopping each car that crossed. Still two hundred yards from the line, he spotted a dirt road to his right. He turned onto the dirt road, following it several miles as his mind assessed the situation. The police had never been this close. He pulled his car to the side of the road and looked at his appearance in the rearview. Streaks of blood covered his face. He reached into his travel bag, changed his clothes and wiped the blood off his face. Ne needed a diversion.

Diversion

Frank's phone rang only moments after Evan left the crime scene. He and Burkhalder piled into his truck, choosing to drive. The South Carolina border not far from their home. Several hours later they entered the city of Belleview and Frank called his friend.

"We're in town."

"Meet at the house."

Frank handed Burkhalder the phone as his friend rattled off directions to the house. She took notes. "Take a left at the next light." An Ebert's Pharmacy on one corner and a Corny's Chicken on the other, he pulled into the left turn lane. Static fuzzed through the speakers, Burkhalder pushed the tuner button and scanned through the channels. Stopping when she got a news station. "At the corner with the white church, make a right." *Two found dead at the house fire…* Alice increased the volume on the radio. *A car lost control, plowing through the family room. The charred remains of a male driver found inside the car. The cause of the fire unknown.*

Alice and Frank swapped glances.

They arrived at the house, Frank's buddy, Tyler, dressed in a blue suit, walked towards the truck as they stepped outside it. Wisps of his thinning hair blew in the wind and dark, velvet brown eyes greeted Burkhalder.

"Agent Hopps."

"Alice Burkhalder."

"I finally meet the woman who stole my friend's heart and started this man hunt."

The light caught a twinkle in her eyes.

Agent Tyler Hopps turned on his heels and headed into the house. "There are some inconsistencies. You'll see. Careful where you walk. There's blood in every room. You need to see it. What a bloody mess."

They followed him through the house, stopping in the living room. "We found the father propped on the love seat. There's no recliner, so that must have been his second choice." Caked blood covered the flowery fabric. "We found the girl cuddled beneath that end table." He pointed towards it. Agent Hopps continued through the house.

"Who was the photographer?" asked Burkhalder, studying the beach pictures filling every wall.

"The girlfriend. So that's different. He always picks married couples. Also we found a fifteen-year-old. The boyfriend's son. I suspect he didn't plan on that kid being here. She divorced her husband a year ago. He's slipping, losing his edge."

Flashes of each bloody crime scene and dead body ran through Burkhalder's brain. Lilly's hair flowing beneath the rubble. Tiny

241

Eilida's death grip and every other little girl left homeless by the monster. "I wish. Has he been found?"

"The locals put up road blocks and checked every car leaving the county. No sign of anyone fitting the profile. They took down the road blocks after only a couple hours. A car ran through a house. Burned it to the ground. The locals dispatched their officers to that scene. A single occupant burned beyond recognition inside the car, his teeth shattered on impact so we can't even match dental records. We put a team on it, could be him."

"We heard on the radio. So they took down the road blocks?"

"They had no other choice. My team was en route."Agent Hopps pushed open a door. The familiar outline of a body lay across the floor. A lamp and other objects covered the area of the floor by the dresser. "He didn't go down easy. At six foot, two hundred pounds, he fought him."

"Big boy."

"Yeah, not big enough or skilled enough," piped Frank.

Agent Hopps took them through each room filled with pools of blood and outlines of bodies. When they got to the bedroom, even Burkhalder wasn't sure what to think.

A semi dry lake of crimson covered the carpet around the headboard but the bed itself was a shade of pink. "What the...?" questioned Burkhalder.

"We found an empty bottle of hydrogen peroxide. Here's where we get lucky. A sliver of a common latex glove was stuck inside the lid."

The glimmer of a smile tugged at Burkhalder's lips. "He got caught! Peroxide mixed with blood causes a chemical reaction. His blood is on those sheets, maybe even the floor."

"We've sent everything in for testing. If there's any remnant we'll find it." Agent Hopps tugged at his chin.

Frank hadn't said much through the entire tour. He walked around the room, taking note of the bloody hand prints. "This is messy. Too messy. There's no struggle in this room. He's on top of the woman. Someone sneaks up behind him and smashes his skull." Frank threw his arm in the air and swished as if hitting someone on the head. "Knocks him out and escapes from the house. The perp wakes up, angry but in control. He doesn't think about his head, instead he goes into the bathroom." Frank walked to the master bath. "See everything on the floor. He tosses it, finds the peroxide then pours it over her neck. He's bleeding, but how bad? He doesn't take a chance. How soon did this get called in?"

Agent Hopps checked his notepad. "Two thirteen. A 9-1-1 call came in. A woman, but the number is unknown. My team is running it."

Burkhalder lifted her pointer finger. "Hold up. When he woke up the cops were on their way. He didn't have time to clean. Did anyone question the girl?"

"Her father won't let us. She's a traumatized two-year-old." Tyler shrugged.

"And the only witness we have." Burkhalder knew how it went with the girls. Either too small to talk or too scared.

Frank studied the blood pattern on the ground. "The drops are leading out of the room, down the hall and out the back door." He talked as he stalked through the house and opened the back door. "If I wanted to get away without being caught, I'd hide in that shed."

"We thought of that. The owner says his overalls are missing but the neighbors didn't see anything. They were all gawking at the police in front of the house. Let's get to the other scene."

"Not yet." Burkhalder stepped outside the house and walked towards the shed. She scanned the area, trees, and bushes. She walked the perimeter. Frank and Agent Hopps followed her movements.

"What are you looking for? My team's been over this area with a fine toothed comb."

She leaned towards a single bushy pampas grass and shifted the leaves, revealing a slim leather rope. "This."

Agent Hopps walked towards her and peered inside the bush. He reached into the front pocket of his shirt and pulled out a pen. Then used it to tug the rope free of the bush. He held it in the air. "A bloody arrowhead. I can't believe they missed this." He shook his head, wisps of his hair flailed in the breeze.

The group drove to the second scene to look at the charred remains of the house. Pieces of frame stood alone. The roof completely gone. Chunks of scorched wall hung off the strips of frame. "What did this? Even the Mora house didn't look this bad."

"The fire department is still determining but uh... not much doubt an accelerant was used."

At the morgue they looked at the bodies, replicas of all the others, except the ginger headed teen.

Frank and Burkhalder stayed in town. She knew more about the murders than anyone else. They worked around the clock, discovering a partial print on the arrowhead. The best match, a Tennessee man by the name of LeRoy Homer. Burkhalder insisted they run it against Evan's.

"He was a resident of a mental facility for eight years. His prints are in the system," she argued.

The Calm Before the Storm: Evan's Sins

The tech ran his against the partial, none of the points matched. She dropped her head into her hands and looked at Frank. "Have I been chasing the wrong guy?"

He pulled a chair beside her and grasped her hand. "There's never been evidence before. He got sloppy and now we have a lead. You wanted it to be Evan. After everything you told me, and everything we found, I wanted it to be Evan. Maybe he's truly a victim."

"I'm never this wrong." Her eyebrows sunk towards her eyelashes.

"This guy, Homer, he's fifty-one years old, he lived in North Carolina in the early '90s. Not far from Billows Hollow." He rubbed his thumb over the back of her hand.

She pulled at her lips, fixing her eyes on Frank's soft, loving ones. "When does the DNA analysis come back?"

"They're having a difficult time with that. Everything they've tested is blood from the victims and the peroxide sample is corrupted." He remained silent for a few seconds before breaking the good news. "It's not all bad. The car burn victim is a 30-40 year old male. Approximate height 5'5. His bone structure suggests he was a stout man."

A Convenient Fall Guy

Agent Tyler Hopps's team brought in LeRoy Homer for questioning. Burkhalder took in the harsh lines running across his face and thick, webbed creases along his eyes. His dark hair thin and disheveled. When he spoke, yellowed teeth and a pasty tongue sickened her stomach. Even behind the two-sided mirror he was an ugly man who looked as if he lived a hard life.

Agent Hopps slapped a file onto the metal table between him and Homer. "Where were you July thirteenth?"

"I was at my house. I live alone." His tone condescending.

"You didn't go anywhere that day?"

"Hell no! Disability doesn't pay me enough to have a life."

"Mr. Homer, any neighbors you may have spoken to?"

Mr. Homer glared at Agent Hopps. "I said I live alone. Is that a crime these days?"

Agent Hopps planted himself in the seat across the table. "No. Do you know a Samantha Khan or Jasper Miles?"

Mr. Homer leaned his back against the metal framed chair. "Never heard of them. What's all this about?"

"We found your fingerprints associated with a crime scene."

"I don't know anything about it. Like I said, I was home."

Mr. Hopps tapped his pencil on the table then opened the file. "You were arrested in 1995 for domestic battery?"

Mr. Homer's eyes shot bullets at Agent Hopps. "That was a long time ago and I paid the price. You can't stick that on me again."

"Just getting my facts straight is all. So you were home July thirteenth, live alone, no alibi, and you have an arrest for domestic battery?"

Mr. Homer slammed his thin arm on the table, bouncing Agent Hopps's pencil across it. "We already established that!"

Agent Hopps closed the file, grabbed his pencil, stood and pushed his chair in. "Thank you, Mr. Homer." He strolled to the door and opened it.

"Wait a sec. What the hell? You gonna leave me here?"

"We'll release you soon. I just need to double check the facts with my team." He closed the door behind him and took a stance beside Burkhalder. "What do you think?"

She swished her lips, her eyes focused on Mr. Homer. "I don't know. Let me talk to him?"

"He's all yours. Watch that nasty attitude of his." He smiled, already aware she was more than capable of taking care of herself.

Burkhalder exited the room, stopping at the coffee machine. She pressed a couple buttons. The dark coffee spilled into each cup. The dark liquid sloshed as she walked towards the interrogation room, a folder beneath her armpit. Agent Hopps opened the door for her, keeping his body out of Mr. Homer's line of sight.

Bare gray walls and the stench of body odor filled the room. The plastic baseboards loaded with dust and bright florescent lights flickered above her head, giving the room a depressing ambiance.

She took a seat across from Mr. Homer. His temple pulsed rapidly as his eyes narrowed, scanning her. "Good morning."

"It ain't no good morning sittin' in this pit."

She noted his nasty attitude and smiled. "You're right, this room is depressing." She leaned forward as if telling him a secret.

"No kidding. So I already told the other cop everything. What the hell you want?"

"First, I have coffee." She slid a steaming Styrofoam cup towards him. "I hope you like it black."

He took the steaming cup and held it between his hands. "Mr. Homer. As agent Hopps stated, your fingerprints were found at a crime scene. A gruesome crime scene." She cleared her throat, then shuffled inside her folder pulling out the photos and spread them across the table. She wanted to gauge his reaction. "I'm not a police officer anymore. I dropped that hat several years ago. I'm not an agent either. I own a consulting firm and have spent the past decade and a half looking for one man. He could be you."

Mr. Homer glanced at the pictures then shifted his eyes away from them. "I ain't never murdered no one. I beat the hell out my wife 'cos she was a bitch and a whore. She got what she deserved. I left her very much alive."

She noted his reaction. He wouldn't look at the pictures and jumped to his defense. "I have another picture." She pulled out her sketch of Evan and laid it over the crime photos. His eye glanced towards it. "Have you ever seen this man?"

"Lady, I can barely see it. Do you have a pair of reading glasses I can use?" His voice calmer, with a hint of interest.

"I'll see what I can do." She walked out of the room, leaving the pictures on the table, then came around the double sided mirror and observed his actions. He sipped his coffee and stared at the wall refusing to glance anywhere near the table full of gruesome pictures. "I don't think it's him. Look - he won't even look at them. If it was him he'd wear a smug look on his face and suck in his handy work."

"I have to agree with you. Everything we know about this guy suggests a narcissist."

"I need the arrowhead. Oh, and reading glasses."

Several minutes later, Burkhalder returned to the depressing room and took a seat across from Mr. Homer. She handed him a pair of glasses. He unfolded them and pushed them over his long nose then picked up the sketch. His eyes avoided the bloody pictures. He held the picture for several minutes before speaking.

"Yeah, I met someone looked like this guy, but his head was shaved. It was after that wicked hurricane. Uh… started with a C. Anyways I picked him up and gave him a ride to Horn City."

Burkhalder mulled it over. "Hurricane Chloe?"

"Yup, that's it. I cleared out of the Billows Hollow area day after that storm. Landed in Tennessee. So I met him at a diner. He needed a ride home. I didn't know where I was going so hitched him a ride."

So that's how he disappeared from Billows Hollow. "Anything else you remember about him?"

"He was a run-of-the-mill kid, friendly. Ugly as sin, but conversational." He slipped the reading glasses off his eyes.

251

She lifted the evidence bag with the arrowhead in it. "We found your prints on this."

"Hell, had one of those but lost it years ago. Haven't seen it since North Carolina and it didn't have blood on it."

Ideas filled her head. It sounded as though Evan framed him, stealing the arrowhead and planting it at the scene, but their encounter had been so many years ago. *Did he keep the arrowhead as a way to throw us off should he ever get caught? How many more items has he stolen throughout the years?* She gathered the crime scene pictures, slipped them into the folder then pulled out a picture of Gala. "Do you know this girl?"

His eyes rested on her picture. He lifted the reading glasses back to his eyes and focused on her. "She's a looker. I wish I could say I do, but I ain't never seen her."

"Thank you, Mr. Homer." She stood, gathered her pictures and slid them into her folder.

"Now hold on. I gave you everything honest. When do I get outta here?"

"Mr. Homer, I don't decide that. I'm just a consultant, but your information has been very helpful and I'll make a recommendation to Agent Hopps. That's the best I can do." She turned on her heels and left.

Frank called soon after she left the dingy interrogation room. He and one of Agent

Hopps's team visited the last known owner of the charred car.

"What did you find?"

She sensed a smile and happiness in his voice. "Good stuff. This guy is still very much alive. It wasn't him in the car. He'd sold it for three grand, cash, the day before. The guy he sold it to, a Nyle Weatherbee. I showed him Evan's sketch from my phone. He identified him as the man who he sold the car to." Satisfaction plastered across Frank's face. "It gets better, Nyle Weatherbee doesn't exist."

☾ ☾ ☾ ☾ ☾

Evan lifted his legs across the sectional, an arrogant smile across his face as he watched the evening news. Jupiter brought him a blast of self-esteem and confidence along with Mars ruling his fifth. Ego overinflated. He stuffed the closest look-a-like to him he could find on short notice inside the car and let him burn alive. The bastard felt nothing as his system was loaded with sleeping serum. He and the family inside the house, unfortunate casualties of Evan's war - the *ruthless storm*. His self-preservation. His scapegoat LeRoy, sure to be interrogated. Transiting Venus in the twenty-ninth degree of Leo showed a permanent ending with legal implications by squaring his ascendant as well as the seventh house of relationships. His permanent ending and need to defend himself seen with "killing" himself and framing another while taking a lick to the back of his head. The media would sway, the public feel safe. The Hurricane Killer dead. He'd change his pattern, confuse the authorities. The lunar nodes crossing his midheaven signified something new entering his life while something else departed. Old ways left behind.

A sharp pain from his healing head wound reminded him of his close call and curiosity ruled his mind as he considered the only part of the lunar report that didn't make sense: Venus's ominous position while ruling his eleventh house of goals and friends as well as his seventh house of relationships. *Who?*

While She Slept

2009

Birds chirped and fluttered in the bright afternoon air. The chill of fall sent shivers up and down her exposed arms, or maybe it was the coldness settling in her heart as she watched her grandmother's casket being lower into the ground. She was the one person in her life, a Leo, who filled the void. Astrology was something she and her grandmother spent time learning about. She'd even taken Eilida to her first convention only months before her death. Eilida squeezed her parents' hands as tears rolled down her cheeks. She loved them but missed her grandma who could never be replaced. Sadness swelled inside nineteen-year-old Eilida's heart.

Evan stood thirty yards away, perched against a tree. The bill on his black baseball cap pulled over his eyes, his lips wearing a smug smile. He'd been easy on Grandma, wanted to make it look natural. The police never questioned, never investigated - just an old lady who dies peacefully in her sleep. Eilida's back to him, she never saw him.

After the funeral, at home, she and her best friend Sage took a walk to the lake at the end of the property and hung their legs over the side of the pier. The icy water felt good to Eilida, numbing the pain.

Sage smoothed the dark waves of her friend's hair layering across her back.

"A heart attack in her sleep. That's what they said. She felt no pain." Her voice quiet. She didn't get it. Her grandma had always been healthy, spunky. She lived in the woods alone and took care of herself.

"I hear your thoughts. I loved your grandma too. It's the most vibrant people who go without warning, like they don't want a big fuss. Remember the summers we spent at her house?"

Eilida nodded her head, lifting her feet onto the pier.

"Like the time we thought we were lost in the woods when we just got turned around. Your grandma's house was behind us."

Eilida turned towards her friend. "We had a lot of adventures. I remember breaking into the vacant house across the street. Grandma said the owner died and we wanted to see a ghost?" She chuckled.

"No ghost! Just two teenagers who jumped at every creak in the house and went running back when the crazy neighbors at the end of the road starting shooting at targets!"

"We thought it was someone coming after us for breaking in." Both chuckled.

"I'm always here Lida. I'll miss her too, but we always have each other."

Eilida twisted her body and leaned the back of her head against her friend's shoulder. She grabbed her arm, folding it across her chest. "You have to join me at Astrology conventions now."

"Really, I've always wanted to go. I never asked because I felt like I'd be disturbing your time together."

Eilida lifted her head and narrowed her eyes, zeroing in on Sage's face. "You never told me that."

Sage shrugged. "Now you know."

☪ ☪ ☪ ☪ ☪

A week later, Eilida and her parents sat in a lawyer's office listening to her grandmother's will. She picked at the small hole in the leather chair she sat on, twisting her pinky finger into it. Her father glanced towards her. She pulled her finger out and slipped her leg over the hole.

"Eilida," said the lawyer in a nasal tone. Thicker than usual facial hair and a short bob cut displayed the lawyer's double chins.

Eilida clamped her lips and looked towards her but not at her.

"Your grandmother left you her house. It's paid for, but you'll be responsible for the taxes and insurance." The lawyer glanced to Eilida's parents.

"The house? She left it to me? I'm only nineteen."

"It's your grandmother's wishes dear."

Thoughts of all the happy times she had in that house made joy swell in her soul. Living in the house, she could stay close to her grandma, close to all the good times. Eilida's most loved memories was the fairy tale her grandmother always told. *A handsome King and his Queen, more beautiful than any woman in the land, had a beautiful baby. Her hair black as a raven, eyes blue as sapphires. One day fire breathing dragons flew over the kingdom. The King, his princes and his knights fought them off with all they had but couldn't defeat them. A good witch found the beautiful princess hiding in a chest. She wrapped her and snuck out of the castle escaping to the countryside. The little princess grew and grew becoming just as beautiful as her mother, the queen.*

Sage and Eilida moved into her grandmother's house at Fifteen Eclipse Lane that summer. Eilida took a job at the Chesterville Star, writing for the advice column she named Dear Delilah. Sage took a job at a jeweler's in town. They both enrolled in classes at the local community college.

Tommy

2010

Evan took a job pedaling pharmaceuticals. He didn't need the money, but the traveling made for a good cover as he stalked families. Since the incident during Hurricane Edward, June twenty-seventh 1998, with the Moras' house, he plotted his families more carefully, and no one questioned his time on the road. Saturn quincunx Pluto warned him of a disciplined change in direction of his covert activities. He resorted to the use of syringes to dispense drugs and the added challenge of the Hurricane Killer now a household name spurred by Carrot Top Cop's meddling. Being forced to vary his methods made his *killings* more interesting and stimulating. Every season more and more people evacuated and fewer families were prone to helping a *stranger*. Evan enjoyed the challenge and became more ruthless in his methods.

He had no family of his own but the Kurl's glances were always questioning and accusing. He kept them at a distance, unlocking the main house door once a week for Mrs. Kurl to clean. His private office closed off and locked. A giant map with every home, every family, marked in pin and marker. A shelf lined with various stuffed toys. All worn and loved. Fond memories of each little girl danced in his head. Every toy an affectionate memory of the little girls he *saved*.

In his gold Camry rental, he watched with interest as one of his *families* packed their car - backpacks, tents, sleeping bags, and other various camp gear. A teenage boy walked up the steps to the house across the street from Evan's position. He observed the gangly teen for a few seconds then diverted his attention back to the family. The father, tall with a round middle indicating he drank substantial quantities of beer, closed the back of the van. The mother, medium height and build, leaned into the car strapping in her daughter, one-year-old Vanessa. The minivan pulled out, Evan waited until they were out of his eyesight.

He twisted the key in the ignition, bells dinged, then movement from the house in front of him, the house the teen just entered, caught his eye. A woman stood in front of the curtain, her back to the outside. Her arm waving in anger, muffled shouting drifted through the air. Evan leaned his chest across the steering wheel and squinted his eyes, trying to witness the scene. The teen boy he'd seen only moments earlier swung something long and black towards the woman. It hit her alongside the head dropping her sideways. Evan found himself stimulated by the teen's actions. His hand stroking his cock. He didn't see his *mother*. His mind replayed the incident he witnessed. The long object meeting the woman's head just above the ear and her body thunking to the ground. His fingers undid his button and unzipped his pants. His mind heard the loud thud as she hit the floor and saw blood curdling from her head. Without warning a euphoria washed over him as he ejaculated. He'd gotten off killing his mother for two decades. He stared at the white cream soaking into his pants and grinned.

A breakthrough moment. The teen's violence gave him something he desired, coveted. A need he wasn't aware of until the moment the object hit the woman's head. He fumbled inside his travel bag, pulling out a new pair of pants. Noting his surroundings, not a soul on the street, he pushed his seat backwards and changed his pants. He wanted the boy and waited for him to exit the home.

Close to an hour later, the teen wheeled out a suitcase and popped the trunk of a compact car in the driveway. His long, skinny frame struggling against the weight of it. Evan took that as his opportunity. He walked up to the boy, his eyes narrowing with Evan's approach. "Looks like you need a hand."

"Yeah, uh… thanks." Evan helped push the heavy suitcase into the trunk. The boy pushed down the lid. "Thanks." His eyes pointed downward to the road, he took a couple paces and opened the driver's door and took the seat behind the wheel.

Evan blocked him from closing the door. "Slide over," he ordered, his knife to his side.

The boy's Adam's apple popped out as he gulped, glimpsing the shiny knife. He followed Evan's orders and slid into the passenger seat. The keys already in the ignition, Evan started the engine.

"I watched you. In that suitcase isn't clothes, it's a body."

The boys wide blue eyes drilled holes into Evan. His long, stringy, blond hair falling over his shoulders. "It's not what you think."

"I don't care what it is. I enjoyed what I saw. So where are we dumping your trash?" asked Evan, his expression void.

"I... I maybe the river."

"You've got a lot to learn. We have thousands of wide open acres and you want to dump it in a river where it's sure to turn up downstream? I have a better idea."

"What makes you think a body is in that suitcase?"

"I observed you hit that woman on the head. What was it, a fire poker? Her body fell. You killed her. My theory it was self-defense, always nagging you, telling you how worthless you are. Did she abuse you as a child?"

"Who are you?"

"Your best friend and worst enemy." The clusters of homes grew further apart as they drove into the woods. The men sat in silence for many miles.

"What's your name, kid?"

"Tommy." Filled with nervous energy he twisted at something beneath his shirt.

"Nice to meet you, Tommy." He turned off the county road onto a dirt road. They followed it for several miles.

"Well, Tommy, whose car is this?"

He swallowed hard. "The woman in the trunk."

Evan shook his head, not surprised by the statement. "Tommy, we not only need to get rid of the body, we need to destroy the car."

"Why are you doing this? Anyone else woulda turned me in."

"Because I like you. You stood up for yourself and rid the world of another abusive parent. My mother and father physically harmed me every day." Images of a leather belt high above his fake father's head, squealing as it whipped through the air, pounding against Evan's bare flesh. His mother washing his wounds, fondling his privates. He cringed and shook the image from his mind.

"What's your name?"

Evan mulled over Tommy's question. What name should he give him? He avoided the question until he felt he could trust the kid. "I'm the man saving your ass."

The Calm Before the Storm: Evan's Sins

The car weaved through dirt roads, stopping at a lake. Evan looked towards Tommy. "This lake is miles deep." Evan got out and popped the trunk. Tommy came around and helped him unload the suitcase. Vibrant colors bounced off the lake as the sun set and a cool breeze swept over the men as they pushed the suitcase up the cliff above the lake. The chilly fall mountain air not enough to keep sweat from beading on Evan's bald forehead. Tommy's stringy blond hair stuck to his face and neck.

Boulders scattered about the cliff. Evan gathered several and sent Tommy back to the car to find something to tie them with while he sat on the suitcase catching his breath.

Once they tied a couple heavy boulders to the suitcase, they pushed it towards the edge and let it drop. The water splashed and gurgled as it sank. Tommy fell to the ground, breathing heavy.

"No time for a break, kid. We still have the car to get rid of."

"Here?"

"No. I have something else in mind. I have a lot to teach you." He offered the breathless kid his hand, pulling him upwards. The more time he spent with Tommy the more he liked him.

They circled back to Evan's car. The house lights off and the neighborhood quiet. Evan pulled the car over and threw Tommy the keys. "Remember, you follow me. I catch you deviating I will double back and find you. You'll end up the same place as the body we dumped, understand?"

Tommy nodded his head confirming he understood.

They weaved through the mountainous roads, passing few cars. Evan stopped his car, nothing but trees and mountains surrounding them. He motioned for Tommy to pull alongside the road onto the dirt shoulder.

Both men exited their vehicles. Evan pulled his knife, handed it to Tommy. If Tommy tried anything, Evan knew he could twist his skinny frame with his bare hands. "Slide under the car and jam it into the gas tank."

Tommy did as asked. Evan threw his dirty jeans under the vehicle, gasoline poured onto them, and handed Tommy a matchbook. "Light the pants."

Tommy struck the match and tossed it but it burned out before reaching the puddle soaking into the pants.

"Try it again. Don't fear it."

Tommy's hands trembled as he struck another match.

"Control it. This is yours," Evan coaxed as Tommy moved the glowing match closer to the pants. The flame walked up the match towards Tommy's fingers. He flinched but held it steady, dropping it when the flame lapped his skin. The fire caught and grew.

"Throw the match book into the fire then run to my car and get in."

Tommy swallowed. He tossed the matchbook then ran, jumping into Evan's car.

Evan stepped backwards, watching the fire rage. He stopped by the driver's door of his rental, took one last look then got into the car, started it up and drove further up the road. He pulled over, engine still running and watched the flames lap high around the car.

"What are we doing? Won't it explode?" Tommy asked with a shaky voice.

Evan turned to Tommy, fire glowing in his eyes. "We have to make sure the car is destroyed." His voice steady.

They headed off the mountain and onto the freeway. Miles passed before Evan broke the silence. "How old are you?"

"Just turned eighteen."

"You have family?"

My dad died when I was eleven and my mom... well... you already know." He looked at his shoes pulling his hands to his lap.

"You ever been southwest?"

"Like Colorado?"

"More like New Mexico?"

Tommy shook his head.

The sun rose above the horizon. Crimson, indigo and gold filled the sky. Evan pulled the car into a 24 hour diner. He turned towards Tommy. "People love sunsets but they don't compare to dawn. The sun edging over the horizon – crimson filling the sky." He stepped out of the car, gazing at the brilliant panorama before him.

Tommy walked to his side. They stood in a silent moment of bonding, until the brilliant sun filled the sky.

"Hungry?" Asked Evan.

"Yeah. I could eat the biggest steak on the menu."

My Protégé

Evan spent his life distancing himself from others, even the Kurls. They lived on his property but had to abide by his strict rules. He brought Tommy home, set him up in a suite inside the house and gave him a job. Mr. Kurl was getting too old for yardwork. He expected him to collapse any day in the extreme New Mexico heat.

Evan stood at the sliding glass door watching Tommy scoop debris out of the pool. His gangly arms filling out from the yard work he stayed busy with and the protein meals they ate. Tommy leaned over, one knee on the pool deck, the other leg propped on his foot. Sweat glistening on his bare chest, his arm muscles flexing as he dragged the pool robot closer and lifted it onto the deck. Evan's hand strayed towards the bulge forming in his jeans. He stroked until he realized what he was doing and that the open curtains exposed his actions. Conscious of his infatuation with Tommy and his sudden urge, he hurried to his room and locked the door. He stripped his pants off, tossing them like a horny kid and stroked until he reached euphoria. The release his body begged for and kept *Mommy* away.

He hid from Tommy his erotic feelings, unsure how the boy would take it. The last thing he wanted was for Tommy to think him a freak and leave. Instead he manipulated him, giving the boy everything. He'd win his love instead of forcing it.

Evan showered, erasing his indiscretion and sauntered down the stairs into the kitchen. He grabbed a water bottle from the fridge and brought it to Tommy swimming in the pool.

"Thirsty?"

Tommy swam to the side, hanging his arms onto the pool deck. "Thanks!" He grabbed the bottle, twisted the top, gulping until a few drops swirled in the bottom of the bottle. "Jump in. The water is refreshing!"

Evan felt a twitch in his groin and the familiar rise of his jeans. He dropped onto one of the pool chairs, hoping Tommy didn't notice. He needed to get him out of the pool before his desire overrode logic and he did something he didn't want. "Get in the shower. Let's take one of the cars for a spin. You drive."

"Yeah, really?" Tommy lifted his body out of the water, propping his ass on the deck. "OK, let me shower." He swallowed the last of his water and tossed the plastic bottle into the recycle bin on his way inside the house.

Evan sighed relief, waited a few minutes for Tommy to get into the shower then ran back to his room to take care of his erection. If he didn't it would drive him to madness.

"Which one?" asked Tommy, basking in the excitement of driving any of Evan's classic, pristine vehicles.

"You choose," replied Evan, admiring Tommy's youth. A low rumble sounded through the garage as Tommy pulled it out onto the drive. It purred like a contented cat as he shifted, following the curves of the road. Pulling onto highway 40 they cruised over the Rockies.

"This car is incredible!" Tommy's face grinning from one side to the other. His pony tail whipping against his cheek.

"It sure is." The wind whipped against their faces, making conversation difficult.

Tommy pulled the rumbling car into a parking space at Pizza Heaven. He turned to Evan. "At night the lights of Albuquerque sparkle in the sky like a blanket of stars on Earth. On the other side of the mountain is almost a blank."

"You're poetic."

"What? I am?"

"When we get back, I have books full of classic poetry. You should read them."

Tommy scrunched his brow. "OK." He smoothed his pony tail then stepped out of the car.

Pizza Heaven wasn't much, but the pizza curbed Tommy's appetite. Evan didn't like greasy food, however he ate with Tommy, studying how he shoved large bites into his mouth. Tommy finished the last slice and wiped his mouth, setting his napkin down he said, "No matter how many times I see it, this place always surprises me. Back east the mountains are hills."

Evan grinned, listening to Tommy's young mind at work. "Mmm… They are much older."

"No hurricanes either, seldom rains, and people have to try and make grass grow."

"Why do you say that?"

"What part?"

"No hurricanes." *Does he know?*

"I never been west until you brought me here. I guess I figured everywhere was the same."

Evan recalled the first time he set foot in New Mexico. It was an entire new world, almost like being on an alien planet. "I first moved here about your age. I just turned twenty-one."

"Where did you grow up?"

"North Carolina…" Evan thought for a minute before he continued. "My parents were cruel so I left as soon as I could."

"How about sisters and brothers, did you have any?" Tommy rested his left elbow on the table.

"I did but they are all dead now." *Except Emily.*

The Calm Before the Storm: Evan's Sins

Lady Gaga's *Bad Romance* played from the jukebox. The music loud enough to irritate Evan but not enough for him to leave.

"I'm sorry."

"No need, they were little. And I'm not sorry. At twenty-one I found my fortune and life here."

Tommy's eyes shifted towards the table as he spun his plate.

Evan placed his hand on Tommy's. He stopped spinning the plate and looked at his caretaker/employer. It was time to *test* Tommy outside the gates of Poppy Hills. "I have to leave on business and I need you to come with me. There are things that need to be done while I'm working." *Emily things.*

18 Eclipse Lane

2011

"**E**ric, we can't stay here I don't feel safe!" Emily's voice quivered as her husband wrapped his arm around her.

"Honey."

She buried her head into his chest, through muffled voice she spoke, "Since the first letter a pit of blackness sunk to my stomach, then the black roses, the truck running us off the road. Now a pink pacifier with the name Erin written on the bow. Who but us knows the baby's name? It's a simple pacifier, but it makes the butterflies in my stomach flap like they're on steroids!"

"I know." He caressed her hair.

She perked her head upwards. "There is something dark in my past. I felt it since the first letter. I've never wanted to know about my biological family. The idea makes my heart flutter and scares the shit out of me. My parents fell in love with me from the first time they saw me and adopted me as soon as the courts allowed. Do you think... never mind."

Eric rubbed his hand across his lips and mustache, a few hairs sprung upwards as his fingers brushed over them. "It's not safe here but I don't yet know the solution. I hate for this freak to run us out of our own home."

Emily grabbed a booklet off the coffee table. "Maybe we can move. I found this today in the grocery cart. I was going to throw it away, but the circled one caught my eye." She handed him a Chesterville real estate guide.

"Chesterville, that's a hike every day and no telling the psycho won't follow us."

"Can we at least look? In the mountains, away from all the freaks here in the city. I looked at the schools and they're better than anything here. They could grow up breathing fresh mountain air and watching the stars. I made an appointment with the realtor Saturday." The tranquil blue in her eyes replaced by a blue so dark it reminded him of foreboding clouds.

He smoothed stray blond ringlets behind her ear. "I love you."

"Does that mean yes?"

"Yes. I'll stop at nothing for you and the boys."

Saturday, the Turnwell family set out for Chesterville to meet the realtor at Eighteen Eclipse Lane.

"Hi, Mr. and Mrs. Turnwell." She leaned forward, giving them each a quick shake.

"Good morning Mrs. Jarvis," offered Eric.

She stretched her lips into a forced grin. "You ready? As you can tell, the road is quiet, secluded, but only a few minutes from town. And the schools here are third in the state." She looked to the Turnwell boys then Emily's swollen belly.

Emily shrugged. "Ready."

The group followed Mrs. Jarvis up the steps and into the house. "Wait till you see the view from the back deck. Uh… it's breathtaking. And there's plenty of space. Four bedrooms and a spacious master, one for each of your boys and a nursery." She droned on, showing each room and feature in the house from the stainless steel appliances to the master suite spa tub.

The boys exchanged glances to each other as they eyed the custom swing set in the backyard. "Dad, can we play?" asked the oldest son.

Eric nodded. "Go, test it out."

"What do you think?"

Emily loved the house. She turned to her husband, sparkles twinkling in her blue eyes.

He swallowed. "Mrs. Jarvis we love the house, but need to discuss this as a family. We'll give you a call."

"Did I mention the owner is letting it go at a bargain? He hoped to use it as a home away from home getaway, but recently learned he'll be leaving the country indefinitely and so needs to sell as soon as possible."

The Turnwells arrived home late in the evening after spending the rest of the day enjoying quality time at Bouncy Kingdom. Emily ushered the boys upstairs and tucked them in. She kissed each of their foreheads. "Night." She flipped the light off and closed the door, leaving it cracked so the hall nightlight could shine into their room.

Eric sat on the couch, his brows creased into a V. Emily recognized Eric's trouble face. "Not again, no." Panic bubbled in her gut.

He swallowed hard then cleared his throat. "It's Flash."

Water puddled in the corner of her eyes. "What do you mean Flash?"

"We're making an offer on that house and then we'll figure out how."

A steady stream of tears rolled down Emily's cheeks. "What's wrong with Flash?" She padded towards the kitchen.

He shook his head jumping off the couch to block her path. "No!"

From the corner of her eye she saw a matt of hair covered in blood. She pummeled her husband with her fists. He pulled her to him and walked her to the couch. "What did the bastard do?"

He sucked in a deep breath. "He mutilated him."

"We are out of here. Pack the car, we're going to my parents!" Emily shouted.

That night, after the police left, Eric buried their dog. His mind a flurry of dread and anger. Dirt clods flying through the air. Each time they called the police, filed a report, and no results - nothing. The creep left no trace. He patted the dirt over Flash's mangled body. *If I find the psychopath I'll kill him for scaring my Emily, for threatening my family.*

The following day the Turnwells made an offer on the house. Eric drove his family to her parents' home where the couple sat across from each other at a butcher block table, Emily held a calculator in her hand while Ted went through their expenses. "It'll be tight until this house sells." A stern look in his eyes, his voice firm.

"We have to do this. Maybe my…"

Eric interrupted. "Your parents."

She nodded her head.

He lifted his head to the ceiling, raking his fingers through his thinning hair, lowering his head he looked into Emily's eyes and took her hands in his. "I only want their help as a last resort." Eric worked hard for everything he earned in life. Unlike Emily, his family was poor. He made straight A's to get into college on a scholarship. He never took handouts, but his family had to come before his pride.

Her fingers wiggled in her husband's hands. "I've told my parents everything. They only want us all to be safe" She wiped the tears beneath her eyes.

"I'm scared too. All I want is my family safe." His quivering voice gave away his own fear. "We can do this and we'll ask them *if* we need help."

She nodded and feared Eric staying at their home alone all week while he worked. Her parents' home was just too far for his daily commute. "Can you stay with Lucas?" Lucas was Eric's longtime friend.

"Would you feel better if I did?"

"Yes. We shouldn't ever go back to that house."

Eric bolted upright with excitement. "Maybe we can rent it?"

Emily shook her head back and forth, fear rising inside her. "No. I want no connection. If we rent, then we have to check on the place, our names, our new address tied to the house."

"We can go through a rental agency. They take care of everything."

"No. This stalker whoever he or she is… is smart, calculating. I want a clean break."

His eyes drifted to her belly, and he imagined their perfect daughter growing inside her womb. He stood and padded behind her, tripping on a Lincoln Log. "What the…" He picked up the toy, placing it on the table, images of his rough and tumble boys sprinted through his mind. She was right, they had to get away clean, no ties to this life. From behind, he snaked his arms around her neck laying gentle kisses on her cheek. "You're right. I'm a proud man and if we can't figure this out - if we can't sell the house right away - we'll ask your parents."

His kisses worked their way to her lips. She parted her mouth, accepting his tongue.

A week after their house went on the market it sold, a very generous offer.

Three months later, they closed the deal on their new home and moved their growing family to Eighteen Eclipse Lane in Chesterville. The horrific incidents ceased, their lives became peaceful and Emily gave birth to a baby girl, Erica.

Poppy Hills

One of Frank's connections came through, confirming Evan's home address, Poppy Hills, no surprise to Burkhalder. He'd used a fake name, even a fake ID, peddling drugs didn't require a license. For years the cover worked well, hiding his true identity. Burkhalder buzzed the button outside the heavy black gate surrounding Evan's home like a fortress. She knew she had no true evidence against him but hoped to strike fear, or at least police acknowledgement, into his narcissistic head. Maybe if she got lucky he'd let something slip. Frank kept his distance, but wasn't about to let her do this alone. The man was a cold blooded serial killer.

Evan heard the buzz. Not expecting any visitors, he glanced at the monitor. Carrot Top Cop stood beside a truck outside the gate and a large figure loomed behind the wheel.

Amused, he pressed the button. "Be there in a minute."

Evan got into his golf cart and headed towards the gate, climbed out and walked towards it.

"Can I help you?" asked Evan. His eyes twinkling in the sun.

"I'm former Detective Burkhalder." She moved closer to the gate. "I would have called first but…"

He interrupted. "What do you want, Detective Burkhalder? I'm a busy man." Closer, he identified the large figure behind the wheel as a man.

She noted his sharp tone, pleased that at least she disturbed his day. "I want to thank you for saving that little girl's life."

Tommy spotted a red headed woman talking with Evan at the gate. He eased closer to listen, careful to keep his cover behind a large tree.

"I didn't do anything anyone else wouldn't have and I don't think you came all the way here to thank me."

She pushed her sunglasses on top of her head. The bright sunlight blazed in her eyes but she wanted him to look in them.

"Mr. O'Conner, I know what you did to Gala and to all those families."

"That's why you brought Mr. Beefy. Oh, you thought I couldn't see him in the driver's seat?" A smug grin plastered across his boxy face.

Tommy craned his head further around the tree as a large man came into his view.

"I'm admiring your slice of heaven. You've done well for yourself. From Windy Oaks nuthouse to here - impressive." Frank shielded his eyes as he observed Evan's land.

"Nice reuniting, sorry I can't invite you in." Evan ambled towards the golf cart.

Burkhalder couldn't let him go. Not yet. She needed something, a morsel. "How's Emily?"

He halted, rotated to face her again. His demeanor calm and cool as an ice cube. "I wouldn't know. I haven't seen her since the horrible night an attacker... Have a good day."

"You did an excellent job faking your death, very clever. Even down to your fake ID. How long have you been using it?"

Evan shifted and froze. "Would you want to be associated with the death of your family? Have people always wondering and whispering behind your back? Windy Oaks was a traumatic time for me, coping with the murders of my family. I choose to live a peaceful life without the nightmare of my past rehashed every move I make."

Frank hit a chord and went with the flow, probing for more information. "That's odd, seems you only started using the name Kevin Flank after June thirteenth 2007. Where were you that day?"

Evan narrowed his eyes as the blackness crept across his irises. His instincts told him to stop, but powers beyond his control begged him to continue. It took all his energy to climb into his golf cart and head towards the house.

Tommy, still plastered to the tree, overheard the entire conversation. The couple walked towards the truck. He turned and sank to the ground, blowing his straight blond hair out of his face. The creak of the truck door opening then a sudden stop in their movements forced him onto his hands and knees. Mrs. Kurl's sweet voice sailed through the air.

"Can I help you?"

Burkhalder stopped mid stride, and turned. "Hello." She smiled, small lines webbed from her eyes. "Maybe you can. You work here?"

"Yes, for many years, long before the current Mr. O'Conner."

Burkhalder wasn't sure how to broach the subject when Frank stepped in.

"Frank Roy. We work for a cable channel that wants to do an interview with Mr. O'Conner. From poverty to wealth." Frank continued charming Mrs. Kurl as suave words spilled from his tongue. He eased in the date of July thirteenth.

"Mr. O'Conner travels a lot, makes remembering the times he's home easy. He was here."

"You're sure."

"Oh yes, positive, Mr. Roy. Mr. O'Conner is a private person. I doubt he has interest in doing an interview, especially one that will be televised."

"I understand. Thank you for your time."

Burkhalder slid her a card through the gate. "Should he change his mind."

"I'll be sure to pass this along, but don't expect an answer."

Burkhalder stepped inside the truck and leaned back into the seat. From the corner of her eye a thin blond frame moved from behind a tree twenty or so yards away. She twisted her head but the form vanished. "Did you see that?"

Fate's Destiny

Eilida yelped at the chance to make the OPA conference and her chance to meet nationally renowned Patrice Renard. The 9th annual professional astrology retreat in Myrtle Beach, South Carolina. She flew down the stairs and flopped her body on the couch next to Sage. Leaning her head against her friend's shoulder she blurted her news. "I did it. We're in!" She lifted her head to gauge Sage's response.

"OMG!" The two women leapt off the couch and jumped up and down like two school girls going to see their favorite band. Both women believed there was more to life, something brewing beneath the surface, or in this case above the surface - dictated by the stars and planets of the vast universe.

Sage and Eilida arrived at the convention center and took the nearest escalator to where the conference was being held. They stepped inside the vendor room, eyes soaking in the activity around them. The huge room was divided into several aisles with more vendors lining both sides as well as the perimeter. Astrology related materials, from jewelry to crystals, were everywhere. As they strolled the aisles, Eilida tried not to be too obvious ogling the name badges of those around them, looking for someone whose name she'd recognize. Some astrologers looked appropriately weird in long, flowing skirts matched only by their hair, with more rings than fingers while others were in jeans and others still in business dress. The men were mostly in casual dress, though one in particular was wearing a kilt. Her eyes took in his strong, muscular legs and sent a quiver bounding through her as she imagined the kilt tossed on the arm of a chair and... She shook the image from her mind.

The pair perused the plethora of goodies, Eilida dragging her friend by the hand when she saw a crystal table, spending a good bit of time examining the many offerings. She felt drawn to certain ones, slips of cardstock the size of a business card accompanying each one describing the stone's influence.

She stood there a while, admiring one in particular for its odd shape. The card said it was a desert rose, good for transmuting hatred into love and healing past conflicts. She took it in her hand to see how it felt. It felt good but she could see the vendor guy was occupied with other customers so set it back carefully, deciding to come back later.

Another table caught her eye, this one apparently occupied by an astrologer. The lady behind it had shoulder length salt and pepper hair, maybe a bit more salt than pepper. Her genuine smile and attentiveness to those talking to her attracted Eilida. While other patrons talked to the astrologer Eilida browsed her books, one of which was entitled *Whobeda's Guide to Basic Astrology*. She picked it up and flipped through the pages, reading sporadically.

As much of an astrology buff as she was, most of it really confused her. Written in terms that made sense, Eilida decided to buy one and waited in line to get it autographed.

At last it was her turn and she handed over the book, grateful no one was behind her so she could chat a bit.

"Hi," the woman said with a smile. "Would you like me to inscribe it to you personally or leave it plain so you can sell it on eBay when you're done?"

Eilida laughed. "I wouldn't do that!" she responded.

"Yes, you would," Sage muttered, giving her a friendly nudge.

"Not this one," Eilida insisted. "So make it out to me. Eilida." She spelled it out, knowing most people gave her a blank look if she didn't.

"So are you Whobeda?" Sage asked. "That's a pretty unusual name, too."

The woman chuckled, laugh lines crinkling the corners of her amber-colored eyes. "Yes and no,' she responded. "It's my mystic name. Some of us prefer to operate behind some degree of anonymity. Some of the people I work for in my day job wouldn't be amused if they knew I was an astrologer."

"Really?"Eilida responded. "What's your day job?"

"I work in the aerospace industry," she answered, but before Eilida could prod her for more, Sage pointed at her watch.

"We better get going over to the auditorium if we want a good seat," she prodded.

"Oh! You're right! Nice talking to you, Whobeda," she said with a smile. "Thanks for the autograph! And I promise I won't sell it on eBay!"

The pair left the vendor area and strode down the broad, carpeted corridor to the auditorium where they slipped through the chunky double doors held open by metal door stops and found two open side by side seats. Both women beamed with excitement as they waited for Patrice Renard, slated as the next speaker, to take the stage.

A few seats behind them a shaven headed Evan took his seat. In the thickness of the crowd, neither was aware of the other. Throughout Patrice's speech the women soaked in her every word. Anticipation building as Eilida determined she would meet her face to face.

Her speech and Q and A session over, everyone filed out of the auditorium. Evan, a few rows behind, conveniently left the room before the two women. Light reflected off the baldness of his head catching Eilida's attention. A cold breeze swept over her and tremors of fear coursed through her body.

"What's wrong?" urged Sage as Eilida stood frozen and ghostly white. She took her hands and guided her to the closest seat.

"I... I... I'm not sure. A feeling, like doom is waiting for me outside those doors."

"Take a deep breath and we'll wait for the crowd to leave. We haven't eaten yet, let's grab a bite." The pair headed for the door behind the diminishing crowd and turned down the concourse toward the escalator and restaurant below.

Eilida knew food wasn't the problem. The fear that swept over her was the same as her fright filled dreams where the bald man with eyes black as a moonless, starless night chased her. In his hand a knife, drops of blood trickling from its blade. "This feeling is like in my night terrors."

"You're awake and we're safe."

Eilida remembered the flash of light reflecting from the man's scalp - the same flash that identified him in her dreams as the moonlight danced across his barren head. Feeling dizzy again, she dropped down in a chair across from the vendor room and concentrated on where she was, looking intently at the different booths beyond to ground herself back in the present. Her gaze fell upon the crystal table and it was as if a bolt of lightning struck. She got up and headed for it with purpose, Sage right behind her.

"Where are you going?" her friend asked.

"The crystal table. I have a feeling he might have something to help me."

They waited for what seemed forever before the man behind the table made his way over to her.

He greeted them with a kind smile. "Good afternoon, ladies. I'm Mike. Can I help you find something specific today?" He was older, probably fiftyish, medium build with a full head of hair that was probably blond at one time but now mostly grey.

"Oh, yes, I hope you can!" Eilida spilled out. "Which ones are good for protection?"

His expression went from friendly to concern, as if perceiving her desperation. "Are you in some sort of danger?" he asked.

"I don't know. I feel as if I am. I keep having these awful nightmares and feel as if they're some sort of message."

The man frowned, his gaze drawn to the zircon ring she'd bought at the last conference. "Do you realize that your ring may be drawing whatever you fear to you?"

"What? How could that be?" she asked, taken aback.

"A tetragonal structure is considered an Attractor. If you want to keep something or someone away, you need something that has an entirely different crystalline structure. One that's monoclinic and serves as a Guardian or a Barrier that's triclinic. That zircon is tetragonal, entirely different."

Horrified, she slipped it off her finger and handed it to Sage. "Here, you always liked it. You can have it!"

Sage stepped back, shaking her head. "Not if it's bad luck!"

"Not necessarily," Mike explained. "It's great for bringing something you want into your life such as a new relationship but not so good if you're looking for protection."

Sage smiled. "Cool! Then I'll take it!"

"So what do I need?" Eilida prodded.

"It depends on what you want protection from. Guardian talismans help protect something of value while Barrier talismans keep away undesirable situations. Perhaps you could use a Guardian to keep you safe and a Barrier to keep you away from danger, or perhaps it away from you."

"Yes! That sounds like exactly what I need. What do you have?"

"I should have just the thing," he said and turned toward a cabinet at the back of the booth where he searched through a couple drawers before returning with a pendant set in silver which featured a round, dark green, iridescent stone about an inch in diameter, accented by four smaller stones of a similar color but lacking the rainbow effects.

"The center stone is moonstone, an excellent Guardian, and the smaller stones are kyanite, a traditional Barrier," he explained, handing it to her.

She intuitively closed her fingers around it and held it to her heart, eyes closed, sensing its energy. Her heart rate slowed as a sense of peace settled around her. She expelled her breath in a sigh and opened her eyes.

"Oh, yes, this is wonderful. I must have it. How much?"

The price was a bit outside her budget but she pulled out her credit card, knowing she would have paid a lot more.

Behind her, a man cleared his throat indicating her turn was up. She twisted sideways to give him the evil eye. He glared back under eyebrows resembling squirrels' tails.

The following day, Eilida and Sage waited in line nearly forty-five minutes so Eilida could get her natal chart and reading from Patrice Renard. A mass of dragonflies flew through her stomach as her turn approached.

A short lady with a bob strolled out of Ms. Renard's room. Eilida looked at Sage, smiles plastered across their faces. "Our turn!" voiced a giddy Sage.

Eilida took Sage's hand and they marched into the room like two schoolgirls. No crystal balls or tarot cards, instead a full figured Patrice, her fiery hair curled just above her shoulders. But they weren't there to see a gypsy and have their palms read.

"Ms. Renard. It's so wonderful to meet you. I follow your stuff." As the words dropped from her mouth she felt stupid. *Follow, she's going to think I'm a stalker.*

Eilida and Sage talked with Patrice a few minutes. Her round figure reminded Eilida of her mother, warm red hair and confidence further eased Eilida's nervous stomach. Once she had their dates, times and places of birth, she typed everything in and the computer generated their charts. Eilida's flew off the printer first. Ms. Renard looked from it to Eilida then slid it to the side as she studied Sage's. She laid it in front of them and explained the position of the planets and their meanings. Sage's horoscope was filled with happiness, longevity, and success.

When it came time for Eilida's, she laid the natal chart on the table facing Eilida and sucked in her breath. Eilida's eyes went directly to the blue triangle in the center.

"We call this blue triangle a yod or the finger of god."

"What does it mean?"

"A fated life, but let's get through all of it before you decide what that means. This blue line ties Pluto in the 3rd house to the Sun in the eighth house. This implies that you crave

293

powerful experiences and are attracted to the unfathomable. You commonly hide your interests, except from your closest friends and family. Uranus and Neptune in the fourth house indicate your home life, growing up may have been unstable in some way. You may be searching for an ideal home. The darkness in your eyes reveals the truth in these words."

"I love my family but I've always felt like an outsider except with my grandmother, umm… until she passed. Sage feels more like family than my parents sometimes."

Patrice's bubbling personality spilled over. "At your age, most of us feel that way."

Eilida's anxiety eased again as Patrice continued.

"Mercury in Taurus and in the 8th house show you tend to be very methodical and have an interest in investigating the supernatural."

Eilida's lips curled into a smile. Her interest in Astrology centered on her interest in the "otherworldly"

"Pluto in Scorpio, the twelve year group you're both part of, loves mystery and the macabre."

Both girls chuckled, they lived off zombie and suspense flicks.

Patrice smiled, then her face grew stoic. "There is something in your past, maybe a natural disaster that changed the course of your life. It might be related in some way to the death of your grandmother."

Zombie-like, Eilida lifted her chart from the table and stood to leave. The dragonflies morphed into dragons breathing fire into her innards, aching to get free. As Eilida exited the door the chatter and noise in the convention center quieted as her mind focused on *something in your past*. What could possibly be in her past? Her parents were the most "normal" people she'd ever met and she had a picture perfect childhood, no siblings, everything she needed and most of what she wanted. Her parents and grandmother spoiled her. Yet a feeling she didn't quite belong always lingered in the back of her mind, followed by a sinking feeling of dread in her belly.

She turned and took a step back into the room, asking another question. "Is all the bad stuff in my past? Does my future look better?"

"Here's my card, feel free to call." Eilida noted her solemn expression.

Eilida lay in bed tossing and turning all night. Her mind a flutter of curiosity and fear, replaying Patrice's words over and over, '*a fated life... there is something in your past*'. Her fascination of mystery drove her imagination. The man in her nightmares flashed in static against her fleshy brain. Light glittered from her pile of clothes on the floor. Her pendant!

The Calm Before the Storm: Evan's Sins

She reached down and clutched the pendant, cradling it in her hand. Peace bathed her body and she fell into a restful sleep.

In the Stars

Evan loved when everything in his world came together. The first day was hit and miss, he'd thought maybe he'd been wrong then he saw them. Tommy was magic. Evan kept his distance, hidden behind a booth, pretending to read an astrology book he just purchased.

"I'm a klutz, so sorry," said Tommy, while collecting the items from Eilida's bag that fell when he *accidently* bumped into her.

"Accidents happen."

"Let me buy you both a coffee. It's the least I can do."

Eilida threw her bag onto her shoulder and gazed towards Sage. Talking through their eyes, Sage agreed.

"Sure!"

The group walked away from the heavy booth area towards a quaint coffee shop inside the convention center. The aroma of fresh brewed coffee filled the air and paintings of mugs hung on the walls. "I'm Tommy, by the way."

"Sage."

"Eilida."

"Like your names. Most girls are Ashley." He grinned.

The Calm Before the Storm: Evan's Sins

"My parents would have been hippies if they'd been born a decade earlier." Sage laughed at her own joke.

"What do you like?"

"I'll take a mocha latte," voiced Sage as she slid into the booth.

"I'll take the same," Eilida parroted, sliding onto the seat beside Sage.

Tommy smiled and strolled to the counter, returning with three coffees.

He handed each their coffee and slid into the booth opposite the girls. "You both into this stuff?"

"Yeah. I love it! I think there's so much more to life than what we see on the surface." Eilida lifted her drink and sipped at the steaming liquid.

"What about you? You're here."

Tommy smiled. "My uncle believes in this stuff. He drug me here. I'm not so into it."

"We had our readings done yesterday and OMG! They were on the level," voiced Sage, tracing the rim of her coffee.

"See this pendant?" Eilida lifted the pendant from her chest. "The center stone is a moonstone. It acts like a guardian, protecting what I value. And the smaller stones." She leaned forward so Tommy could see better, "They're kyanite." He leaned forward in response. "They are a barrier, keeping away danger."

"That's pretty cool. Does it work?"

"I can feel its soothing energy."

"Are you in some kind of trouble?"

"Not exactly. I sometimes have a bad recurring dream or get a feeling of doom in the pit of my stomach. Since I've been wearing this, everything's been peaceful."

"Maybe you have past life trauma like reincarnation and shit. It's coming back to haunt you."

Sage choked for a second on her coffee then set it on the table. "Look, just because we believe in the possibility of Astrology doesn't mean we believe in everything considered kooky. There is a real basis to it that should be taken seriously. Reincarnation isn't truly possible. I'm not going to die and come back as a fly. My energy, though, may recycle and my essence may trigger thoughts in those of the future."

"You really believe that?" Tommy's face serious.

"I don't know, but the possibilities are endless."

Eilida piped in keeping a straight face, "Think about it. We are a series of neural pathways and chemical bonds. When we die, those bonds breakdown. Do our neural pathways cease? It's possible they reach out to others as energy is released. Don't you ever watch ghost shows? Ghosts communicate with us through television, radios, lights - energy."

Tommy furrowed his eyebrows. "That's deep. I never thought of it like that."

Sage bit the side of her lip to keep from laughing. "We're just messing with you. But, hey, humans don't know everything so anything is possible. You just have to think outside the box."

"Point taken."

"This ring." Sage placed her hand in front of Tommy. "Eilida bought it at the last convention. Yesterday we found out it may be drawing what Eilida fears because of its structure. It's no good for protection but great for bringing something you want into your life. Eilida slipped it off her finger fast. For her it may have been bad, for me it's good."

Sage gave Tommy an idea. He hoped Evan didn't know anything about stones and their energies.

Eilida changed the subject. "You know my deepest darkest secret. What about you?"

"Well, I work for my uncle. He's got a big ranch out west. My parents died when I was little."

"I'm sorry." Eilida's eyes gazed downward to the table.

"Look, I was young and my uncle is a pretty cool guy. He's got these hot rides he lets me drive whenever I want. What about you, what do you girls do?"

"I run an advice column, Dear Delilah. Some of the crap people ask is ridiculous."

"My job isn't as interesting as Eilida's. I work at a jeweler's."

"Tommy, thanks for the coffee. It was fun meeting you but we gotta get going, don't want to miss tonight's celebration. You going to be there?" Eilida said, slipping out of the booth.

"I might. Should I?"

Sage clutched her purse, pushing herself out of the booth. "Of course."

"I have to check with my uncle. Not sure when we're leaving but if I make it I'll find you there."

Eilida shrugged. "Maybe we'll see you there. Oh... and get to meet your cool uncle." The girls left and went to their room to shower and get ready for the celebration. Tommy slipped out of the booth and found Evan.

☾ ☾ ☾ ☾ ☾

"Walk with me, Tommy," ordered Evan, peering at Tommy under the brim of his black cap. Keeping a safe distance and using the crowd as cover they followed the girls.

"What did they say?"

"They are going to be at the celebration tonight. They asked me to join them."

Evan nodded in agreement. "You should. That'll give me time to slip into their room."

"Sage has this ring. It's cool and used as a guardian and barrier against evil." Tommy lied.

Evan halted. "Really." He wasn't sure if he truly believed in stones but knew Astrology hadn't failed him yet. And the ring might ward off his mother from ever returning.

"Yeah. Maybe I can get it without her noticing." His eyes filled with excitement.

"You do that. I think I want it."

That night, while Tommy met up with Eilida and Sage. Evan snuck into their room. He sifted through Eilida's suitcase, pulling her dirty clothes towards his nose to inhale the scent of her innocence. His mind flashed to Hurricane Chloe, how he couldn't find her during the storm and the look on her terrified face when he opened the chest. Her turn was coming soon but first, Emily. Nothing was more important than following chronologically, keeping order.

In the bathroom two towels hung damp on the bar. He felt Eilida's energy reach out to him as he drew his hands against his sides and across his chest, his eyes closed. Nowhere did he find the ring, meaning the girl took this stuff as seriously as he did and had it on her finger. The thought of them having something in common forced his lips to curve into a smile and a chuckle to escape his thoughts. He'd have to leave it to Tommy to get the ring. His good luck boy. Since meeting his protégé, mother hadn't visited once. The closeness he felt towards Tommy was more than he'd let on. He wanted the boy in a more than friendship way and spent the time since they met grooming him, giving him a suite inside the house, allowing him to drive his cars. The time was coming soon when he'd let Tommy know how he felt.

Evan slipped out of the girls' room to make his appointment with Whobeda. He never trusted the computer reading he'd done years ago and wanted a true reading from an actual astrologer. He entered the private room and her amber eyes greeted him with warmth. He took a seat across the plastic table from her and fed her the location, time and date of his birth. Within a few minutes she had his chart. Her eyes narrowed as she glimpsed the information and laid it on the table and explained the meanings of each connecting line.

"You are a passionate, intense person. You're also idealistic and take a mystical approach to life. That explains your interest in Astrology." She smiled. "You have strong attachments to your family and are driven by your feelings." She slipped a shawl over her arms as a sudden chill entered the room. "You have strong attachments to your past, your heritage, family traditions and may be unable to step out of the habits and roles you learned as a child. Your tie to your mother is very strong." Blackness devoured Evan's eyes. She shuddered and wrapped the shawl tighter around her shoulders.

He sat quiet, the anger inside him spilling into his eyes. The mention of his mother and his inability to stop killing her and his family. The role he learned as a youth. The damage his fake father and mother placed upon his soul thieving his childhood. Hearing Whobeda's eerily accurate words made him realize the stars and planets guided the path of his life since birth. Born when Mars conjuncted with the Moon in his 4th - predisposed for his mother's violence towards him. Pluto in the tenth house affirmed the secrets related to his father. The one who raised him a bogus replacement for his true father. *Does my own father have more secrets?* She continued to speak, the words filtering through his mind. He blamed his mother for giving birth to him at such an unpleasant time, cursing his life. His mother flashed in static, not fully taking form, she never reappeared. He sensed the astrologer's uneasiness, upsetting him further. A sympathetic moment. The woman's easy style and soft tone in her voice relaxed and consoled him. She was merely the interpreter of the bad news.

The chill in the room followed Evan outside the door and Whobeda took a deep breath. Never had she received such a frightening vibe from a client.

☾ ☾ ☾ ☾ ☾

Tommy milled through the crowd until he found the girls. "I thought I'd never find you in this crowd."

"You made it!"

Eilida looked around. "Where's your uncle?"

"He wasn't feeling good."

The girls scooted further in line towards the refreshment table. "Get in." Sage waved her hand signaling for him to step between them in line.

"Oh, thanks." He looked at Eilida's pendant hanging from her throat. "How's that necklace working? Can you still feel its power?"

"Nothing bad has happened." She grabbed a plate.

They moved through the line, filling their plates, grabbing drinks then took seats at a table.

"Your uncle doesn't know what he's missing, especially if he's the junior astrologer in your family."

"After our discussion earlier, I've been thinking. I don't know, maybe this stuff isn't so crazy." He sipped his soda.

The guest speaker took his place and the crowd quieted as everyone's focus turned towards him. His speech was a wrap up session for everything discussed during the lectures. From the corner of his eye, Tommy noticed Sage fiddling with her finger. The speaker finished and opened the floor for questions. Sage slipped the ring off her finger and rubbed the spot it previously sat. He took that as his opportunity and stacked their plates, hitting the top of his glass. Soda poured everywhere. "I'm so sorry. That's the second time in one day." He grabbed a handful of napkins to soak up the spill, clutching Sage's ring inside them.

Sage scooted away from the table to avoid the soda spilling onto her dress. "Being a klutz isn't a cardinal sin." She chuckled.

Tommy grinned and asked. "You sure?" As he took the full napkin, his hand beneath it, he let the ring drop into his palm then threw the wad into the trash. He slipped the ring into his front pocket as he wiped his hands on his pants.

The distance to the table a straight shot, Tommy's long legs took three strides. "I gotta go. My uncle's asking for an antacid. Thanks for the night."

Sage scrunched her perfect nose. "Oh, I hope he feels better. Thanks for joining us."

"See ya later." He tipped his forehead and left, returning to his room.

Sage stood, her eyes scanning the floor. "OMG it's gone!"

"What?"

"My ring. The one you gave me. I set it on the table because my finger felt weird, tingly."

Eilida helped her search. "It's gone."

"Oh well. I think it was turning my finger green." She lifted her finger and shoved it into Eilida's face.

"Your finger is not green."

C· C· C· C· C·

Tommy returned to his room. Evan lay on his bed reading through a stack of papers. Tommy threw him the ring.

Evan caught it midair. "You got it." He turned it between his fingers and shoved it onto his pinky. "It's a little small but after reading my natal chart I need it." Evan's mother hadn't made an appearance in years, now with the ring she'd be gone forever.

Trust

As far as Evan was concerned Tommy had proven himself and earned his trust. He'd terrorized Emily. Except the dog. Evan took care of Flash himself. He wasn't sure if Tommy was ready yet. *Soon, he'll be ready soon.*

Tommy lay on the sectional, his legs propped on a matching footrest. In his lap, a notebook PC. When he saw Evan he threw his legs off the footrest and scrambled into an upright position. He glanced at the clock. "Let me get your bag." He rushed to Evan's side and reached for his bag.

"I got it. I'll be back by Saturday. You have my number should you need me for anything."

Tommy nodded his head in agreement. Evan left.

It took Tommy time but he'd earned Evan's trust so much he no longer lived in the guest house but the main house with Evan. The next morning, Tommy disabled the cameras throughout the house. Manipulating them to still frames. In the kitchen, Evan kept latex gloves under the sink he used for cooking. He slipped a pair over his hands and hauled himself up the stairs, two at a time, and picked the lock to Evan's office door. He'd never been inside Evan's room. Nobody went in but Evan and Mrs. Kurl once a week and Evan kept a close eye on her while she cleaned it.

Inside, he looked around. Everything neat and in order. Living with Evan, he'd learned to think like him. Stretching his hands against the door frames, he felt for a lever or something out of place. He slid the furniture away from the walls - nothing. He walked into the closet. It was empty except for a chest. He opened the lid of the trunk. It was empty. Frustrated, he fell to the floor, holding his hands around his knees he blew blond strands out of his face. He watched the hair fly into the air and a hairline crack above the chest caught his eye. He scooted towards it and ran his finger along it. It was definitely a crack, smooth and purposeful, reaching towards the ceiling. He pushed the chest out of the way and felt along the crack. He stood and pushed against the wall. His foot slid backwards and hit something hard under the floor. The wall in front of him gave and he tumbled into another room.

He pushed himself up and gawked at the room. A huge map spanned the wall straight in front of him. Mesmerized, he zombie-walked towards it. Pins and names covered the eastern seaboard. A red pin with a string stuck into Horn City, written beside it, *Emily*. He traced the string to Billows Hollow

The Calm Before the Storm: Evan's Sins

Hurricane Chloe Cat 4 Eilida Tate. So that's his interest in her. Then near Pensacola, Florida another pin and again and again. He followed the string to nine different locations, various hurricanes and girl's names. He stumbled backwards falling on his hands. Above him a long shelf. He stood and eyed the stuffed animals and baby dolls on the shelf. Each had a numbered tag around its neck. He followed the numbers with his eyes, ending with eight. *He never kept anything of Emily's?* Beside the map were lunar charts all matching the dates of each hurricane, except one dated June ninth 2007 with a note scribbled below it, *no good Jacksonville, FL, storm died before touching land.*

Fumbling in his pocket he took out his phone and snapped pictures of the map and toy lined shelf. Below the shelf on the carpet lay a photo album. Inside a baby picture and on the next page a woman with two different colored eyes. He closed and laid it down exactly where he found it. Creepy crawlies running the length of his body, he slipped out of the room. Before closing and locking Evan's door behind him he glanced around, sure Evan would notice even the smallest detail out of place.

The open bathroom door gave him an idea. He eyeballed it looking for something, anything, that might contain Evan's DNA. A single small pubic hair in the shower stood out like a black bunny in a patch of snow. A

wide smile creased his thin lips. *Gotcha!*
Collecting the hair, he left the room and stole
to his room, sending each picture in a text. He
sat on his bed and waited, then a follow up
text *u rock dil.* He turned his phone off and
stuck it back in the ceiling vent.

When Evan returned a few days later
Tommy's nerves climbed the walls and his
heart beat out of his chest as Evan entered his
room.

2010 and 2013 Came and Went

Burkhalder lay on the couch, her head resting on Frank's arm. "What happened? Did he stop? The season is officially over."

"The press is all over it, maybe he's changing his pattern."

She sat up and turned to face him. "You can't believe that. In two decades he's never varied his pattern. He stays one step ahead of the nation."

He leaned forward, placing his hands on his knees. "Maybe that was him in the car. The body was destroyed beyond recognition. Or maybe he's laying low, planning a new strategy. Let's think like him. All this is about the women. He butchers their necks and rapes them. He thinks they're his mom and leaves the youngest, always a girl. Why? Because of Emily?"

"That's it!"

"What?"

"The girls. What do we know about them?" She pulled their names out of a file and ran through the names. "The only one of these girls I've checked on is Eilida. She doesn't know about me, but I've spoken with her aunt and uncle throughout the years. I begged them to tell her about her parents but they refuse. I get it they don't want to trigger bad memories. What about the others?"

"So we find each of the girls. Which ones are grown?"

"Emily is thirty-two, Eilida is twenty-two…" She ran through the list and they determined the ages of all the girls.

"He is a man of patterns. We have to find Emily. What if he already has?" Her green eyes filled with worry as she looked into Frank's soft, calming eyes.

She hopped onto the computer. Frank picked up his phone and called a friend. Within twenty-four hours they had compiled a list. Five months later, they had the whereabouts of each girl, including Emily. She'd taken them the longest to track.

May 7th, Burkhalder sat on the living room carpet, her back against the couch, in disbelief at the information in front of her. Talla, visiting, sat cross-legged on the floor beside her helping her sift through the piles. Both sets of eyes froze, then looked towards each other. Burkhlader grabbed her phone and dialed.

"Frank, we found it! And you aren't goin' to believe it."

"Pullin' in the drive-way."

The Calm Before the Storm: Evan's Sins

Click. Each hung up their phone. Frank rushed through the front door, sliding to her side. "What is it?"

She pointed to the map in front of her. "Emily and Eilida live across the street from Emily, Evan's sister. They are neighbors."

He looked at the map.

"It gets worse, Emily has three children. The oldest two are boys. The youngest a girl... Erica. She's two years old."

☪ ☪ ☪ ☪ ☪

Mr. Fritz walked into his house after a long day. He poured a brandy and loosened his shirt. Sinking into his chair, he flipped on the TV. His eyes lowered to his fireplace. The stone looked out of place. Setting his brandy on the side table, he padded to the fireplace. The stone wasn't flush. He slid it aside. *No! No! Where the*...The knife Evan used to slaughter his family was missing. His body stiffened and he looked around, wild eyed. Every creak, every noise, made him jump. His car keys lay beside the door. Without wasting a moment he grabbed them and bolted out the door.

May 8, 2014

Eilida lifted her head from the
pillow. Her pendant clasp loose.
She stood, shaking out her long
brown curls. The pendant landed on her pile
of clothes. Jay lay sleeping, his brown hair
tousled over his face. Covers wrapped around
his middle, his feet hanging off the side of the
bed. *You sexy thing!*

She grabbed her pile of clothes, the
pendant slipping to the floor, and dressed.
Eilida slipped her feet into her shoes, kicking
the pendant under Jay's bed. Clutching her
purse, she stole out the door. Arriving home
about one o'clock, she snuggled into her own
bed and fell asleep. She tossed and turned.
Inside her dream she ran for the chest, a man
with a glinting knife in his hand chased her. A
river of blood trailed after him. She dove for
the chest. Her eyes flew open, her heart
beating out of her chest.

She swiped her hand across her forehead,
pushing her hair out of her face. Her other
hand grabbed for her pendant. Patting her
chest and her neck she panicked, realizing it
wasn't there. She jumped out of bed tossing
her clothes, emptying her purse, and yanking
her sheets off her bed. It was nowhere.

Defeated, she fell backwards onto bed and hoped she lost it at Jay's.

☾ ☾ ☾ ☾ ☾

Evan clicked send to his response to Eilida's *Dear Delilah* advice column. *Delilah, she remembers my song.*

Tommy rested beside the rented car. Evan threw him the keys.

"Where we going?" Tommy asked while climbing into the driver's seat and starting the ignition.

"I have a job."

Evan directed Tommy up the mountain to Eclipse Lane. "Meet me here in four hours."

"OK."

Evan exited the car, his pharmaceutical bag over his shoulder, slipped through the trees and trudged up the road to Eighteen Eclipse Lane.

"Hello," said Emily Turnwell as she opened the door. Erica tugging at her leg.

"Good afternoon. I work for Nox Pharmaceuticals and we have a free package we're handing out. All it costs is allowing me to do a small demonstration."

Something about him seemed familiar to her. She couldn't place why. "I've never heard of drugs pedaled door to door."

He smiled. "They're not prescription drugs in here. Allergy medications - over the counter."

She thought for a minute. Her oldest son suffered from hay fever. Every spring he spent miserable, watching the other kids playing outdoors. "My son has allergy problems. He's ten."

I know that. "Safe for children."

"Alright, alright come in." She held the door open. He went through his salesman spiel and gave her a ton of test samples.

"What a beautiful house. I bet you have an amazing view of the mountain from here."

"We do." Erica ran to her pile of toys.

"Do you mind if I take a look?"

"No, the kitchen and deck is through here."

Evan slid his hand into his bag, pulling out a syringe, and followed. Her neck close enough to stuff the needle into it. But he wanted something more. She let him inside yet had no recollection of who he was. All these years, he'd waited and planned. He lived a few streets over in the group home and often took walks, observing the area. He learned Eilida's grandmother lived on Eclipse Lane. When her neighbors moved across the street he took the opportunity as an open invitation to buy the house, remodel it and sell it to Emily at a bargain price. He even bought their old home. Soon after, he slipped inside grandma's house and gave her a special dose of his own heart attack medicine, cementing the deal. He wanted more! "Emily."

About to turn the door knob, she slid her hand to her side and turned towards him. She hadn't given him her first name. His eyes blackening and suddenly everything flashed through her mind. She backed towards the table where a heavy rolling pin lay. She made a quick plan to hit him on the head, grab Erica, and run to the neighbors. "Who are you?"

"You remember, don't you?"

"I... I... don't know."

"Sure you do." He stepped closer, watching her hands behind her back.

He reached his free hand towards her arm and touched her. "I'm your brother. I spent years searching for you."

She swung the rolling pin with her other hand. He ducked and lunged forward, knocking her off balance. Her head hit the table, stunning her. The rolling pin fell to the floor.

"Mommy, mommy." Erica ran into the room.

"Go to your room!" shouted Evan.

She ran around the corner, stuffing her thumb into her mouth and slid against the wall in the hallway.

Evan jabbed the syringe into Emily's neck, giving her a small amount. "This won't hurt, but it will keep you quiet." Her body

went limp in his arms. He looked around the
house. Finding pantyhose, he tied her onto
the chair and stuffed a sock into her mouth.

A car crunched over the gravel road.
Evan slithered to the window, gloved his
hands, then picked up another syringe. He hid
behind the front door. The knob turned.
Evan waited for Eric Turnwell to come
through the door. As he closed it, Evan
shoved the needle towards his neck. Eric
pushed against Evan's chest. They fell to the
floor. Eric grabbed Evan's hand holding the
syringe and beat it against the floor. Using his
strong body, Evan rolled Eric over and
slammed the needle into him. He dragged his
body into the kitchen and tied him into a chair
facing Emily, shoving a sock into his mouth.

Evan leaned towards Erica still sitting in
the hallway. "Erica, I'm your uncle. Can you
show me your room and toys?"

She nodded her head, stood, and walked
down the hallway.

"Is this it?" He pushed the door open.
She continued sucking her thumb as she
entered the room. "Do you know how to play
hide and seek? I'm going to hide and you find
me?" She looked at him with big blue eyes,
clutching the edge of a ratty pink blanket on
her bed as he closed her door. He carried one
of the kitchen chairs into the hall and placed
the back beneath the doorknob to her room.

Small feet pounded the gravel road. Evan slid his knife out of his waistband and flicked it open. Two boys burst through the door. "Mom, Dad," called the oldest, running into the kitchen. He stopped short when he saw Evan holding a knife to his mother's throat. The youngest boy rushed to his brother's side.

The oldest pushed his hand to the side to guard his brother.

"No need boys. Come in, take a seat."

"Who are you?"

"I'm your mother's older brother."

"No you're not."

"Shut up kid, get in the chair and I'll tell you the story. Run and your mother is dead."

Both boys shuffled into the kitchen. Evan shoved them into chairs and tied their hands.

"Ready? You want to hear the story?"

The youngest one looked at Evan wide-eyed. "I don't think so."

His brother threw him a *shut up* face.

"Too bad because I'm going to tell you. When your mommy and I were little we had evil parents who hurt me. They beat me and did things to me you can't imagine. One day the grim reaper visited and took their lives. We had a brother but the grim reaper took him too. You see, one day he would have faced the same torment I did. The reaper allowed me to live and Emily hid under her dresser so he couldn't find her. Emily and I were separated. We never saw each other again until today."

"You're the *reaper*!" shouted the oldest son.

"You little ass." He slid the blade across the boy's throat in one quick movement, causing the boy's head to droop. Blood flowed into his lap. The youngest boy screamed. Evan slid the syringe into his neck and drug the blade across it. Evan lifted his head. The boy gurgled on his own blood. His eyes fluttered. "You weren't as much an ass as your brother." He dropped his head and it slumped onto his chest.

Emily wiggled in her chair, tipping it over. Tears flowing across her cheeks as each of her precious boys died in front of her. Helpless and tied to a chair, she couldn't help them. He held his knife to her neck. The blade sticky with blood. "What do you think of the house? I picked it out for you. It's secluded. You can scream and no one will hear you." He took the sock out of her mouth. "Go ahead."

Gasping for air, tears running down her cheeks she looked at her precious boys. She needed to get to Erica before Evan killed her too. "Why? Why are you doing this?"

"Because I can. It started to keep mommy away. I killed her eight times and still she came back. Then I met someone and she went away. Poof that was it! Now I'm doing it because I enjoy it. I want you to feel the pain I felt every time she touched me."

He walked towards Eric, reading the horror in Emily's eyes as he ripped the blade fast and quick across his neck, his murky eyes glaring into her soul. Emily scrunched her eyes, unable to watch the terror. *Erica! Why didn't I ever ask about my past?*

"She never harmed you. She would have hurt Elfred. That was mercy. It had to be done, but you." He grabbed a fistful of her hair. She whimpered, tears streaking her cheeks. "You were special."

"I don't remember. I was a baby. I didn't. I…" She screamed and he stuffed the sock back into her mouth.

Holding the blade against her flesh, he twisted slowly. She whimpered and closed her eyes. "I, I, I, That's always been it. I, you… You care only for yourself! Open your eyes!" Her blue eyes popped open. Her only thought as Evan's blade, cold and stiff, rested against her throat, *Erica, sweet baby.*

A sting erupted from her neck as Evan twisted the blade further. He slashed again and again until Emily's whimpering stopped and her eyes stared blank and still. He untied her and raped her corpse.

Final Chapter

Eilida pulled into her driveway and entered the house. She ran upstairs to her room, slid the mouse of her computer. Her work email on the screen. A message from Ted blinked. She read while pulling off her pants and slipping into her jeans.

Dear Delilah,
This is Ted again. I want to thank you for your advice. I have been in touch with my sister. In fact, I will be meeting her and her family tonight. Thank you, Ted.

Eilida sat on the edge of her bed, tying the laces on her sneakers, and smiled. *At least something good comes out of my job. My editor err… is a jerk. I'm happy for you Ted.* She jumped up, gathering her dirty clothes and hurried down the stairs. Tossing her clothes in the hamper, she grabbed her keys and jetted out the door to walk off her steam. Her boss/editor never took a moment to say a kind word to anyone. He spent his time dictating and belittling.

A few dark clouds hung in the distance.

C C C C C

The crunch of gravel outside caught his attention. He twisted his head to peer out the window. *Eilida. Your daily walk. Tsk tsk. Don't be long.*

Evan untied Emily and lifted her body out of the chair, propping it against the wall. He looked at Eric. "Hmm... you put up a struggle so let's make it look like you tried to defend your family." Evan untied his hands and gave him a push out of the chair. A hand towel lay beside the kitchen sink. Slipping off his bloody gloves and putting on a fresh pair he searched through the house looking for bleach. He soaked the rag in it and wiped everything he'd touched with ungloved hands.

Sliding the chair from beneath Erica's door knob, he wiped it down, placing it in the kitchen. He walked through each room he'd been in, collected his knife - wiping it with the bleach rag. In his head he counted the number of used syringes versus the number he came with, sure he got them all he placed them in a garbage bag wrapped in the bleach rag and tossed the pantyhose and his used gloves inside. He opened Erica's door and waited for Eilida to return.

☾☾☾☾☾

Something was different about the Turnwells' but she couldn't place it. The house looked normal, a shadow passed the front window, meaning they were home. Eilida marched up her drive way, stopped and peered across the street, ignoring her paranoid mind, she went inside the house and jumped in the shower.

☾☾☾☾☾

Evan exited the Turnwells', stole across the street. Lifting the rock the girls kept an extra key hidden under, he clutched it and an evil grin spread across his face. He snuck around to the back door and let himself in. Her purse lay on a table beside the front door. He tossed it to the couch then proceeded upstairs where he heard water running. Stopping to look, Eilida standing naked, her hair wrapped in a towel. She leaned over, swathing her legs in lotion. "You're next," he whispered to the air, then slipped downstairs and out the back door, placing the key underneath the rock.

He slipped through her yard to the patch of trees at the end of the road. Tommy waited as Evan asked him. Evan was too preoccupied with his kill and self-absorbed ego to notice

Tommy's eyes glancing through his side mirror and hand motion through the open window.

"Got us a room in Salvation Cove. You know the way?"

Tommy nodded and pulled the vehicle onto the main road.

☾ ☾ ☾ ☾ ☾

Eilida opened her car door, gazed at her neighbor's house and realized her mind wasn't paranoid. The shadow she'd seen earlier from the window wasn't a Turnwell. The clouds above thundered and lighting exploded from the sky as Eilida snuck around the back of the Turnwells' house, her keys still in hand. She climbed the steps of their back deck. An internal force driving her. She opened their back door and peered inside. Their lifeless bodies, the bloody mess, forced her family's murders to blast into her conscious mind, flooding her emotions. She ran, tears flooding her face as her mind played and replayed the black eyed man sliding his blade across her parents' throats. Her brothers laying in pools of their own blood, a sticky mess on the floor between them. The scary, black eyed man standing within breathing distance of her, hidden behind her mother's dresses. Scrambling into the chest, his face haloed by

326

the sun the first thing she saw as the chest lid opened. The rain pelted against her, soaking her body as she ran unaware through the woods, her foot sinking into the wet ground, she reached for a tree limb, her car keys dropping from her hand. She tripped and tumbled headlong as her body somersaulted down the mountain. Evan's face, a grin full with malice and his beady eyes the last thing she saw as her head hit the boulder, halting her body's motion beside River Freedom.

A hand reached into the mud and lifted her keys, trudged up Mount Wilde, got into Eilida's car and cranked the engine. Rain ripped through the air and against the windshield, making driving off the mountain treacherous. Once safely away from the mountain roads, the driver picked up a cell, calling 9-1-1.

$$C \cdot C \cdot C \cdot C \cdot C$$

Burkhalder crawled up Mount Wilde in her SUV, passing a small maroon coupe headed off the mountain. The rain unrelenting. She reached the Turnwells' road. Her phone rang, Frank's number flashed across the screen. "What did you find?"

Frank reached the mountain before Burkhalder, in time to watch Evan slide into the passenger seat of a gold car. Not wanting to lose him, he turned his truck around and followed the vehicle off the mountain. He kept a safe distance and used his truck's height to his advantage as he slipped in and out of traffic. The gold car exited the freeway, continued left along a winding road and pulled into a motel in Salvation Cove that rented cabins. He pulled alongside the road as Evan exited the vehicle and went inside the office. Frank scrunched his eyes trying to get a look at the driver, all he could make out was long blond hair drawn into a pony tail. *A girlfriend?* he questioned. Evan exited the office, a key in hand and hopped back into the car. The driver turned and spoke, masculine features. *A boyfriend?*

He allowed them to pull out and follow the road, waited five minutes, then followed. Each cabin secluded amongst its own grouping of trees. The gold car parked outside a cabin. A tall, blond, skinny man exited the driver's side and walked around to the trunk while Evan exited the vehicle and opened the cabin door. They disappeared inside. Frank called Burkhalder.

"I'm outside a cabin in Salvation Cove. Umm... The place is called Hideaway Lake. Evan's here with a young man, protégé or boyfriend, I'm not sure. I may need your back up."

"On my way." She turned her SUV around and headed back down the mountain.

She'd catch up to Emily after they destroyed Evan.

☾ ☾ ☾ ☾ ☾

Evan admired Tommy's smooth, youthful skin as he caressed his body. Excitement rushed through him as he was finally going to *have* him.

"Roll over, allow me to pleasure you." Tommy whispered in Evan's ear, nibbling his ear lobe.

Eager to feel Tommy's hands on his awaiting flesh and his manhood harden and welcome Tommy, he rolled over. Tommy caressed Evan's flesh and bit at his back. His right hand reached beneath the rolled covers and pulled out a syringe. He kissed the small of Evan's back, making his way upwards. The syringe edging closer to Evan's neck. He slid it in. Evan screamed, "You bastard!" and tried to turn over, but Tommy held him down. All the work he'd done for Evan over the past few years had developed his muscles. Evan's strength wiggling beneath him, using all the force in his arms, chest and back he pushed against him until his body stopped. Evan's breathing slowed and Tommy knew the drugs had taken effect. The last conscious thought Evan had: *I shouldn't have challenged the stars and planets. I should have heeded my lunar report.*

Tommy jumped off the bed, rummaged through Evan's luggage for his gloves. Once he found them, he slid them on his hands and grabbed a knife, caked in flaking dried blood, out of his own bag. He mounted Evan from behind, lifting his head, placed the knife to his neck. Sage's ring on a chain caught the knife. He whipped the blade and the chain fell. "This is for Mark and every other little boy, parents, and little girl whose life you destroyed."

☪ ☪ ☪ ☪ ☪

Burkhalder pulled up beside Frank. They got out of their vehicles and edged towards the cabin, guns in hand. Frank peaked inside the cabin through a crack in the curtains. A puddle of red saturated the sheets. He motioned for Burkhalder, who joined him. She gasped. "Whose blood?"

"I dunno, but we're going to find out." He pulled out his Swiss army knife and fiddled with the lock until he heard a click. He pushed the door open. Burkhalder, on the other side of the door frame, her gun in front of her as she entered the cabin. Frank, gun in hand, moved to her side. They exchanged glances then proceeded inside the cabin. Frank pushed the door with his gun while

Burkhalder walked into the restroom - empty. She slid her gun into its holster.

"Bathroom's empty."

He pointed towards a back door, proceeded towards it, and went outside. Combing the area around the cabin, finding not a soul in sight. He returned inside the cabin.

"It's over," she said, staring at Evan's dead body lying face down on the bed. The light reflected off something buried in the blood. She moved closer. A zircon ring on a chain was submerged in a pool of his blood.

"Should we call it in?" asked Frank as he wrapped his arm around Alice's waist.

"Let him rot, just the way he did his victims." She dropped her hand into his back pocket.

"Nature vs. nurture," muttered Frank. They exited the cabin, she drew her lips to his and snaked her tongue inside his mouth. He returned her kiss and skated his hands across her back. He pulled away. "You ready?"

A smile tugged at her lips as she opened her car door, her eyes towards the bright moon glowing overhead. *A gibbous moon... I wonder what the astrological meaning is... Maybe a time for cycles to end.*

She followed Frank home, no longer worried for Emily, Eilida, or any of the other girls, as Evan could never harm anyone again.

Epilogue

"Your one o'clock is here."

"Thank you, Angelica," voiced Mr. Fritz.

A thin woman with slender curves walked into his office, dressed in a sleek fitting black dress. On her head, a wide brimmed Kentucky Derby style hat with a veil. She sat, her slim legs gathered to the side, and lifted her veil. "Thank you so much for taking the time to hear my case."

Mr. Fritz's face turned white as a dove. He stumbled backwards, falling into his chair. One green eye, one amber-yellow eye stared at him from beneath the brim of her hat.

Volume II Ruthless Storm Trilogy

All the Astroloical charts and readings are
courtesy of Whobeda A.K.A. Marcha Fox.
Take a peak at her website

www.valkyrieastrology.com

Evan's Natal Chart- find out how well it fits
him.

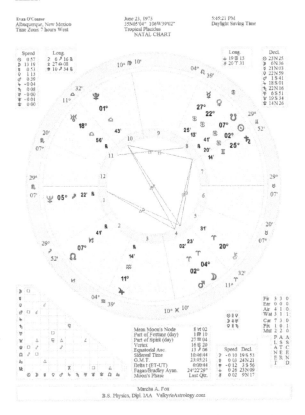

The Calm Before the Storm: Evan's Sins

The Cosmo Natal Report for

Evan the Creepy

June 23, 1973

5:45:21 PM

Albuquerque, New Mexico

Calculated for:

Daylight Savings Time, Time Zone 7 hours West

Latitude: 35 N 05 04   Longitude: 106 W 39 02

Positions of Planets at Birth:

Sun	2 Can 20	Pluto	1 Lib 43
Moon	4 Ari 23	N. Node	7 Cap 41
Mercury	27 Can 25	Asc.	29 Sco 07
Venus	22 Can 13	MC	10 Vir 10
Mars	2 Ari 02	2nd cusp	29 Sag 52
Jupiter	11 Aqu 14	3rd cusp	4 Aqu 39
Saturn	25 Gem 14	5th cusp	11 Ari 32
Uranus	18 Lib 56	6th cusp	7 Tau 20
Neptune	5 Sag 22		

Chapter 1: How You Approach Life and How You Appear To Others

Scorpio Rising:

You are very strong-willed and proud, but intensely private and not easy to know well. Behind your quiet exterior lies a great deal of emotional depth, sensitivity, complexity, and also fierce determination. When you want something you go after it rather quietly but insistently and wholeheartedly - and you usually get it.

You are not a person who lives lightly or superficially. You want to live passionately and intensely and are not averse to challenge, danger, or to facing the darker side of life - human pain and struggle. You function well in crisis situations and often seek them out, for you enjoy the feeling of living at full capacity.

You are very intuitive about other people and especially about their unspoken feelings and hidden motives. You usually have strong, immediate gut reactions, either positive or negative, which prove to be correct. You approach life very instinctively and are not always fully conscious of why you feel or act as you do. You also have a very strong affinity

with animals - an acute sensitivity and a
nonverbal kind of rapport with them.

In relation to others, you are rather
cautious, sometimes even suspicious, until you
get to know and trust them - and trust doesn't
come easily to you. When you commit
yourself emotionally to someone, be it friend
or lover, you are intensely loyal and devoted
to them and you also expect the same kind of
unwavering, undying loyalty in return. If you
are ever betrayed by someone you care deeply
for, you are capable of hating and retaliating
with as much fervor as you once loved.
Nothing is done halfway. In fact, you are
intensely involved and often jealously attached
to whatever you care about, be it person, idea,
or cause. There is definitely a streak of
emotional fanaticism in you.

Because of your natural reserve, others
may see you as something of an enigma. You
are quite self-protective and often defensive.
You are also very magnetic, especially to
members of the opposite sex.

Neptune Conjunct Asc.:

You seem gentle and receptive and often
you do not make a clear, strong impression on
others. You have an elusive and subtle quality,
and people may be nebulous about who you

are. You are easily influenced by others and
somewhat naive. You have a spiritual, mystical
approach to life and are very idealistic and
sometimes impractical.

Chapter 2: The Inner You: Your Real Motivation

Sun in Cancer:

You have powerful emotional attachments to the past, your family, your childhood, those places you associate with safety and security and your beginnings. Maintaining a connection with your roots and heritage and keeping family bonds strong are very important to you. Loyal, devoted, and sentimental, you tend to cling to whatever is dear to you, be it person, familiar place, or cherished possession.

You are sympathetic, nurturing, supportive, and very sensitive to the emotional needs of other people. You like to be needed, to care for others, and you often worry about the people you love. You have a very strong need for a sense of belonging and acceptance, and you center much of your life around your home. You are more concerned about people and their feelings than with power, achievement, or position in society. Kindness, consideration, and tenderness impress you more than any sort of honor the world can bestow.

You are primarily emotional and your views are often dominated by your feelings and by your own personal, subjective experiences, rather than reason, logic, or abstract principles. It is difficult for you to judge situations in a fair, objective manner for your personal sympathies and loyalties usually enter in. You take things very personally, and sometimes build a wall around yourself to protect yourself from pain and rejection. You feel rather shy and vulnerable at heart. You also tend to be moody, experiencing frequent emotional ups and downs. You need to have a place and time in your life to withdraw, introspect, dream, and replenish yourself; otherwise you become cranky and unhappy with those around you.

You function in an instinctive, nonrational manner and like to immerse yourself in creative activities where you can express your feelings, imagination, and instincts. You often love to cook, since it can be both creative and a way to nurture and nourish others. You also have a great affinity for music, because it evokes and communicates feelings that may be difficult or impossible to put into words.

Your compassion, sensitivity, and imagination are your strong points. Your faults include an inability to release the past and go forward, clannishness and prejudice, and a tendency to be self-pitying when you meet hardships in life.

Sun in 8th house:

You crave intense experiences and are attracted to aspects of life that are strange, unfathomable, or taboo. You may hide your interests or inclinations, except from those who know you very intimately. You are rarely content with yourself and your life, and you have an inner urge to be continually going farther or deeper than you ever have before. You also have a strong interest in social power and the role that money and economics play in people's lives.

Sun Square Moon:

You often feel that you are at cross purposes with yourself, for your conscious intentions and desires conflict with your subconscious emotional needs and drives. You are pulled in two different directions. You have difficulty satisfying both your need to be an individual and your need for caring relationships and a sense of belonging. Also, you send out mixed messages so people don't always know how to respond to you or know what you really want, thus creating confusion or conflict in close relationships.

Sun Square Mars:

You are direct, energetic, sometimes aggressive and combative. You often feel that you need to fight to get what you want and you tend to have a "me-first" attitude that angers or irritates others. You are hasty, restless, impatient, and sometimes reckless.

Sun Square Pluto:

You are intensely willful, zealous, and fanatical, though often you hide the intensity of your feelings and your personal motives and desires. You have an infatuation with power and an almost compulsive desire for personal recognition, the desire to be Somebody. You tend to worship Heroes who have powerful personal magnetism and charisma, and often seek to emulate them. You also have both a fear of, and an intense fascination with, death and the hidden, secret, dark side of life.

Chapter 3: Mental Interests and Abilities

Mercury in Cancer:

You are highly interested in inner, subjective, and personal issues, and your thinking is based more on feelings, intuition, personal experiences, and prejudices rather than reason or logic. Intellectual abilities and accomplishments without heart or soul mean little to you. You are empathic and would be an excellent counselor, for you are a sensitive listener and deeply interested in a person's feelings and inner life. In addition to psychology, you are drawn to education, art, poetry, music, or mythology. You are not especially confident about speaking in public, but will open up and share your thoughts in small, intimate groups. You enjoy keeping a diary or personal journal and reading the chronicles of others' lives and personal development.

Mercury in 8th house:

The mysterious and the unknown fascinate you and you may investigate the supernatural or something that is hidden or taboo. You need to know what is going on behind the scenes. You are also deeply curious about or astute about economic, political, or social power, big business, and the motives and powers behind the social facade.

Mercury Conjunct Venus:

You appreciate aesthetics and have a fine sense of form, design, and beauty. You could develop considerable technical skill as an artist, designer, craftsman, or creative writer. You could also sell objects of beauty - artistic products, cosmetics, jewelry, etc.

You have the ability to please and harmonize well with others and tend to ameliorate relationships between people. Your sense of humor, tact, and personal charm are of great benefit to you in any work with people on a one-to-one level.

Mercury Trine Mars:

You speak clearly, decisively, and convincingly, and thoroughly enjoy a vigorous discussion or debate. You would be an effective lawyer or public speaker, a salesman of ideas. Others tend to listen to you and follow your lead, and you have a talent for directing people and making decisions. You also have an aptitude for writing, especially criticism or satire.

Chapter 4: Emotions: Moods, Feelings, Romance

Moon in Aries:

Emotional outbursts are frequent with you due to your fiery temper and emotional impulsiveness. You express yourself very directly and honestly and no one has to guess what your true feelings are. However, you dislike showing any personal weaknesses or needs for support, comfort, and nurturing. You are often impatient with yourself and with others. You abhor emotional dependency and dislike "complainers".

You inspire others to take positive action in their lives by your own enthusiasm and eagerness to meet life's challenges, and are attracted to people who are adventurous, courageous, and independent. You are rather bossy, but you do not like to be with people that you can boss around too much. You enjoy a good fight sometimes. Relationships built upon mutual respect and a good deal of emotional freedom are ideal for you.

You become very cross if you do not have enough vigorous physical activity. You will feel your best if you "do battle" on the tennis or racquetball court (or engage in some other competitive sport) frequently.

Moon in 4th house:

You have strong attachments to your past, the place where you grew up, your heritage, and family traditions. In fact, you may be unable to step out of the habits and roles you learned as a child. Your tie to your mother is very strong and you also seek mothering and protection from your spouse and other family members as well.

Moon Conjunct Mars:

You feel that you must always be DOING something, and become impatient and irritable if you have to slow down or wait for anything. A stormy home life may be the result of your own tendency to fight for what you want, rather than compromise. You may not realize how competitive you are.

Moon Opposition Pluto:

You have intense desires and feelings and your personal relationships are deeply emotional, passionate, and often stormy and painful as well. There are powerful magnetic ties between yourself and those you care about, and you could become emotionally obsessed by another person. Your feelings can become so urgent and compelling that you do things that are not rational. You undergo periodic emotional upheavals and purging, when you must break all ties, release the past and begin anew.

Moon Trine Neptune:

The beauty and harmony of your surroundings has a very powerful effect on your emotions. You are very sensitive and cannot stand to be in an atmosphere where there is discord or dissonance. Gentle, kindhearted, and peace-loving, you will give or sacrifice much in order to avoid a fight and to "make everyone happy".

Venus in Cancer:

Sensitive and sentimental, you are deeply attached to your family, old friends, familiar places, and the past. You are romantic and tender in love, and the remembrance of birthdays, anniversaries, family rituals, and other days of personal significance is very important to you. You seek caring, emotional support, and security in love. You like to be needed, to cherish and protect your loved ones, and you are somewhat possessive of them.

Venus in 8th house:

You crave very intense, deep, emotional relationships, and would even prefer a stormy, tumultuous relationship to one which is smooth but lacking vitality and passion. You love wholeheartedly and expect all-consuming, total devotion and attention from your partner. Casual, light relationships hold no appeal for you.

Venus Square Uranus:

Your love feelings are easily aroused and your romantic relationships begin with a sudden electric attraction, but they often end abruptly, and you may be in and out of love frequently - especially in your younger years. You crave emotional excitement and need to feel spontaneous and free, so you may avoid making firm personal commitments. Unusual or nontraditional forms of love and relationships appeal to you, and you are attracted to unique, creative, or unstable people.

Chapter 5: Drive and Ambition: How You Achieve Your Goals

Mars in Aries:

You have a warrior's attitude - decisive, courageous, and bold. You tend to always want to DO something, even when waiting for an appropriate time or not doing something (simply letting things alone to resolve themselves) would actually be more efficient and effective. You absolutely cannot tolerate being passive or even patient about getting what you want. You feel that it is up to you to take the initiative and you go after your goal or desire very aggressively.

You are also self-reliant, do not depend on others to do things for you or help you along, and you are often irritated when other people offer advice or direction. Cooperation rarely comes easily to you. You are willful and can be quite oblivious to others' desires or feelings when you are pursuing something you want. You are highly competitive, enjoy a challenge or a good fight, and may be downright pugnacious at times. Abounding in energy and enthusiasm at the start of a new venture, you need a very positive response and encouragement to sustain your interest in it. If a project isn't successful rather quickly, you are apt to drop it and move on to something else, rather than rework or refine it. The desire to blaze a trail, to do things in a new way - YOUR way - is very strong in you. You can discover, invent, and initiate new things, but are impatient and may lack the stamina and perseverance needed to complete a long-term project.

Mars in 4th house:

It is not easy for you to show the world at large your angry or competitive side, but your family sees this side of you more often. Temper tantrums, tumultuous family relationships, or a great deal of competition between you and one or more of your relations is likely. You like to be the one in charge in your home and you put a lot of energy into making it the way you want it.

Mars Opposition Pluto:

You have a powerful will and when you want something, you pursue it passionately and relentlessly until you achieve it. You may be so driven by your desire that you lose all objectivity. You often become compulsive, even obsessed, with doing or achieving something, no matter what the costs or how hard you must work for it. Your forcefulness may be veiled or subtle, for often you do not reveal your real aims and intentions to others until they cross you. Intense power struggles and relationships with a strong dominance/submissiveness theme are likely. You have enormous energy reserves, and are capable of extraordinary effort and great achievement if you use your energies for constructive purposes.

Mars Trine Neptune:

You dream up creative solutions to problems and take an imaginative, unusual approach to getting a job done. When difficulties arise you prefer to avoid conflict and confrontation in favor of more peaceful or subtle methods of resolving problems. Working to help others or for a cause that transcends your own narrow, personal interests is satisfying for you. You have an artistic flair and appreciate the colorful, unique, or strange.

Chapter 6: Other Influences

Jupiter in Aquarius:

Your strength lies in your ability to be innovative, open to new progressive concepts, willing to experiment and to reject customs and traditions when they cease to serve any positive function in the present. Also, you have an expansive view of the world, one that includes humanity and not only your own small, personal circle.

Jupiter in 3rd house:

You have a great love of learning and an eager, curious, active mind which impels you to travel and see as much of the world as possible. You read widely, and may excel academically. You love being in a teacher-student relationship and may stay in school for many years, prolonging your studies for as long as possible! You also communicate well and would be an effective, inspiring teacher.

Public relations or any field involving communications and sharing information also suits you very well.

Saturn in Gemini:

You doubt your own intelligence and mental capacities, and you may work very hard at studies in order to compensate for this. You are often overly serious and disinterested in light or superficial conversation. Spontaneous communication, social give-and-take, and making small talk are likely to be difficult for you.

Saturn in 7th house:

You take your commitments to others very seriously, especially in close one-to-one relationships. Your strong sense of responsibility to the other person makes you a trustworthy and dedicated partner, but you often feel that marriage or any binding commitment between yourself and another person is too restrictive and burdensome, and thus seek to avoid it. Close relationships may be more work than pleasure for you and it may seem that you are always "working on" your marriage rather than enjoying it. You will persevere and ultimately grow through the process, however.

Uranus in Libra:

You are part of a 7 year group of people who strive for greater equality in relationships. You treat parents, children, and spouses much more like friends and equals than other generations do, and many of you will experiment with alternative marriage styles that allow for greater freedom and equality in relationships.

Uranus in 11th house:

You have unusual, even eccentric friends, and you are likely to join groups, communities, organizations, or clubs which promote progressive or unconventional ideas, social change, or innovation in some form. You are dynamic and creative in business affairs and in organizations.

Neptune in Sagittarius:

You are part of a 14 year group of people that are extremely idealistic and farsighted in their dreams. Your age group is very liberal and expansive in outlook, and consequently churches become much more flexible and more eclectic in their approach during your life time. Religions that do not adapt to the broad-minded attitude of your age group simply are unable to attract very much interest and involvement from you.

A great deal of metaphysical musing and speculation is evident in your age group, and there is a very strong interest in all manner of psychic phenomena, UFO's, prophecy, etc.

The Calm Before the Storm: Evan's Sins

This interest will open many new doors and insights, but will also often lead to a great deal of fantasizing and speculation that is taken more seriously than it should be.

Neptune in 1st house:

You are yielding, gentle, and impressionable. You tend to "melt" into your surroundings, and do not make a very powerful, vivid impression on others. Especially while young, you may not have a very clear sense of identity.

Sensitive and compassionate, you do not enjoy fighting and no matter what you profess, you are a pacifist at heart.

Neptune Sextile Pluto:

The entire generation to which you belong has tremendous opportunities for spiritual rebirth and awakening. This will not be forced upon you or precipitated by unavoidable events, rather it comes from an inner yearning and a natural propensity to seek the depths.

Pluto in Libra:

You are part of a 12 year group of people who are deeply interested in personal relationships. Your age group has a deeply-rooted yearning to see people relating and communicating with each other effectively and harmoniously. There is little egotism and a willingness to hear the other person's side of the story and a readiness to compromise and arbitrate different points of view. In fact, the need for harmonious, peaceful relationships is so strong that there is a tendency to overlook real differences and to focus only on the similarities in an attempt to bring different parties into harmony with each other.

Interest in psychology and sociology is high in your age group. There is a tremendous heightening of awareness of social skills. Your age group will experiment with different marriage styles, family relationships, and even business relationships in an attempt to bring fair treatment and effective communication between people. Interest and appreciation for other cultures is also strong, and your age group will work hard to preserve and support the cultural heritage of all ethnic groups.

Your strong yearning for equitable and harmonious relationships is also reflected in major advancements in trade agreements, arms control, and international cooperation that are designed and implemented by your generation. These agreements and policies foster a much safer and more cooperative environment for all, although there is also a tendency for greedy individuals to take advantage of the conciliatory atmosphere and twist situations to their own ends.

In short, you are part of a generation of individuals who are deeply interested in other people; you are a humanistic and humanitarian group. You will struggle and experiment with personal relationships, and forge new models for how people can relate as friends, family members, and members of nations as well.

Pluto in 10th house:

You have a powerful sense of destiny and may be unusually, even ruthlessly, ambitious. There is a very driven, compulsive quality to the way you pursue your career or other important life goals, which is likely to win you both staunch admirers and vigorous opponents.

There is a very "radical" side to you, and you may want to remake or change the world in some significant way. Depending on other astrological factors in your chart and your own decisions, you can be either very destructive or a powerful force for healing and positive change in the world.

Lunar Return Charts

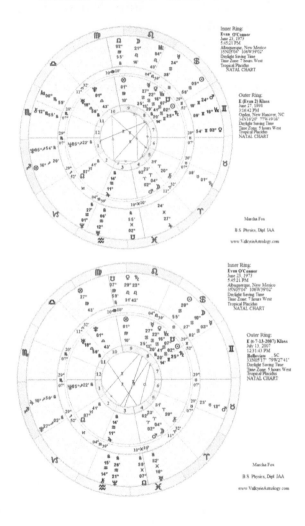

Inner Ring:
Evan O'Conner
June 23, 1973
5:45:21 PM
Albuquerque, New Mexico
35N0504' 106W3902'
Daylight Saving Time
Time Zone: 7 hours West
Tropical Placidus
NATAL CHART

Outer Ring:
E (Evan 2) Klaas
June 27, 1998
3:16:42 PM
Ogden, New Hanover, NC
34N16'20" 77W49'06"
Daylight Saving Time
Time Zone: 5 hours West
Tropical Placidus
NATAL CHART

Marcha Fox

B S Physics, Dipl IAA

www.ValkyrieAstrology.com

Inner Ring:
Evan O'Conner
June 23, 1973
5:45:21 PM
Albuquerque, New Mexico
35N0504' 106W3902'
Daylight Saving Time
Time Zone: 7 hours West
Tropical Placidus
NATAL CHART

Outer Ring:
E (t-7-13-2007) Klaas
July 13, 2007
12:31:43 PM
Belleview , SC
33N08'17" 79W27'41"
Daylight Saving Time
Time Zone: 5 hours West
Tropical Placidus
NATAL CHART

Marcha Fox

B S Physics, Dipl IAA

www.ValkyrieAstrology.com

Continue reading for the first two chapters of In the Midst of the Storm Volume 3 Ruthless Storm Trilogy.

If you're curious what happened to Evan's youngest victims, find their stories in the Evan's Girls series.

I Remember You

October 2016

Tommy sat inside his truck, the sun slowly setting. Inside the large building, he observed Eilida through his binoculars, her head poured over a book. In the past couple months, he'd studied her habits, memorizing her routine, but hadn't yet found the courage to face her.

When they'd last met before that dreadful day of her accident, which he took in part as his fault. The guilt ate away at him. He needed to make it right but didn't want the door slammed in his face. He was every bit as guilty as anyone else that day.

He'd lived with Evan long enough to know his intentions were not above board, even though he'd never actually seen him in the act. He was a violent man on the inside and calm on the outside. But it was all an act. Evan was a controlling, manipulative, and calculating killer.

Tommy scrolled through his phone, his eyes resting on the map. Until that day, Tommy hadn't wanted to believe Evan was the killer, she insisted he was. His eyes rested on the map as he widened the picture with his fingers, staring at the words *Emily* then *Eilida Tate*.

His body shuddered as he'd figured out too late who Emily was, not only that but he'd helped him! Evan was sick and twisted beyond the worst serial killers in history. He'd given Tommy mail and a package to be delivered to a residence, but never a name.

He dropped his head against the steering wheel in guilt and shame. If Eilida never forgave him, he'd accept it, but merely wanted the opportunity to explain himself and beg for her forgiveness.

At the Astrology conference, he'd taken an instant liking to her and her friend. Sage was far bubblier than Eilida, who carried an air of darkness foreshadowing her. The same evil darkness that ate at him -- Evan. He'd destroyed so many lives.

He'd sought Evan's weakness and used it to destroy him, but not before Evan had a chance to eliminate four more lives. Those of his half-sister and her family, leaving only the daughter alive. Tommy tightened his hands into fists until his knuckles turned white.

Releasing the tension in his hands, he grabbed the binoculars and raised them to his eyes. He watched Eilida toss her bag over her shoulder and stroll towards the exit. He started his motor and waited.

The lights overhead blinked on as Eilida looked up from the book she had her head buried in. She glanced toward the window at the darkness creeping over the campus. Checking the time on her phone she sighed and, with one quick movement, closed the book. She picked up her denim bag and stuffed the book inside, pulled out her favorite worn black hoodie and slipped her arms inside it. Then flung the bag over her shoulder as she strolled towards the large double doors of the campus library.

"Goodnight Eilida," called Ms. Rixley, the night librarian. Her soft, round face smiling as she pushed her square-rimmed glasses upwards on the bridge of her nose.

Eilida waved and returned a smile. "Goodnight, Ms. Rixley." She spent so much time studying in the library she considered Ms. Rixley a friend. New to the campus, as she'd only transferred the beginning of the semester, she didn't know too many people yet. She missed Sage to no end and her daydreams drifted towards lusty moments between her and Jay.

Pushing the heavy glass door open, a blast of chilly October North Carolina air swished towards her. She shuddered involuntarily and pushed her hood over her head, tucking her long, wavy dark hair into the collar. With her head down to deflect the wind, she walked towards her car.

Each time she touched the door handle brought back memories of the fateful night her biological parents died. The idea that Evan had been inside the car made her skin crawl, but she refused her parents' insistence on buying her a new one, saying, "A deep cleaning will be fine." Starting the engine, she shifted into drive and left the campus. Within minutes, she pulled her car into a spot outside the apartment building where she lived.

Tapping her fingers on the steering wheel, she decided not to go inside. She'd been studying day and night and wanted a break, needed a break. Leaving her denim bag in the car, she got out and walked towards Flashers. The hot spot all the college kids went to.

She hadn't yet been there even though it was a mere two blocks from her apartment. The blustery wind blew hard against her. *So much for an Indian summer*, she thought. Snuggling her arms around her chest to keep out as much wind as possible, she jaunted the two blocks to *Flashers*.

On the outside, the place was a brick building with a solid neon light donning the bar's name. Inside was loud. Sleek black tables and chairs spotted the floors, while colorful lights flashed overhead. *Pillow Talk* by Zayn played from the speakers. Students filled the dance floor. Spotting an open seat at the bar, she maneuvered through the crowd, dropping her hood and clutching her wallet that contained nothing but her driver's license and debit card.

She climbed onto a black barstool. A young man with thick, dark hair and satin brown eyes turned from behind the bar.

"What can I get you?" he asked. His voice a deep baritone.

"A Heineken."

His eyes swept over her, then he nodded and walked towards the beer cooler. She couldn't help her wandering eyes from watching his jeans move with each stride of his legs. *What a cute ass!* she thought. With her studies, she had no time for a relationship but a booty call -- maybe.

He slid the beer towards her and winked as he turned to help the next customer.

Twisting in her seat, she watched the students grinding on the dance floor and felt herself heat up with lust. She'd made a commitment to Jay, but they agreed on a break until she graduated. He was miles away and she needed it more than once a month or so. However, she wanted to stay honest and true to him. He'd been there for her when she needed him, yet her mind envisioned the sexy bartender and her in a passionate moment. *Stop it, Eilida!*

The Calm Before the Storm: Evan's Sins

A deep voice and tap on her shoulder brought her back to reality. She turned to see a tall, thin, but muscular young man. His straight, long blond hair pulled back in a ponytail.

"Tommy?" she asked, remembering him vaguely from the astrology convention she and Sage went to. They hung with him quite a bit.

"Eilida, right?"

"That's me," she responded, leaning in close to talk above the loud music.

His pale blue eyes twinkled under the lights. "So, uh, I haven't seen you in here before?"

"This is my first time. I'm finishing my bachelors at the University." She cocked her head playfully. "So, what about you?"

"Taking a few classes. Haven't seen you around campus."

"What's your major? Astrology?" she joked, lifting an eyebrow.

He rolled his eyes. "That shit is pretty cool but no. Right now I'm working on a degree in... criminal justice."

Eilida caught his hesitation but ignored it. "Journalism for me. It's my dream."

The gentleman sitting next to her left the bar and Tommy slid onto the empty stool eying her near-empty beer. "Looks like you need another. My treat."

"A girl can't turn down a free beer."

Tommy and Eilida talked for the next couple hours. She enjoyed talking, thinking of something besides her studies, and was relieved to have a friend she could hang with on occasion. They swapped phone numbers and she excused herself.

"I'll see you around," she said, giving him a quick friend-hug.

He returned the hug. "How did you get here? You need a ride?" he offered.

Enjoying his company and fully trusting him were two different things in Eilida's book. She faced too many nightmares in her life. "No, thanks. I live close." She maneuvered the wild, twenty-something college crowd and pushed the door open, pulling her hoodie over her head.

The cold air chilling her to the bone, she walked swiftly towards her apartment. Her mind cloudy from too many beers. A trail through the woods surrounding her apartment complex opened up to her left. If she stayed the course of the street-lit sidewalk, it'd take her longer to get home than if she took the path through the woods that led almost directly to her door. Her body shivering, she decided to take the chance and cut through the woods. Really, it was just a small chunk of trees with a well-worn path that most people used for walking their dogs.

Halfway through the shortcut, she heard voices talking. She slowed her pace and listened but assumed it was a couple walking their dog.

"What the hell are you doing?!" yelled a male voice.

She jumped and on instinct plastered herself against a large tree and scanned the area. Hoping she was fully camouflaged by the thick trunk. She peeked her head around it and spotted two young men. One had jeans sagging past his buttocks and a red jacket. The other wore all black and he held a glinting silver object. Her mind flashed back to the shining object and black eyes that chased her within her nightmares. She breathed deeply, trying to stay calm, and considered her options. The last time she'd run through woods didn't fare well for her and she ended up in a coma for a week.

Running was out of the question. Going forward was out of the question. She felt the cool metal of the pendant against her chest and remembered its soothing qualities. Taking a deep breath, she crouched, using the trees for cover and squat-walked towards the next tree. She couldn't avoid the piles of leaves littering the ground, but hoped her steps were gentle enough the guys would consider them an animal.

The voices moved closer to her and she went into near panic mode. *Breathe, breathe. They're probably just smoking pot and mean no harm*, she soothed herself, but the feeling in her gut sent shivers of horror flying through her body. Bad memories resurfaced and she saw his face, the monster, Evan's face. She closed her eyes, attempting to gather her courage.

Leaves rustled beneath their pounding footsteps, growing closer with each one. No longer able to control her fear, she took her chances and ran.

"Who's there?" called one of the men, as Eilida sprinted through the woods. Not watching where she was going, she ran smack into broad shoulders and a rock hard abdomen. Waves of horror shuddered throughout her body.

I'm Fine

Eilida pushed the solid chest with her hands but it didn't budge, so she side-stepped to run past but he grabbed her arm. "Eilida."

The familiarity of his voice forced her to look into his face. Blue eyes filled with concern and lowered eyebrows stared back at her. Saved by the pendant, it was without it that tragedy struck. His eyes shifted from her towards Saggy Jeans and All Black. "Did you hurt her? Were you chasing her?" he demanded.

They stood at the mouth of the trail and the street lights illuminated their faces. Saggy Jeans met Tommy's glare. "Nah, she just ran. We didn't know anyone was there."

All Black shifted on both feet. "Really, man. He's tellin' the truth."

Tommy narrowed his eyes. "People don't just run, man."

"Nah, we cool. We didn't do nothing."

Eilida watched her innocent *assailants* squirm as if they really had done something. They were high school-aged boys. All Black took a silver object out of his pocket and grabbed something behind his ear. A cigarette and a Zippo. The moonlight glinted off the lighter and was most likely the object he'd held earlier that had struck morbid fear into every orifice of her being.

Tommy let go of Eilida's arm and moved towards the boys, focusing on All Black who took a drag from the cigarette. "How old are you, punk?"

Sweat bubbled on his forehead and his eyes darted past Tommy as if he was considering whether he could run by him without getting caught. After a moment his gaze met Tommy's. "We don't want no trouble."

Eilida stayed put, observing the show. She knew she should probably say something, but watching them squirm was more fun even with the wind pounding against her back. Tommy stood at least six inches taller than either boy and even though he was thin his shoulders were broad and his chest and arms were well developed. He was like a wall when she ran into him.

Tommy grabbed the cigarette from All Black's hand and dropped it to the ground, grinding it into the dirt. "You're not old enough to smoke." The boy scrunched his nose, then opened his mouth, then shut it as his eyes were drawn towards Tommy's side. Tommy raised his shirt enough for the boys to get a glance at a sheathed knife hanging from his belt. Their eyes grew large as UFOs.

Eilida stood on the other side, far enough away, she didn't see it. But the boys did.

"Go, run, before I change my mind," Tommy snarled.

Both boys gulped. Saggy Jeans said, "Yessir," as he jetted across the street. All Black hot on his heels.

Eilida held her hand over her mouth, smothering her chuckle. Tommy glanced at her. "You think it's funny? It was kinda."

She rolled her eyes. "Thanks, I guess I overreacted."

He smoothed his ponytail and stuck his thumbs in his front pockets. "Why don't I finish walking you home?"

She looked into his blue eyes. "Thanks, but I can get home from here." She wasn't sure if she trusted him enough to escort her home. Eilida turned on her heels and took a couple steps, then turned back. Tommy stood in the exact spot watching her.

"How did you know?" she asked. It seemed more than convenient that he just popped up out of nowhere and saved her neck from two delinquents with bad grammar.

"I left *Flashers* a few minutes after you and saw you turn onto this dirt trail. What were you thinking? That could have been worse than two punks."

She twisted her lips. "I live around the corner and walk the trail all the time. People walk their dogs, most of them the size of large rats. It's not scary."

"Then why were you running?"

"Is this twenty questions?" The sparkle in his blue eyes stirred a memory she couldn't quite place. The week she spent in the coma was a week of her life lost, but something about the way he looked at her in that moment carried a memory just beyond her grasp. She flung her arms into the air and sighed. "Walk me home and we'll talk."

He stepped closer to her. "I'm sorry. I can be over protective. But when I saw your face. I saw fear -- real fear."

She nodded and took his hand. "I appreciate it. I do."

A motorcycle passed them as she let go of his hand. She jumped at the unexpected sound and Tommy shifted his stance at her reaction, but said nothing. She took a few steps and he strode up beside her.

"About a year and a half ago, I had a bad accident. It took me months to recover; physical therapy every week and counseling. The accident was triggered by something in my past." She hated people feeling sorry for her and hated being the center of attention, so she gave him the condensed version of the story. If he wanted more he could pick up a newspaper.

"Those boys brought back the memory?"

She nodded in agreement. "Something like that."

"I have a few of those too."

She cocked her heads towards him. "I bet we all do."

The brick building housing her apartment was just ahead. Large trees, nearly bald from shedding their leaves, surrounded the entrance. They turned the corner to her apartment complex and she considered whether she should ask him inside -- he'd just saved her, in a manner of speaking -- or if they should part ways now.

"I lost my best friend in a..." He shifted his lips. "He was murdered. I don't talk about it much, but I get it. That's why I get so over protective. I don't want to lose anyone else, even someone I barely know but whose company I enjoy."

She pondered his words and thought maybe they had enough in common that possibly he was trustworthy. He'd never given her a reason to doubt it and had plenty of hidden, yet easily accessible, weapons in her apartment. "You want to come in? We can... talk."

Tommy smiled. "We will, but not tonight. I wanted to see you home safe." He pulled her towards him, his firm chest against her, and folded her into a hug. "Goodnight."

She wrapped her arms around him, the heat from his body warming her, then let go.

"Goodnight." She turned and unlocked the door.

Tommy watched until she was inside safely, then walked back to *Flashers*.

Eilida pulled her black hoodie over her head and threw it on a wooden table chair. She tossed a bag of popcorn into the microwave and opened a Heineken. Leaning against the Formica counter, she took a swig and thought about the night, about Tommy. The fact that he didn't come inside even when invited impressed her. And she could get really used to his solid chest pressed against her and firm biceps surrounding her.

The microwave beeped and she grabbed the popcorn, padded a couple feet to the living room, stripped to her underwear and snuggled onto the sofa. A fluffy pillow beneath her head and a warm thermal blanket covering her body. Her apartment was a studio. She hadn't wanted to waste money on a place she wasn't living in more than two years and hadn't bothered to hang anything on the white walls.

A picture of her family, including Sage, was propped on the coffee table beside her. She reached past it for the remote and clicked on the TV, then pressed the play button on the DVD player.

Holding her against his body encouraged emotions he wanted to keep hidden. He felt the need to protect her, but at the same time he had a growing attraction. When they first met, he'd ignored it because he needed to be in control. Any emotions and desires for her he'd pushed aside, as they'd have only gotten her killed.

Climbing inside his truck and closing the door, Tommy shuddered from the cold. He slid the heater on full blast and took his phone out of his pocket and typed *I secured the meet*. His finger lingered over the icon a few seconds before he clicked send.

Moments later, a thumbs-up appeared on his phone's screen.

Scarlett

Pseudo

April 1961 5 years old

The sunny day in April carried a light breeze as I jumped off the last step on the bus. No sign that the hot summer was approaching quickly. My blue apron skirt bounced with the spring in my step and my saddle shoes beat against the pavement as I ran towards my mommy waiting at the front door.

She leaned down, her skirt brushing the cement walkway and wrapped her arms around me. "Hi, baby."

"Hi, Mommy. Look what I made today," I said with pride as I lifted a large purple paper butterfly from my backpack.

"Oh, isn't that beautiful," she said with surprise in her voice. "Let's hang that in your room, shall we?"

"Yes, yes," I agreed and rushed toward my room. The white walls garnered many butterflies of every color and size. My twin bed had a lavender comforter covered with purple and white butterflies and lavender curtains hung across the windows. My room was a haven made of my favorite color – purple. I stood by the spot where I wanted Mommy to hang my new butterfly.

She entered the room, her yellow skirt flounced at her knees with each step she took. Her dark hair tied up in a ponytail and her bright brown eyes smiled at me. "This is where you want it?"

"Uh huh."

She took a thumbtack and pinned the butterfly to the spot I pointed at. "There you are. We'll show Daddy when he gets home." Her smile large and full of love.

"OK," I said, bouncing into the kitchen for my after school snack.

The sun lowered in the sky and Daddy came home. As soon as I heard the door open I rushed toward him and he scooped me into his thick arms filled with tickling hair. "How was your day?" he asked, his hazel eyes beamed with joy and sparkled in the setting light of the sun. His blond hair slicked back against his oval head.

"Good. I want to show you what I made."

"I must see it," he said in mock surprise.

"Mommy hung it in my room."

He hoisted me over his head and sat me square on his shoulders as we headed down the hallway. He entered the room.

"Do you see it, Daddy?" I asked.

"No," he said spinning around and making me dizzy. "Is it here?" he asked, stopping and pointing to an old butterfly.

I giggled. This was our routine. "No, Daddy."

He spun again, then asked again before he settled on the new one.

"It's just gorgeous, almost as pretty as you – my little butterfly." He lowered me.

I smiled a partially toothless smile. "I love you, Daddy."

"I love you. Hmm… where is my other love?" he said, asking about Mommy.

"I think she's finishing dinner."

He widened his eyes. "Oh, let's sneak up on her," he said, tiptoeing down the hallway and placing a finger over his mouth.

I stifled a chuckle and followed on my tiptoes. We peeked around the corner and Mommy gazed our way. "Oh, what do we have here?" she said, her eyes wide as if in surprise.

I giggled and Daddy wrapped his arms around her, planting a kiss on her lips.

It was a Friday and Genevieve, our elderly neighbor, came over about seven p.m. as always so my parents could enjoy date night. I couldn't pronounce her name so I called her Gen. She wore her white hair in a bun and had kind blue eyes.

When the bell rang I rushed toward it and flung the door wide open. "Don't you look pretty," she said.

"Thank you," I answered, spinning in my purple nightgown.

"Genevieve, come in," voiced my daddy.

She stepped inside and took a seat with me at the kitchen table. I had the cards already out and waiting. I so enjoyed Friday nights and our card games, which she usually let me win.

My parents kissed my head and walked out the door.

Gen's blue eyes gazed into mine. "One day you will do something great. Very few people have eyes like yours and they give you a special oomph that others don't have."

I smiled. Gen loved my eyes. One was green and the other amber. She and my parents agreed that I was something superior like a fairy. They insisted my eyes gave me special powers.

After an hour of cards Gen tucked me into bed. "Goodnight, Scarlett," she whispered, planting a gentle kiss on my cheek.

I woke up hours later to a large commotion in the house and the sound of Gen crying. Scared and worried, thinking Gen was hurt, I jumped out of bed and scurried down the hallway, halting at the end of it. A police officer dressed in uniform sat beside Gen on the couch. She was OK but where were my parents?

My heart thumped against my ribcage. Another officer walked into the house, his eyes rested on me.

"How are you?" asked the officer. His mustache moved up and down with the motions of his mouth. He steadily walked towards me as I backed down the hallway. Flashes of fear and unidentifiable blood-smeared images rattled my mind.

"I need you to come with me," he said, getting closer with his hand out. I gazed into his dark eyes. There was no sparkle inside them. My heart beat faster when he took another step. Remembering the games I played with Daddy, I side-stepped him. His hand grabbed for mine when I slid underneath his legs, ran as fast as my two small feet carried me and jumped onto Gen's lap. Wrapping my arms around her neck, I clung for my life.

I don't know what scared me so much, but an ominous sensation entered my gut and I knew my life was about to change for the worse. I should have woken up to Mommy and Daddy giggling not Gen's sobs and two unknown people in my house. They wore badges but to me they were strangers.

"Shhh... Scarlett," Gen soothed as I scrambled to plaster myself against her.

"She has to come with us," said the officer in a deep voice.

"She's a little girl and confused. I will go with her," Gen said, her arms wrapped around my trembling body.

"Suit yourself," the deep-voiced officer huffed.

"Where's Mommy and Daddy," I whispered in Gen's ear.

"Oh, Scarlett. You sweet baby. Your mommy and daddy..." she choked back a sob, "they aren't coming home."

I traced the flowered pattern on the couch with my finger as her words sunk in. "Why not?" I asked, my brows furrowed.

"They've gone to heaven," Gen responded in a gentle voice as she caressed the back of my head.

I didn't really understand. "Without me?"

Gen took a deep breath. "Yes but it wasn't their choice. Their time on Earth has passed but you still have a job to do." She lifted the hair above my ear and whispered, "Remember, one day you will do something magnificent."

I leaned back, still planted on her lap and looked into her blue eyes. "Because my eyes give me special powers."

"Yes," she chuckled, "because of your eyes."

Hand in hand with Gen I walked out of my home, never to return, and climbed into the back of the police car.

There were many things that happened within those few moments that I wouldn't understand until a few years later.

Eye Opener

Two years later

I was placed into a home for abandoned and orphaned children. Gen visited every so often for two years than never returned. My heart broke; she was the light in my life, my reason for living. Every day my heart ached for my parents. They loved me and my memories of them are burned into my heart with love.

"Hey, funk eyes," quipped Michelle, "no one will ever want you with those funky eyes. You'll be an orphan forever." She stood in front of me with her legs forming a wide V, preventing me from swinging. Her brown hair hung like limp spaghetti. She was my age, but much larger than me.

I stared at her, trying to tap into the special powers that existed in my eyes. I imagined telekinetically flinging her backwards into the concrete school. Her broken body sliding against it and puddling on the cement playground. I understood full well my eyes didn't really have any special powers but I enjoyed pretending they did.

"You're in my way," I said.

"Make me move," she grunted.

I would if I could. A kickball rolled beside us and she left her stance long enough to lean down and grab the ball. I pushed hard and forced the swing as high as I could make it go in the few seconds I had. It whooshed past her, knocking her to the ground.

"Funk eyes," she sneered, dusting the dirt from her dress.

Ignoring her comment, I continued pumping the swing for the rest of recess. Michelle wasn't the worst. I only had to see her at school. At the home, Dana made it her life's purpose to destroy me. Within the week the home had taken in a few more children, placing Dana and I in the same room. It was small, with barely enough room for the two beds and one tall dresser.

"Catch," shouted Dana as she threw her backpack at me and slid onto the bench school bus seat beside me. The heavy bag felt as though it was loaded with bricks. I pushed it toward her. Since I had to share a room I had to put up with being her mental punching bag. But I had a plan to at least keep my peace with her. She deplored kitchen duty so I volunteered to take her share of kitchen chores.

I loved the kitchen but was sure not to tell her that. It was far better for her to think she had me under her thumb.

Dana's hefty bag took up the space between us on the bus and she sat with her legs in the aisle so she could talk with the other students. Everyone knew we were the orphan kids but she played like she was something more and vied for popularity. She was pretty, with her long, straight, dirty-blonde hair, oval face, and deep blue almond-shaped eyes.

The bus rolled to a stop and Dana stood. "Can you get that?" she asked, pointing to her brick-laden backpack.

I smiled, stood and hefted the bag over my shoulders. The bag hit her in the side, knocking her into the seat on the other side of the aisle.

Her blue eyes glared at me and shot bullets into mine. "Watch it!" she screamed.

I didn't say a word, certainly not an apology; after all, I meant to do it. She thought much of herself and I was a couple years younger and only weighed forty-five pounds but I was smarter than her. I marched off the bus, one step behind her. She stopped abruptly and I almost fell backwards from the weight of her bag but the boy behind me caught the bag, evenly distributing the weight so I caught my balance.

I went straight to the room and dropped her weapon of a backpack onto her bed then jaunted straight to the kitchen. I loved it there as we were the first to taste any treats. I wrapped the smallest apron around myself. It was a couple sizes too big so I had to wrap the strings all the way around and tie it in the front and the bottom hung just above my ankles.

Today's treat was homemade brownies and milk. I piled them onto a plate while Mario, another orphan, grabbed the milk and a stack of cups. I left the innermost brownies in the pan and winked at him. He winked in response as we carried the snack to the others in the dining hall.

Once we dropped it off and served the others we ran-walked back to the kitchen for our brownies, the moistest in the pan.

Later that night, after dinner and clean up, I sat with the others as we watched The Andy Griffith Show and took turns bathing. We didn't get baths nightly since there were only two bathrooms and a limited amount of hot water. The ladies put us on a schedule according to room assignment. Tonight was mine and Dana's night as well as a couple other kids.

Dana strolled out of the bathroom after her fifteen minutes was up with a brush in her hand. She slicked down her wet hair as she took a seat beside me. "Your turn," she smirked.

"Dana, no brushing in the family room," scolded Moira, one of the ladies who ran the place.

"Yes ma'am," she said, seething under her breath and following behind me as I entered the bedroom to grab my bundle of night clothes.

She dropped her brush onto the dresser which she'd taken over. I had nothing on top of it and one drawer at the bottom to put my clothes in. I didn't have many materialistic items anyways, mostly I had memories of the butterflies on my wall and my two beautiful parents.

Not wanting to miss anymore TV Dana scurried out the door without saying a word. I headed towards the bathroom.

By the time I was finished it was bedtime and the ladies scuttled us into our rooms. They were always in such a rush for us to get into bed. It was a routine they never deviated from. Moira poked her head into the room, seeing us both in bed she closed the door and went onto the next room.

Dana turned towards me, I never slept with my back to her as I wanted to see the attack head-on. She folded her pillow and curled her fingers around the edges of it. "I overheard the ladies talking and they said your parents hated you," she whispered.

I knew better. "Why would they say that?"

"Because it's true, dummy. All our parents hated us, except mine. They loved me," she said with a taut smile on her face.

"How do you know? You're here too."

She ignored my question. "Your daddy is in jail and your mommy gave you up."

That's ridiculous, my parents died, I thought but didn't say it. Instead I asked the question again that she'd side-stepped. "What about your parents?"

Still ignoring my question she rolled her eyes. "Your daddy hurt your mommy." She emphasized *hurt* and it stung deep in my soul.

I didn't know at seven what she meant and was tired. She was mean and ugly inside so I shut my eyes.

"Your daddy hurt her and a bunch of other women, that's why he's in jail," the words rolled off her tongue with stingers attached.

I ignored her words and kept my eyes closed. That was the first I learned of my biological parents.

The following day was Saturday and I waited for Cat, the lady who worked in the kitchen directing and teaching us, to disappear for her afternoon walk. I gulped down a little lemonade to wet my throat that was parched from the anticipation of what I was about to do, then left the kitchen and padded down the hall. Making sure no one was around, I peeked my head around the corner of the door to their small office.

The kids were all outside playing a game and Cat was on her walk, easy peasy. I slid into the room and headed straight to the file cabinet. The ladies made sure we understood this room was off-limits but since nobody ever attempted to get inside they'd grown lackadaisical about locking it.

I stood on my tiptoes and thumbed through the folders. Finding mine, I opened it. What I read brought tears to my eyes. Everything Dana said was true. A church lady dropped me off at the orphanage when I was a newborn. It said in bold letters she was a rape victim and wanted nothing to do with the child. My birth certificate was inside the file; Melissa Jones was listed as my mother. The family I'd always thought were my parents took me in at three months old. They filed for adoption when I was five but the papers were never finalized because of their early deaths.

Tears dropped from my eyes and my nose grew hot and leaked. I swiped my face with the apron and stuck my folder into its rightful slot. Rape -- that word didn't exist in my vocabulary. Edging close to the door I leaned in and hearing nothing but the vacant house I went back to the files and found Dana's.

It turns out her mother had her out of wedlock and was forced by her family to give her up. I thumbed through until I found her birth certificate and it listed Sam Courier as her father. I knew that name, I'd heard it somewhere before.

A door slammed and brought my mind to the present so I shoved her folder back into the cabinet and closed it. Female voices and clicking on the floors moved closer to the office. Panicking, I slid underneath the large wooden desk and curled into a tiny ball.

"See you at dinner, Cat," said Moira as she pushed open the office door and took a seat at the desk. Luckily I was small and scrunched into the darkest corner. All I saw was her black heels as they tapped the floor to Chubby Checker on the radio.

What felt like hours went by and my bladder was near bursting. Clutching against myself I fought the urge to pee all over. The glass of lemonade I stole before sneaking into the office was my penance for the wrongs I just committed. A drizzle of pee trickled over my fingers and I knew I couldn't hold it anymore. I looked around and spotted a vent on the other side of Moira's legs but didn't know how to get there without bumping into at least her feet.

Over the sound of the radio, I heard Cat call, "Moira."

The Calm Before the Storm: Evan's Sins

Moira scooted her chair back and stood, offering me the opening I was waiting for. With one hand squeezing my crotch and my bladder muscles tensed to keep it in I scooted with my back against the desk and wall to the vent then pushed aside my soaked panties. The pee burned as it streamed into the floor vent, a little splashing against my legs and the floor. I guessed the vent was for heat but that wouldn't be used in Albuquerque, New Mexico until sometime in the winter. My flood of urine would be dry by then, although it would probably cast an awful odor once used. I shrugged, unconcerned as I felt so much better.

Moira left the office with Cat and I climbed out from under the desk. My wet panties felt cold and gross against my crotch. Scurrying to the door I peeked out. Moira and Cat went around the corner toward the front door. I heard it creak open then closed and seized the opportunity to sneak to my room, hoping Dana wasn't there.

My lucky day, the room was vacant, then I heard voices calling for me. My panties uncomfortable against me I walked bowlegged and wanted to change but thought to wait. I figured they were looking for me since I'd been gone so long. Scooting into the tiny area between my bed and the wall I grabbed a Nancy Drew novel, The Secret of the Old

Clock, and began reading. At seven I read better than any of the students in my class.

The door opened and Moira walked in. "Scarlett."

I cringed. "I'm here," I replied, waving my hand in the air.

"What are you doing? We've been calling you for several minutes now," she said with concern in her voice.

I stood, a dribble of pee from my panties ran down my left leg. "I'm sorry," I said, hanging my head, "I was really into my book and didn't hear." I placed the book atop my bed.

She sighed. "Scarlett, I should have known." She moved to the front of my bed where I was now in full view. "Did you have an accident?"

I peered down my apron, a large wet spot was at the end of it. I must have accidentally peed more than a trickle when I soaked my hands. I shook my head no and responded, "I snuck a glass of lemonade earlier and I must have spilled some on my dress." I didn't want her to know, worried that at some point when they turned on the heat and the smell took over the house that they'd know I was the culprit, meaning I'd been in the office.

"Well come on, let's get that off you."

"OK, Miss Moira." I walked closer to her and she moved back, allowing me the room.

Her eyebrows made a V while her forehead wrinkled. "You don't need to lie."

What? How did she know? Then I saw the wet bubbles shining on the linoleum right below where my butt had been. I thought back and assumed the splashes were more than I thought too.

"Turn around?" she asked.

I did, reluctantly.

"The back of your dress has a wet spot too."

I gulped. "I'm sorry. I guess it happened while I was reading. I didn't even know." I rested my face in my hands and cried.

"It's OK, honey, you're still a young girl and accidents happen. Right now we need to get these clothes off you and get you into something dry. And you need a bath."

After my bath I washed my clothes and hung them to dry. I'd be the laughing stock as everyone would know I peed myself. It was embarrassing, but at least no one knew the reason.

In bed that night Dana teased, "Do you need diapers like a baby? Do you need a bottle too?"

I tried to ignore her but then she said, "The little bastard baby nobody wants is retarded and still pees herself. Wa Wa." Her mocking tone made all the anger inside me rise to the surface.

"I'm not a bastard baby! My parents adored me."

Her eyes widened. "What a big vocabulary you have. Tch," then she turned over and went to sleep.

That night I waited for her to start snoring then left the room and grabbed a small disposable cup from the bathroom. I filled it with cold water and went back to my room and held the cup below her fingertips slowly bringing it as far over her hand as I could and waited a few minutes.

She moved in her sleep so I quickly drank the water as I'd made no plans on how to get rid of it and jumped onto my bed, stuffing the cup into my pillow case.

Dana continued to wiggle in her sleep then jumped out of bed. I kept my head buried in my pillow to stifle my laughter.

"What did you do?!" she shouted.

I turned and jumped in mock surprise. My eyes wide and mouth forming an O.

Within seconds Cat was at the door. "What's going on in here?" she demanded.

Dana looked at her then me and her face grew red. "I... my bed."

Cat's eyes moved across Dana's nightgown. "Dana, you are eleven years old!" she scolded, her hands on her hips.

"I didn't, it was Scarlett," she said, tears in her eyes.

"Scarlett did not pee your bed. Grab those sheets and get a clean nightgown. You will take a bath and make your bed with new sheets. First thing in the morning you'll wash them."

Dana harrumphed, "But…" Cat gave her the stink eye with one eyebrow raised and Dana shut her mouth and did as she was asked.

I curled back onto my side and didn't hide my smile as they headed out the door.

Volume II Ruthless Storm Trilogy

CPSIA information can be obtained
at www.ICGtesting.com
Printed in the USA
LVHW051800270220
648406LV00001B/80

9 781951 017088